For Noelle, Isaac, Alana and Elise

CHAPTER ONE

I discovered the dead body three days after my fiancée, Leyla Bennett, joined the cult.

At the time, I thought it was a hunting accident. Later of course, I knew what really happened. If I had known it all before, I might have said something different when Leyla proposed that she become a certified, sandal-wearing, vegetable-eating, ohm-chanting member of the Forest Way.

~

It all started about two weeks after Thanksgiving. Leyla and I were eating lunch at Dylan's, my favorite waterfront café in Grand Lake. The café was in a strip that looked across the street to the Grand Lake waterfront, which, at this point in the year, was actually an ice-front. The name of the place came from the Minnesota North Shore's favorite son, Robert Zimmerman; better known to the world as Bob Dylan. Dylan of course, had spent more time in Hibbing, Minnesota than the Lake Superior Coastline, but it was close enough. More importantly, the café named after him had excellent food and service.

Alex Chan was there too, along with Julie, who was the part time secretary at both the church and Chan's law office.

"One of you is paying for this," said Julie, looking first at me, and then Chan. "I don't care who."

"She looked at you first," said Chan, chewing his food and hardly glancing up.

"That's just because he's so easy on the eyes," said Leyla, patting my cheek, and then staring at me with a ridiculous expression of sickly adoration. I slid my eyes at Julie and then returned Leyla's look.

Julie made an indelicate noise. "You two make me sick. Get a room."

"We gotta get married first," I said.

"Yeah, when is that happening again?" asked Chan, taking a drink of Coke.

"New Year's Day," said Leyla, rearranging her napkin.

Julie looked at me out of narrowed eyes. "You planned it that way just so you'd remember your anniversary, didn't you?"

"I have no idea what you're talking about," I said blandly, concentrating on a french-fry that I intended to eat.

Leyla laughed. I never got tired of hearing that sound. "Don't worry, Julie, I know all about him. I'm sure that was part of it. But we also agreed that we loved the idea of starting out new with each New Year. And I always wanted a winter wedding by candle-light."

"Barefoot in the spring," said Julie firmly.

"That's so cliché," I said. "Everyone wants that. We're doing barefoot in the snow." For some reason, Leyla kicked Chan under the table. He yelped and spilled a little Coke on the table.

"Oh my gosh, I'm so sorry," said Leyla, putting her hand on Chan's arm. "I meant to kick Jonah."

"You ever play soccer?"

"No, but she's been practicing on me for quite a few months now," I said. "She's also got quite a punch. My shoulders are black and blue."

Everyone watched Leyla while she slowly unclenched her raised left hand and used it to play with her thick, dark long hair while looking innocently out at the falling snow.

I took a sip of coffee and leaned back. I felt warm and happy inside, enjoying the company of dear friends, my love and good food. The whole world was right.

"I want to join the cult," said Leyla.

CHAPTER TWO

When the love of your life tells you that she wants to join a cult, there are a number of appropriate and helpful responses. I just couldn't think of any of them at the moment.

"What?" I said, maybe a little more sharply than I intended. Several other people in the restaurant turned to look our direction.

"The Forest Way?" asked Chan. He looked interested, like someone had cited an obscure precedent in a trial.

"Oh honey," said Julie, leaning toward Leyla and patting her hand, "Jonah's not that bad, really, once you get to know him. It's not worth joining a cult to get out of the marriage." She looked at me thoughtfully. "And if you really can't handle Jonah, there's always Alex here," she nodded at Chan.

Chan gave her the look that he liked to think made him appear to be an enigmatic Chinese man of mystery. I thought it made him look like he had gas.

"Are you OK, Alex?" asked Julie. "Does your leg still hurt?"

He gave an exasperated sigh.

"Never mind," I said to him.

Leyla laughed. "I don't mean join the cult for real, you silly people. I want to do an investigative report. A couple people from Grand Lake have joined. They have their kiosk, selling tea in our mall here." Next door to Dylan's was a small converted warehouse with some public space and several shops. It wasn't really a mall, but it was a popular spot in the winter in Grand Lake. "I've seen them in Duluth too. In the six months since the cult moved here, there's been a train-load of rumor and speculation. Some say they're brainwashing people. Others say they are just sincere but misguided people. I'd like to find out the truth for the people of the North Shore. Besides," she added, "If I do a good job, it could get picked up nationally."

Leyla was the editor for the bi-weekly Grand Lake newspaper. A couple of years ago, she had been a television reporter on the rise. I guess she still had the itch for a good story, and the desire to break a big one.

Chan frowned. "Nobody really knows much about them. Couldn't it be a little dangerous?"

"Yeah," I said. "I don't want you becoming some cult-leader's twelfth wife before you marry me."

"I'm not going to get brainwashed," said Leyla, tossing her hair.

"I'm not so sure," said Julie. "Look how easily Jonah convinced you to marry him."

"That's a valid point," said Chan.

"In all seriousness," I began, "I – "

"We *are* serious," said Julie, interrupting.

"In all seriousness," I said again, "there are techniques to brainwashing, and many cults have learned them. It isn't always as easy as just saying 'I won't believe them.' It's even partly chemical. The reason most cults are vegetarian is because protein helps you think more clearly, and they deprive you of it to make you more vulnerable." I took a big bite of my hamburger, to demonstrate my point. "You can't very well join the cult, and then say, 'but I'm going to keep eating meat.'"

"Are the Forest Way people vegetarian?" asked Chan.

I shrugged.

"Nobody really knows," said Leyla. "That's part of why I want to do this. We hardly know anything."

Chan frowned again. "But Jonah does have a point. You need to do this safely."

"Look," I said to Leyla, "you are your own person. I can't tell you what to do."

There was a snort and a mumble from Julie's direction. I ignored it.

"But could you agree to some precautions, to ease my mind?"

"What did you have in mind?" she asked.

"Could we set up some kind of a messaging system? Maybe some kind of code that lets me know you are doing OK, and are of sound mind?"

"If they *are* into brainwashing, I doubt they'll let her keep a phone or use a computer," said Chan.

"I think they have a strip of land that goes down to the Shore, but as I understand it, their main complex is up in the hills," said Leyla.

"So what's your point?"

"Well," she said, "you like to ski and snow-shoe. Maybe we could arrange a kind of drop location – somewhere in the woods near the complex where I leave you a message."

We chewed on this for a bit, and agreed to go over some maps and find an appropriate location.

"Are there any legal ramifications?" I asked Chan.

"Could be," he said. "Sometimes people who have been brainwashed claim they don't want to leave the cult. Sometimes they donate all their property to the cult."

Leyla sighed. "OK. Maybe you could draw up some kind of legal document where I say that I'm only doing this as an investigative reporter, and any decisions I make after I join the cult are invalid."

Chan leaned back in his chair. "I don't think that will hold up," he said. "But maybe we could create a waiting period on certain decisions. For instance, we could say that you would have to have no contact with the cult for a month, before any transfer of property could be finalized."

"Maybe we could get her to agree to a longer waiting period before she marries Jonah, too," said Julie.

That was Julie, being herself. But it wasn't too long before I wished we had all paid more attention to the brainwashing angle.

CHAPTER THREE

I was skiing through a December blizzard. The snow would swirl around me and wrap me in a little bubble where I could only see five or ten yards. And then after a while it would lift for a few moments to show me the glowering gray clouds hovering over the sad, pine-clad hills. A lot of times I can embrace the cold and gloom and thick, quiet snow, and even kind of enjoy it. But that day, I was just cold and wet. I was only out there for the sake of love. As soon as I was done, I would be sitting in my cabin in front of a fire, sipping hot cocoa and brandy, listening to Bach, or Beethoven, or maybe Steely Dan. But first I had to check the drop location for Leyla's safety message.

I was coming through a little pass between two ridges when I heard the echo of the shot. I didn't think much of it. It was deer season, or near enough. A lot of North Shore families supplemented their diet with venison. If they happened to take a buck a day or two on either side of the weekend, no one up here raised much of a fuss.

I tucked my poles under my arms, crouched over, and swooped down the slope into the next valley. The trail wasn't groomed or maintained in any way. It was just one of those back country hiking or hunting trails that wander through the hills above Lake Superior. That meant it was kind of narrow, and not always suited to skiing, but it was good enough for my purposes. I picked up some decent speed.

As I neared the bottom, I saw a colorful shape lying on the trail in front of me. I tried to do the Telemark style stop, but I overcompensated and went flying just as I heard another shot boom out. I landed in the snow next to the shape, which I now saw was a man. His right hand was clutching a rifle. There was red in the snow all around him. He wasn't moving.

Every year hunters are shot by mistake during deer season. I shouted, presuming that my human voice would tell the hidden hunter that I didn't have antlers. The snow descended again in a thick flurry, smothering visibility just as a second bullet whined by and smacked into a tree behind me. I snatched the rifle from the prone man. It was a bolt action gun with a scope, maybe a Remington 700. I worked the bolt and then fired into the air. "There! Deer don't shoot back you insane idiot," I muttered. "Plus, they don't wear blaze orange." I was wearing a vest of that color to avoid this very kind of accident. I fired again, and just in case, awkwardly scuttled into the trees next to the trail. I snapped my skis off, and crouched in the snow, waiting.

I'd never been near a hunting accident, but I assumed that usually what happened is that after the shooter realized what he'd shot, he felt awful and tried to give assistance.

There was a vast silence. The snow swept noiselessly down, obscuring the hurt man only five yards away.

"Hey!" I called.

Nothing answered.

"Man down!" I yelled. I might have felt funny saying it in other circumstances, but watching the motionless figure on the trail, it seemed kind of serious. There was already a little veil of snow on him. I pulled out my cell phone, but to my utter lack of surprise, I had no signal.

I crawled back out onto the trail, holding on to the rifle. The injured man was face down, lying completely still.

"Hey," I said, gripping his shoulder. "Hey, someone's here, it's going to be OK."

Carefully, I pushed him onto his back. I sat on my haunches and stared at him. I was right. Depending on his theology, of course, everything *was* going to be OK for him.

Just not in this life.

The bullet had hit almost in the center of his chest. The snow was stained with bright blood. His eyes were lifeless and staring. He looked to be in his early thirties and he had a scraggly, spotty, reddish beard on his cheeks.

I waited. It wasn't long before I got very cold. It got darker as the snow thickened and the sun, somewhere far away, considered just giving up for the day. After about fifteen minutes I decided that whoever shot him was too scared to come and see what had happened.

Maneuvering the body, I got it into a fireman's lift and staggered to my feet. I sank to my knees in the snow, lost my balance, and pitched the body forward. It landed, legs and arms crossed, half buried in a frozen drift. I tried again. As I lifted him, his stocking cap slid off his head and dropped to the snow. I considered, and immediately dismissed the idea of bending down to get it. This time I managed to take five steps before I hit a deep spot again, once more dropping the dead man. He must have weighed almost two hundred pounds.

"I've got more of a fast strength, than a brute strength," I said to the general vicinity. No one replied. I waded through the snow to where the body had landed, and laid him out on his back, hands folded, in best funeral parlor position.

"Good thing I'm a pastor," I said to him. "I'm authorized to do this stuff. Sort of."

I considered the possibility that I was cracking up. I decided it was pretty likely. Then I floundered through the snow, snapped on my skis and slipped back up the trail. I didn't have cell phone reception at any point when I stopped to check. I reached my car at the trailhead three miles later, but still did not have a signal.

After packing up my gear, I drove six miles to the top of the ridge that overlooks Lake Superior. The snow was already several inches deep on the road. There was no view of the water that day, and it was almost dark anyway. But I finally had a cell signal.

My first call was to the county Sherriff's department. I told them what I had found, and where, and gave them the location of the trailhead where I had parked.

"Bring snowmobiles," I said. "It's more than two miles back in there, and the snow's pretty deep."

Next I called the Grand Lake police Department. "Chief just heard it on the scanner," the dispatcher said to me. It's been a slow day here, so he's going out to assist." I thanked him, hung up and drove back to the trailhead.

The snow settled on my windshield and covered it up like thick drapery. I got cold and decided to drink coffee from my thermos to warm up. After that was gone, I got cold again, so I started the car and ran it for about ten minutes.

After about forty-five minutes it was full dark. I saw headlights cutting through the driving snow and two trucks pulling trailers swept into the parking area. Several patrol cars followed. I got out of my car to greet them.

A tall slim man stepped from one of the cars. He had an iron-gray mustache that was trimmed with impeccable precision. His nose curved down like a hawk's, and his blue eyes were habitually colder than the winter around us. He stalked over to me and stood there for a second in the glare of the headlights. Then he shook his head.

"Borden. I should have known." His voice was crisp and hard.

"Jaeger," I said. "Been awhile." Jaeger was one of the chief investigators with the Sherriff's Office.

He considered that, blinking through the snow. In the background people were calling to each other, backing up trucks and unloading snow machines.

"Maybe not long enough," he said.

We never did get along very well.

Another figure entered the bright circle of light. He was also tall, but clean shaven. A little reddish-blond hair showed under his Grand Lake PD stocking cap.

"Jonah," he said, sticking out his gloved hand. We don't take gloves off to shake hands in the winter in Minnesota. Too many people have lost fingers that way.

"Dan," I said. Dan Jensen was chief of the Grand Lake Police force. Technically, this wasn't his jurisdiction, but being in rural Minnesota, the Sherriff's office and the Grand Lake town police worked pretty well together.

"What's up?" he said.

While the snowmobiles were unloaded and prepped, I told Jensen and Jaeger what had happened.

"You know how to drive one of these things?" asked Jaeger, gesturing at a snow machine.

"Sure," I said.

"OK, lead the way."

The snowmobiles had headlights, but even so, I took it slow. We were in the middle of a real blizzard now, and visibility was awful. Finally, we reached the little pass where I had heard the first gun shot. I eased the machine slowly down the hill and started scanning for the body. I knew it wasn't going to be easy, because enough snow had fallen to cover it with at least a few inches. I came to the place where I thought I had left him, and pulled up. Jensen, Jaeger and three more Sherriff's deputies stopped behind me.

"Around here," I shouted over the noise of the machines, gesturing with my hand. I moved down the trail a little more, and then I saw the area where the body had laid initially. The fresh snow had almost covered it, but I could faintly see the hollows where I had churned up the area, trying to help the dead man. I pulled beyond it, turned the snowmobile around and shined my headlight back toward the others. I cut the engine, leaving the light on.

The others got off their machines and walked over.

"He was shot here," I said.

Jensen and Jaeger squatted at the edge of the faintly disturbed snow. Another man came up with some camera equipment, and took a few pictures. Then Jaeger stepped forward and started brushing through the snow.

"Did you leave anything here?" he asked.

"Not intentionally, but I didn't search the area," I said. "Something might have fallen out of his pockets, maybe."

He grunted and poked around some more. Jensen was walking further down the trail beyond my snowmobile, the powerful beam of his flashlight jabbing into the darkness.

"Sure this is right?" asked Jaeger. "You said there was a lot of blood. I don't see any here."

I stared at the snow. He was right. "I don't know. We're in the right general area. I tried to carry him out, at first, and I dropped him twice. Maybe this is where I dropped him." We walked further down the trail, but I couldn't find any bloodstained snow.

"It's probably dropped two or three inches in the last hour," I said after a while. "It could have been anywhere along here."

"You can't remember," he said.

I doubted anyone could have remembered, what with the new snow and the dark. But I held my tongue as Jensen came up to us.

"Snow's a little rough down the trail, like maybe other people walked around here this afternoon. Did you notice tracks when you were here before?"

"I don't know," I said. "I was a little preoccupied, what with being shot at, and discovering a dead body."

Jaeger snorted. I wondered if it would be juvenile and un-pastorly of me to rub his face in the snow. "OK," he said. "The scene's a bust. Let's get the body."

I led him over to where I had laid the dead man out on his back. The snow looked like it had been stirred up, but there was no body there.

"I thought it was here," I said. I looked around. There was another place it might have been. I walked over and started shoveling snow aside with my hands. But there was nothing there. "I was sure I put him there," I said, pointing back to the first place.

Jaeger plowed through the thick snow and stood a little closer to me than was necessary. "What are you pulling here, Borden?"

I straightened and stood eye to eye with him. "What're you saying, Jaeger, that I brought you out here for the fun of it?"

We glared at each other for a minute. The tension grew. I really, *really* wanted to rub his face in the snow.

"You think you can take me, Borden?" The steam from his breath swirled around my face.

"Act your age, Jaeger," said Dan Jensen, cutting in. "I think all three of us know that Jonah could take you to pieces, what with his black belt in Tai Bo, or whatever, and also that his weird sense of honor would never let him do it."

"Tae Kwon Do," I said.

Jensen shook his head like he was irritated. "I thought you two had worked out your differences."

Jaeger's face, what I could see of it behind his mustache and scarf, remained expressionless. His cold eyes flickered momentarily. Then he sighed. "Sorry," he said, slapping me on the shoulder. The word, not the blow, almost knocked me off my feet in surprise. "Old habits die hard, and I'm not thrilled to be out here in the cold and dark."

"It's OK," I said. "It's not enjoyable and that's a fact. And I don't understand. The guy was here, and he wasn't long dead. In fact, he was still warm."

A shout interrupted our thoughts. A sheriff's deputy waddled up to us. "We just found a little spot of snow with some blood in it. Also, we found this." He held up the dead man's stocking cap.

"That's his hat," I said. "It fell off when I was trying to move him."

"He must have walked," said Jaeger.

"He was dead."

"Says you," said Jaeger. Jensen glared at him. "I'm sure you thought he was dead," Jaeger amended more gently, surprising me again. "But maybe he was just out cold, with the shock and everything, and after you left, he got up and made his way out. You said he was still warm."

"OK," I said, trying to keep the peace with Jaeger, even though I was certain the man I left had been dead. "Then where did he go? We didn't see him on the way in."

"Where's the trail go to?" He gestured north, where the path continued on into the hills.

I shrugged. "I think it's several miles before it hits another road. I don't really know."

Jensen called to the other deputies and asked, but no one knew where the trail led. There are dozens of paths like that in the Arrowhead region of Minnesota. Some were made by loggers, others by snowmobile or dirt-bike enthusiasts. The government makes some trails too, but those are usually well marked and well maintained.

"Omdahl," said Jaeger to one of the deputies, "you and Petersen take a couple machines and see if you can find where this trail comes out." He blinked up into the thickly flying snow. "Be careful, stay in radio contact and come back if this gets any worse. Don't take any stupid risks. You get stuck out here tonight, you might not make it back."

Jaeger turned back to me. "I don't s'pose you took his wallet, or driver's license or anything before you left him?" He sounded resigned.

"No."

No one said anything.

"Well," said Jaeger at last, "if he's alive, he'll get medical treatment, and we'll find out about it, and your little mystery will be solved."

"If he's dead, he's got to be here somewhere," I said.

"But he's not here," said Jaeger.

Jensen spoke up. "Jonah, if he is dead, and he's just buried under the snow around here, someone will report him missing, and we'll find out then. It's too bad for the family, but we can't do anything about it."

"Well," said Jaeger, "let's give it one more try, while we wait for Omdahl and Petersen, and then get out of the cold."

But the deputies returned within five minutes.

"There's a tree down across the trail, about a quarter mile farther on and around a bend," said deputy Petersen. He waved his hand in the snowy air. "In this stuff, it's impossible to find a good way around it."

Jaeger grunted his acknowledgement. We spent another hour out there in the cold dark hills while the snow piled up around us. We looked all up and down the trail, but we didn't find anything else.

The body was gone.

CHAPTER FOUR

It took a long time to get home. The snow was thick and the roads were slippery and I was thankful that my heavy, front-wheel drive Volkswagen had a manual transmission to help me coax it through the bad places. The worst part was my own driveway, which was more than a hundred yards long. Obviously, no cars had been on it and it hadn't been salted or plowed. When I finally bulled my way through a drift into the garage, I heaved a sigh of relief.

I stripped out of my soaking clothes, found my bathrobe, and then went into the living room to start a fire. My cabin sits on a few acres about a mile and a half from Lake Superior. It's high up on the first inland ridge, so on most days and moonlit nights, you can see far out into the pristine, cold reaches of the world's biggest freshwater lake. My living room faces the lake with two-stories of windows surrounding a fireplace and chimney, but there wasn't a chance of seeing the water tonight.

Melanchthon, the orange, fluffy cat, bounded into the room, skidded to a stop on the wood floor and stared at me with wide eyes and huge pupils. Purring loudly, he launched himself at me, attacking my hands and legs until I quit messing with the fire and began to stroke him.

"All right buddy," I said. "Who said a dog was man's best friend?"

Melanchthon bit me.

After the fire was roaring and the fan was blasting warm air, I flipped on some music and went into my kitchen, which is separated from the living-room only by a counter and a couple pillars.

I put some water on to boil while I seared a steak, and then sliced onions, peppers and mushrooms. When the water was ready, I threw in some linguine and olive oil and cooked the steak with the vegetables, some red wine and a bit of herb-butter. When the meat was medium-rare, I sliced it into short strips. Draining the pasta, I added the steak and vegetables with their pan-drippings, some more herb-butter, fresh basil and garlic and some shredded Parmesan cheese. I ate it at my counter with a bowl of salad and a glass of muddy-tasting Merlot. I set out a dish for Melanchthon. He ate the steak and lapped up the juices, but he ignored the pasta and vegetables. Snob.

Afterwards, I sipped hot cocoa in front of the fire, listening to Handel's Messiah. Occasionally, I got up and flipped on an outside light to look at the snow coming down outside. It had turned into a genuine blizzard. Snow before Christmas feels different than snow after the New Year. Before Christmas it feels like snow is setting the scene. It's fun and peaceful. But by mid-January, it is just a nuisance again. For now, however, it was kind of cool to be sitting in front of the fire while the white powder piled up outside. In fact, two years ago, this would have been an ideal evening. But tonight, something was missing. I was restless. It was Leyla. With her here, it would have been perfect. But she was out there somewhere, maybe not entirely safe, and so I couldn't quite enjoy myself.

That was when I remembered that in all the excitement, I had never checked for her message.

I called Jensen on his cell phone. I had left before the police, because they still had to load up the snowmobiles. They had four wheel drive vehicles, and Jaeger had told me to take my sissy-car and get home before I couldn't.

"Hey, Dan," I said, "You still up at the trailhead?"

"Long gone, Jonah. What's up?"

"Dang," I said. "In all the confusion I forgot to check for a note from Leyla." Jensen knew all about her investigative venture.

"You at home?" he asked.

"Yes."

"Well, don't bother trying to get back tonight. We barely made it back to the blacktop in four-wheel drive, and even the highway wasn't much better. You'd best wait for the plows to go through tomorrow."

There was a short silence.

"She'll be fine, Jonah," said Dan.

"Yeah, I know," I said. "I got a note from her yesterday, and before we started, we agreed that I shouldn't worry until the third day of not hearing from her."

"There you go then. Go get the note tomorrow."

I hung up. Melanchthon jumped up and unceremoniously sprawled on my lap, purring loudly. I petted him, and he grabbed my hand with both paws, and licked it.

"Yeah, you're beautiful," I said. "But not as much as her."

CHAPTER FIVE

The next morning began as bright as an ice-cube glittering in the sun, only not as warm. Bright sunshine after a blizzard in Minnesota means bitter cold, and that day was no exception. Even so, it was beautiful. White powder clung to every tree branch and twig. Down the ridge, a mile or two away, Superior sparkled with a brilliant, deep blue.

I stepped outside into snow that came up to my knees. I went back inside and called Julie on her cell phone.

"Julie," I said when she picked up, "it's going to take me a while to dig out. You'd better cancel all my morning appointments."

"You don't have any appointments," she said.

"Really? I mean, I know I sometimes forget things like that, but I was sure the Iversons were coming in today, and isn't the quilting group this morning too? I usually say 'hi' to them."

"No way," said Julie. "Today is a snow day. Everything is shut down, and that includes Harbor Lutheran Church. I canceled everything already."

"When were you going to talk to me about it?"

"I just did."

Sometimes I think Julie is confused about the nature of the boss-secretary relationship. Alex Chan had reported similar findings.

"OK," I said. "Well, call me if you need me."

"You know anything about *Angry Birds*?"

"No."

"Then I won't need you."

Even using the snow-blower, it took a good chunk of the morning to clear my driveway, shovel my walks, and rake the roof. When I was done, I was wet from flying snow, and I couldn't feel my toes or my lips.

When I was a little warmer, I loaded up my damp ski-gear and got in the car. When I reached the end of my driveway, I saw that the snowplow had come through on the road, and now there was a wall of snow between the driveway and the road, about three feet high and two feet thick. The proper thing to do would be to shovel it out. Instead, I gunned my engine and smashed through it. Later in the winter, I would probably have a large ice-hump to show for my laziness. But I was done moving snow for the day.

In spite of the snow, Lorraine's was open for business. It was a fixture in Grand Lake, and Lorraine served the best breakfast on Lake Superior. A lot of regulars gathered there, including several members of the Grand Lake Police Department.

"Hey Jonah," called someone as I walked in, "find any disappearing dead bodies lately?"

There was a ripple of laughter.

"I heard he pulled a Jesus, and raised the last one," commented someone else. This got a better response. I smiled, in spite of myself.

"Can you do my funeral?" asked a third. "I'd like the resurrection package."

"I don't know about that," I shot back. "But I do have a heck of a life insurance policy I could tell you about." The man in question, a cop named Ingersoll, pointed a figure at me as we all laughed. One or two people clearly didn't get it, however.

I slid into my regular booth. "The usual," I said to Lorraine as she placed a pot of coffee and a mug on the table. The usual was the Superior Skillet – hash browns, mushrooms, peppers, spicy sausage and eggs over-easy, topped with hollandaise sauce, accompanied by two plate-sized pancakes. Moving snow is hungry work.

Two pots of coffee and an ungodly amount of food later, I left. The highways were clear, and though the back-roads had a layer of snow on them, it was obvious that they had been plowed at least once during the storm. The parking area at the trailhead wasn't cleared, however, so I parked against the side of the road – which was now a hefty snow-bank – and geared up.

On un-groomed, fresh snow, cross-country skis sink down several inches, and the going was a little more work that day. The activity warmed up my core, but my face began to ache with the chill, and it hurt to breathe too deeply. Looking at the trail that morning, you would never have known that snowmobiles had been up and down it the night before.

At last I skied into the little valley where I had found the dead man the previous afternoon. I turned off the cleared path by a large white pine, and wound my way through thick trees until I came to a lightning-blasted birch tree. The top of the tree was broken off, and the center was split and blackened. At that point I was about a hundred yards from the trail, and according to the map, maybe half a mile from the compound of the Forest Way cult.

Glancing around, I noticed a set of tracks leading to and from the birch tree. Leyla had used the same steps going away from the tree as she had getting there, to minimize the effort involved in sinking into deep snow. She must have borrowed someone's snow boots, because although the tracks were jumbled, they looked big for her.

I reached into the base of the split birch, and pulled out a clear plastic Tupperware container. I could see that there was a note inside. Unfolding, it, I could see that it read,

I've got to be quick. I'll write more later.

Everything is fine.

Love,

L

I pushed it into my jacket pocket, and in its place I left my own note. Breathing a sigh of relief, I made my way back up the trail and to my car.

CHAPTER SIX

I was in my office listening to Christina Perri a few days later. I felt kind of silly about it, but the girl had talent. It was unfortunate for her that people kept confusing her with Katy Perry. I apologized to the shades of Stevie Nix and Christine McVee, but I left the music on.

The phone beeped.

"Chief Jensen on line one," said Julie.

"Julie," I said, punching the speaker button so she could hear the music, "this will be considered classic rock someday, won't it?"

There was silence. "It's kind of girly," she said at last.

"You don't think she's kind of the modern, female, Steven Stills, only completely different?"

"Why don't you ever consult me with simple questions about Greek, or the meaning of suffering in the world?"

I grinned happily. Confounding Julie was a rare pleasure.

"Don't worry," she added, "I won't tell anyone you listen to girly music."

Ah well. At least I'd had two or three seconds of triumph. You gotta take what you can get. She broke the connection, and I punched line one.

"Hey, Dan," I said.

"Hey, Jonah, any chance you could come down to the hospital?"

I'm the police chaplain, so this wasn't an entirely unusual request. I counseled with paramedics and cops, and sort of considered them my second congregation. "If you give me an hour to

29

finish up a few things, I can," I said. "What's up? Someone get sick, or hurt?"

"No, nothing like that," he said. "But we may have found your body."

We set up, and an hour and a half later, I pulled into one of the two parking spaces reserved for clergy at the Grand Lake General Hospital. It wasn't particularly near to the main entrance, but it made me feel special to park there, so I did.

Jensen shook my hand when I got inside the main door. "Thanks for coming, Jonah," he said.

We went through a maze of corridors. For some reason, hospitals can never seem to lay things out in an orderly and intuitive fashion. I'd been in some hospitals that actually changed wards around if it was too easy to find your way. At last we found ourselves in the basement, in the small morgue.

After we signed in, a white coated orderly took us into a chilly room. One wall was lined with little steel doors that looked like the fronts of file cabinet drawers, only a little bigger. He pulled one open. Inside, on a long drawer, was a dead body. The skin was paler and empty of life, but the hair and scraggly beard were still ginger. I looked carefully at the face.

"That's him," I said.

Jensen nodded at the orderly, who closed the drawer, and we walked back out.

"Wanna grab some coffee?" asked Jensen.

"What kind of question is that?" I asked. "Have I ever turned down coffee?"

"Do you have time?"

"That's the only question," I said. "In this case, I do."

We drove over to Dylan's by the harbor.

"Where'd you find him?" I asked sipping my coffee.

Jensen gave me a funny look. He blew on his steaming mug. "Now, Jonah, I trust you," he said. "But I'm a cop. I gotta do my job. I don't want to be accused of despotism or whatever."

"I think 'nepotism' is the word you're after," I said.

"Whatever. I gotta treat you like anyone else. Just 'cause you're my friend doesn't make you exempt from questions."

"I get it, Dan. You're a good cop. Shoot."

"Tell me your story again, how you found him."

I told him. He looked at a little notebook while I talked, nodding at certain points. He added a couple of scribbles.

"You ever see this guy before?" he asked.

"No."

"You didn't know him?"

"No."

"Do you know someone else who knows him?"

"No." It was tedious, but I appreciated Jensen's commitment to impartiality.

"So, you first found him down on County Road Seven?"

I looked at him closely. "What are you talking about? You were there. It wasn't anywhere near County Seven. It was up off the Flintlock Trail."

"You didn't see him on County Seven?"

"I haven't been down that way for months," I said. "You know very well I saw him up near one of the forest roads, a few miles off the Flintlock."

He nodded with satisfaction, and closed his little notebook. "That's what I thought. Thanks, Jonah."

"What was that all about, Dan?"

"We found him down on County Seven, five miles south of town."

I stared at him.

He nodded. "That's right. So either he wasn't dead when you found him, or someone moved him."

I digested this for a moment.

Jensen sipped some coffee and then said, "You sure he was dead when you found him?"

"Yes. He'd been shot in the middle of his chest. There was a lot of blood. His eyes were open, and stayed open without blinking. There was no pulse. He didn't respond in any way when I tried to carry him, when I dropped him, or when I laid him out."

"Your fingers could have been too cold to feel a pulse."

I thought back to that afternoon. Everything I had already said was true. But I had figured he was dead as soon as I turned him over, before I carried him, before I checked the pulse. Why had I been so sure? I took a sip of coffee, which is an excellent way to stimulate thinking. As if to prove my point, I suddenly knew.

"This time of year, your breath makes a lot of steam in the air. But his didn't. No breath."

Jensen nodded. "Actually, I think he was dead where you found him, too. Down on County Seven there was no evidence at all that it was the kill site. Everything looked to me like he was killed elsewhere and dumped there."

"Why?"

Jensen shrugged. "Someone may know that the killer was hunting in the area where you found our guy. If the body shows up elsewhere, there's no connection to the trigger happy hunter."

"But he had to know that someone found the dead guy," I said. "He must have seen me moving and thought the deer was only injured, because he shot at me too, remember? Then I shouted, and fired the victim's gun in the air so the hunter would quit. There'd be no doubt in his mind that someone else was there."

"Someone else? Or just our John Doe, shouting and shooting before he expired? The killer maybe thought it was him. You were gone by the time he got to the body, remember?"

"Wait a minute," I said. "John Doe? You don't know who he is?"

Jensen shook his head. "No wallet, no phone, no hunting license or papers of any kind. You didn't happen to look at a wallet before you skied back to your car, did you?"

I called for a third refill on my coffee. "I'm sorry, Dan. It just didn't occur to me."

"It's not your fault, Jonah. No reason you should have. Just a wild hope that maybe our mystery was solved after all."

"So, you think the shooter, or whoever moved him, cleaned out his wallet and stuff to make it harder on you?"

"That's what I'm thinking," said Jensen. "The only reason to remove John Doe's ID is if he is connected to the killer somehow. So it wasn't just an accident between strangers."

I didn't want that to be true. I didn't want there to be some kind of conspiracy and intrigue so close to the cult. It was bad enough already that Leyla was there. "I don't know," I said at last. "I mean, what if it was just opportunity? He could maybe sell the ID to professional identity thieves. I'm sure he'd appreciate whatever cash he got. Hasn't anyone been reported missing yet?"

"Nope. Could be the storm threw things off. If a guy was off on a hunting trip, maybe his loved ones would figure he got caught by the storm and stuck for a few days. Cell reception isn't great around here. We may hear from someone in the next day or two."

"But you don't really think so."

"How do you do that?" he asked. "I'm proud of my cop face."

I shrugged. "It's an intuitive thing. Maybe even a God thing. So you don't think John Doe was a regular hunter."

He shrugged. Something about this guy isn't right. You hunt sometimes, right?"

"Got a ten-pointer hanging in my home office," I said.

"Okay. This guy had no hand warmers, no toe warmers."

"Maybe he was just a rookie, a greenhorn."

"He smelled nice."

"Okay Dan," I said, "I know you are a happily married man. This is a little weird."

"No, I mean, he was wearing cologne, or strong deodorant. His hair must have been recently washed with smelly shampoo."

"Oh, I get it. He didn't care about spooking the deer with his smell."

"Right, Reverend-detective. No estrus or odor neutralizers on him. Plus, he didn't have a knife."

"No hunting knife?"

"Exactly. What was he planning to do once he shot an animal?" We drank a little coffee, which was God's gift to both the righteous and the wicked, just to show us he loved us.

"Okay, Dan, but what if the shooter took those too? If he's just an opportunist, he might want a good hunting knife and some hand-warmers. And maybe the victim was a rookie, who didn't know about shampoo, and estrus and all that."

Dan thought a little bit. "Well, I guess it's like this. If it was a random shooting between two unconnected parties, and the shooter was just an opportunist who took all that stuff from the victim, I'm screwed. As a cop, I mean. Cases like that almost never get solved. If I assume there is no connection between shooter and victim, I might as well quit right now. That assumption is a dead end. Coincidences do happen, but believing in them never helps you solve a case. So, the only way to pursue this is to assume the connection. Now, tell me truthfully, what does your intuitive-thing say about that?"

I wasn't happy, but I knew the answer. "My gut tells me you're right."

Jensen nodded. "One more thing, Jonah. Was he wearing blaze orange when you found him?"

I thought back to that day. "I can't remember for sure. Now that you mention it, I don't think so. But I'm not certain."

"We found his stocking cap, remember, when we went back there with you?"

"Yeah?"

"It was black."

Hunters were supposed to wear a blaze orange vest, as well as something of the same color on their heads.

"Maybe he was poaching," I said. "It isn't actually firearm season for deer, is it?"

"No. But you can take deer with muzzle-loaders right now. Plus, other species are open for firearms, like bobcat and coyote."

"His gun was definitely not a muzzle-loader. It was some kind of bolt action, like a Remington 700."

"You said you fired it into the air? How was the recoil?"

"I honestly don't remember. Could have been anything between .223 for coyote, and a .308 for big game. I just don't recall how it felt."

"The bullet that killed John Doe went on through."

"So what does all this tell us?"

Jensen looked frustrated. "I don't know. I just know it doesn't feel right. It looks like a hunting accident and a cover up, but it *feels* like something different. I just don't know what. I was hoping you could help me get a handle on it."

"Wait," I said. "The bullet in the tree."

Jensen looked at me expectantly.

"I told you the mystery-shooter fired twice after I was on the scene. I'm pretty sure one of the shots hit a tree by the side of the trail. We might be able to find it and dig it out."

"It won't tell us about John Doe, but it might tell us something about the guy who shot him," said Jensen. "It's something, anyway."

CHAPTER SEVEN

I was a little unsettled by Chief Jensen's speculations. Dan was a hard-headed, no-nonsense kind of cop, and if he thought something was odd, it probably was. But that meant that instead of a simple hunting accident and cover-up, there was something bigger going on, and it was happening very near to the property owned by the Forest Way cult, very near, in fact, to where Leyla was.

I led Jack Jaeger and a team down the trail again to look for the bullet.

"You sure it hit a tree?" asked Jaeger when Jensen and I approached him.

"No," I said, shortly. For some reason Jaeger brings out the worst in me.

"You better not be wasting my time," said Jaeger. His face was as expressionless as always, but I knew that for some reason, I brought out the worst in him, too.

"Yeah, because your time is worth so much more than mine."

"I stop crime and put away bad guys with my time. I serve the people; I don't fleece them and abuse them."

"The only person I've ever been tempted to abuse is standing right in front of me," I said. I had to consciously relax my hands, which were clenched into fists.

"You two are like a couple of dogs, circling each other, growling, sniffing each other's butts," said Jensen. "Jaeger, Jonah's a pastor. But he's a good guy too, so get over it. Jonah, Jaeger doesn't like you. Live with it. Life isn't a popularity contest."

"Whatever," said Jaeger.

"Fine," I said.

"Okay, then let's go," said Jensen.

We took the Sheriff's department snowmobiles again. When we got down to the level spot in the little valley, I stopped, and cut the engine.

I stepped off the machine, sinking deep into the snow. I wandered a little bit, looking around, trying to place exactly where I had been and what had happened.

"Somewhere around here," I said, gesturing toward the right-hand side of the trail. Jaeger, Jensen and the two other investigators fanned out, looking at the trees. I noticed a little pine tree. It seemed familiar.

"I think I took shelter behind that," I said.

Jensen moved over. Suddenly he straightened and stared at a white birch tree standing next to the pine. Slowly, eyes up, he struggled through the snow until his nose was almost touching the trunk. He put his hand up to a spot where the wood was chipped and splintered. Slowly, keeping his hand on the spot, he moved around to the other side of the tree, which at that point was about eighteen inches thick.

He walked all the way around. "Still in there," he said with satisfaction. Then he raised his voice and called out to the others.

They all swarmed around the tree. I stayed back, but I could see the little splintered spot clearly. It was almost exactly in the middle of the trunk.

"I agree," said one of the Sheriff's deputies. "No exit hole. It's gotta be in there."

"It's gonna have to come down," said Jaeger.

"I'm afraid so," said another one of the deputies, a short, thick man named Jordahl. He went back to one of the sleds and opened up a kind of saddle-bag that was strapped to the machine. He came back bearing a small chain saw.

The tree had to be cut about five feet up from the ground.

"Don't cut your hand off," grunted Jaeger.

"Gee, thanks," said Jordahl. "I was planning to do that, but I guess now I won't."

"Don't let the tree fall on your head," said one of the other deputies.

"No, I'm gonna bring it down on *your* head, Swensen. Might make it work better."

The helpful advice continued until it was cut off by the roar of the saw. After more than five minutes, Jordahl leaped aside and the birch crashed down parallel to the trail.

"All right, let me look," said Jaeger.

After close examination, he pointed to a spot just below the cut on the trunk. "Cut it here, about four inches thick. They can dig it out of the slice back at the lab."

While the chainsaw roared to life again, I crossed the trail and made my way to Leyla's drop-box. It was rough going through the deep snow, and my socks were saturated long before I got there.

The box was empty. I pulled a note out of my jacket. I was concerned about the suspicious shooting so close to the Forest Way compound. In my note, I encouraged Leyla to finish up and get out as quickly as possible.

Since it hadn't snowed for the past few days, her trail was still clearly visible, stomped into the powder by over-sized boots. It seemed so simple to just follow those tracks back to the compound, collect Leyla, and bring her back to normalcy, to safety, to me.

But I knew better. She was her own woman, and she loved investigative reporting. I couldn't spoil such a big story for her. But I wished I felt better about her situation.

CHAPTER EIGHT

On Sunday, in honor of my name, I preached a whale of a sermon. It was hard to tell how many people fell asleep, because it was cold out, and some people cheated by keeping their scarves on, but I bet it was less than six. My record was thirteen, but that time was a funeral, and there were a lot of old people attending who were worn out by grief and late nights of watching *Wheel of Fortune*.

Of course, it was always hard to tell the sleepers apart from the Norwegian Lutherans, not to mention the dead people. They all tended to express the same amount of emotion. I consider myself an elite preacher, because I regularly inspire a few Lutherans to nod in agreement when I'm speaking.

After the service, Mike Slade caught me. He was an attorney, but I kind of liked him anyway.

"Hey Jonah," he said. "We're putting out the ice-house today. You wanna go fishing?"

"Ice-fishing?"

"Only kind of fishing you can do at this time of year."

I shook my head. "Sorry, Slade. I don't drink hard enough for that."

He laughed. "Hey, I'm sober three years, remember?"

"People ice-fish sober?"

"*I* do. A nice heater and Satellite TV in the ice-house helps."

"That's like fishing in your living room," I said.

"Exactly," said Slade.

I needed to check for another message from Leyla. The last time, the box had been empty. "I appreciate the offer, Mike," I said. "Another time, maybe."

He smiled, shook my hand, and left.

~

Like every Sunday afternoon, I was desperately tired, but I limited my nap to twenty minutes, so I could get up to our drop box before dark. Leyla had been gone a week, and the original plan was for her to experience a week of life in the Forest Way, and then get out and write her report. Of course, if she ran into something particularly interesting, she might stay longer to investigate more, but I expected she would tell me that in a note. My hope was the Forest Way was actually more boring than C-SPAN in July, and her note today would tell me to come pick her up.

After my nap I drove through light snow to the trailhead, and took the familiar trail down to our drop location. At the old birch I pulled out the plastic box and found a note. It said:

Everything is fine.

Love,

L

I stared at the little scrap of paper for a long time. The more I stared, the less I liked it. I didn't expect a sonnet or even an epistle, but this seemed entirely inadequate. My last note had informed her of the shooting nearby, and warned her to get out soon, just in case it was related to the cult somehow. Nothing in her terse reply indicated that she had even read my message. I would have at least expected her to tell me something of her plans.

Frustrated, I shoved the note forcefully into my jacket pocket and skied back to the road.

Melanchthon nearly tripped me when I came in the door of my cabin.

"Hey buddy," I said. He rubbed up against my leg and commented.

"True," I replied. "How about peanut chicken tonight?"

I built up the fire, and then went into the kitchen. I sliced an onion into rings and put water on to boil. Cubing some chicken breast, I sautéed it with the onion, mushrooms and garlic, and then made a sauce with white wine and peanut butter. I always felt like the peanut butter was cheating, but I didn't know any other way to make it. Combining the chicken, sauce and onion rings, I ate it over linguine at my counter. Melanchthon ate it sans noodles and left his onion untouched. He lapped up every bit of the sauce though.

After supper, I turned on the news from Duluth. Leyla used to work for channel thirteen there. I knew I wouldn't see her, but it felt like maybe there might be some sort of connection.

There wasn't. University of Minnesota Duluth was building a new athletics center. A local politician was in some sort of scandal trouble. The meth problem in Duluth, Thunder Bay, and the entire North Shore was worse than it had ever been. As if to spread the guilt, they then did a piece on the meth problem in Europe. Some expert even thought that the US was exporting it. I started to get depressed, and turned it off.

Melanchthon jumped on my lap, purring loudly. He pushed at my hand so I would remember to pet him.

"How did we let her get under our skin like this?" I asked him. He gave a little mew. "Yeah," I said, "I guess that's what love does."

The next morning I found Chief Jensen at Lorraine's.

"Jonah," he said, waving a hand at the chair across from him.

"Hey, Dan," I said. The server, a girl who had been part of the church youth group for four years, put a pot of coffee and a mug down in front of me before I could say a word.

"Thanks, Mindy," I said. The first sip of the morning is always the best, and this was no exception.

I pulled Leyla's note from my pocket and laid it on the table in front of Jensen. He glanced at it. "From Leyla?"

"Yesterday," I said.

"Brief," he said.

"You too," I said. "But I don't like this, Dan."

"You two usually write all the lovey-dovey stuff?"

"No, it isn't that. In my last note to her, I told her about the shooting. The more I think about it, the more I think the cult may be involved somehow. No one knows who the victim is. Maybe it was a cult member." I drank some more coffee. I take comfort wherever I can get it. Usually, I get it from coffee.

"So, you expected more response from Leyla," said Jensen.

"Well, yeah. Plus, the general plan was she'd be there until yesterday. It was flexible, of course, but if she's staying on, I would have expected her to say something about why, or when she wants me to come get her. This note is nothing."

Jensen cocked his head at the note. "Is this her hand-writing?"

"Yes," I said. I could see him struggle with it. Dan liked Leyla; most people did. His cop's instincts probably told him there was nothing wrong, but his friend-instincts were troubled.

"What do you want to do?" he asked at last.

"I don't know. Do you think I should just go in there and get her?"

"If you mess up her investigation, she might be kind of pissed," he said. "She says everything is fine."

"Something isn't right," I said.

"If I was doing this as an investigation," he said, "I wouldn't go in yet. Not enough evidence. But this isn't police work, and you have a pretty powerful intuitive thing, and she's your fiancée."

"So you're saying it's up to me."

"Welcome to adulthood, Jonah."

"Gee, thanks," I said.

"What are you gonna do?"

"I don't know yet."'

"Let me know if you need any help."

"Sure, Dan. Thanks."

CHAPTER NINE

As I drove home, I decided I needed to go see Leyla. I might be able to visit her without blowing her cover. And even if I did blow it, she could still use all the information she'd gathered so far. As Jensen said, it wasn't a police investigation. She didn't have to build a court-case.

As soon as the decision was made, I felt better. I plugged my iPod into the stereo system and played *Seventeen*, by Stevie Nix. For some reason that song always made me feel pumped up and ready to swing into action.

The first wild action I swung into was to study the text for the week. I was soon lost in Greek verbs and moldy commentaries. It's an exciting life, but someone has to lead it.

For lunch I met with the four members of our community outreach committee. We each brought our own meal, and gathered in the church conference room, which was a nursery with a table in it.

Mike Slade was on the committee, along with my friends John and Susan Olsen, and a woman named Dagmar.

"Whatcha got for lunch there, Pastor?" asked Dagmar, as I brought my food in from the office microwave.

"Leftover spinach lasagna and a side salad with Caesar-cilantro dressing," I said.

Dagmar shook her head in disbelief, and both Olsens threw up their hands. Slade just grinned. "Pay up," he said.

"You cheated, you had to have," said John Olsen.

"Hey, I didn't get the dressing," said Slade. A few dollars changed hands.

"You're betting on my lunch?" I asked.

"It's a small town," said John. "And it's winter. At least we aren't drinking ourselves senseless."

"Good point," I said.

~

After lunch I drove up into the hills to the Forest Way compound. It was a different road than the one I took to the trailhead. Two years ago, the Forest Way had quietly purchased and renovated an old summer camp, thus acquiring one of the few large pieces of private land in the area. A gravel drive, now covered in snow, led off the road onto the property.

As I turned in, I notice two prominent signs, one on either side of the drive. Both signs said: "Private Property. No Trespassing." A few yards later, just before a curve in the little road, another sign said: "Trespassers will be prosecuted." At least they seemed friendly.

I rounded the curve and found myself facing a padlocked chain-link gate. There was a sign on this too. It read, "No Admittance." I appreciated the fact that they chose different wording for each sign. It showed they were probably creative and loving people, like Jonestown, only in the North.

I put the car into park directly in front of the closed gate. Beyond it the road curved again. I got out, and opened my trunk to pull out an old pair of snow boots that I kept there during the winter months, along with my sand and a winter survival kit.

With my snow boots on, I scouted into the woods at the edge of the road. The fence didn't go very far, maybe only twenty yards from the drive. It seems it was mostly there just to discourage idle snoopers. Since I was a serious, rather than idle, snooper myself, it didn't seem to apply to me. I floundered through the snow around the end of the fence, and walked back to the road, coming out near the gate, but on the other side of it now.

A few yards later, the road opened up into a parking area next to a large, wooden building. With my expertise in architecture, I would have called it some kind of lodge-type structure. It looked nice, like it had been recently renovated. Several other wooden buildings were in sight, all of a log-cabin type of construction. It was hard to tell because of the depth of the snow, but it looked like the buildings were all connected by shoveled walkways. A large sign curved over the front door of the nearest building. This one had a new theme. It said, "The Forest Way."

I knocked on the door and waited, stamping a little bit to ease the cold. After a moment, the door opened. A startled middle-aged man stared at me from the doorway. He was of slight build and his balding head was cropped short. He wore thick, shapeless, trousers, a large square, cotton shirt that hung below his waist, and a kind of cape or cloak thrown around his shoulders. I thought maybe this was how Afghanis, or maybe Pakistanis, dressed in the wintertime. All his clothes were sort of a drab, cream color. He wore wire glasses and his clothes could not hide the fact that he looked like an Midwestern accountant. For some reason I had expected the Forest Way to be made up of people who looked like hippies. I guess maybe even hippies needed the occasional accountant.

"Who are you?" said the man. "What do you want?"

"My name is Jonah Borden," I said. "I want to see my fiancée, Leyla Bennett."

"Hmm. Well. You aren't supposed to be here," he said. "Didn't you see the signs? How did you get through the gate?"

"Can I come in?" I asked. "I'm getting a little cold out here."

I saw him hesitate, and rather than risk his decision, I stepped boldly past him into the building, stamping the snow off my feet.

"Hey," he said, but he didn't do anything else. After a moment, he sensibly shut the door before it got too cold.

The room I was in was clearly some sort of welcome and reception area. There was a little counter to my right with a glass window that walled off a room with a desk and a telephone and some office equipment. Directly in front of me was a little sitting space with a couch, two chairs and a couple bookshelves. Directly in front of the couch was a large stone fireplace. A blaze crackled, filling the room with a pleasant, wood-smoke smell. A hallway continued away from there. To the left a stairway disappeared. The floors were wooden, with some thin rugs thrown down.

"Hmm. Well. You're lucky I was walking by," said the accountant, puffing up with self-importance. "I don't usually spend time up here, but I just happened to be in the area when you knocked."

"I always feel blessed to meet people such as yourself," I said. It wasn't very pastoral, but I was having an off-day. It didn't matter though, because the man's sarcasm-lobe had apparently been removed. He flushed with pride, which made me feel like pond-scum.

"Hmm. Well, I can see you are a good man," he said. "But we're not really supposed to have visitors. Someone must have left the gate open."

I made a kind of grunt that may have meant "yes," or "no" or "I wish to decline the collision waiver." I can't help it if he seemed to get the idea from it that the gate had indeed been left open.

"I would like to see my fiancée please," I said again. "Her name is Leyla Bennett, and she is staying here."

"Hmm. Well," he said. I could see that expression was going to get on my nerves before long. "I, uh." He stopped. "Hmm," he added.

"I didn't catch your name," I said. "I'm pastor Jonah Borden, from Grand Lake." Mostly it didn't impress anyone when I told them I was a pastor. But every once in a while it helped.

"Hmm. Well. I am called Twig."

"Trygve?" I asked, thinking of the Norwegian name, which wasn't uncommon in the Northland.

"Twig," he said clearly. "We belong to the Forest. We have all taken names from her."

"Right," I said, wishing I had told him I was a lumberjack, not a pastor. "May I please speak with the one who used to call herself Leyla Bennett?"

"Hmm. Well," he said. "I guess you had better wait here."

"I guess so," I said.

After he left, I looked at the books on the shelves. There was a book of weird poems venerating nature and condemning mankind. Another thin book looked like it contained some sort of weird, vague liturgy for worshipping something – nature? Oneness? Peace? I couldn't quite tell.

Another book was titled *The Death of the Masculine Ethos of Wilderness: A Post-Reconstructionist View*. I opened it up. It looked like maybe it was someone's Ph.D. thesis. I bet it was a hot seller in the bookstalls of Paris. It was written by someone named Herman Brown.

I kept thumbing through other books, but the Ph.D. thesis looked to be the most readable and sensible of the entire collection, which wasn't saying much at all. I guess they didn't do much reading in the Forest Way.

A door closed somewhere and I felt a little gust of cold air. A moment later, a medium-sized man walked into the room. He looked about forty. He had thick brown hair, a thick brown beard covering a square, masculine jaw, and deep, warm brown eyes. He exuded charisma and presence. He was dressed, like Twig, in vaguely Middle-Eastern or Indian garb.

"Welcome," he called in a rich baritone. As I stood, he threw his arms open, stepped over to me, and embraced me in a tight bear-hug. After a second, he moved one of his hands to the back of my head and stroked my hair like he was my daddy, and I his little child.

I have to admit, in one way it was nice. His cologne was pleasant and manly, and the head rub felt good; heck, even the hug felt good. But it was all as weird as Scandinavian Lutherans dancing in church on a Tuesday night. I wondered if it would be rude of me to head-butt him in the nose.

At last he released me. "I am Tree," he said, stepping back and speaking in that wonderful warm voice. I could have grown our church to twice its size with a voice like that. I caught myself hoping he would say more.

"I am also Forest," he added. "But you may call me 'Tree.'"

"Tree Forest?" I asked.

He nodded, smiling his warm smile.

"I am Jonah," I said, shaking off a little cloud of bemusement. "But you may call me Pastor Borden." It was rude and uncalled for, but I was having that kind of day, so I decided not to buck the trend.

"Okay, Pastor Borden," said Tree laughing, as if my rudeness had never appeared. His laugh was low and deep. I decided I might hate him. We both sat down on the chairs in the little sitting area.

"Twig says you are here about someone you know, someone who has joined our little community?"

"Twig says right. I would like to speak with my fiancée, Leyla Bennett. I believe she is new here."

Tree shook his head, as if gently correcting an errant child. "She is not *yours*, Pastor Borden. No one can own anyone else." He paused. "Or any*thing* else. We can only enjoy the moment we have in the company of another human being, or tree, or animal."

"So, if you don't own this," I said, waving my hand at the room around me, "you won't mind if I look around until I find Leyla?"

The briefest flicker of annoyance touched his eyes and disappeared. Perhaps he was a human being after all. "I cannot allow that, Pastor Borden," he said. "The one you call Leyla is an Initiate. During this introductory period, it is best that she avoid all contact with her former life." He smiled his warm, engaging smile at me. I realized I was starting to smile back, and I frowned instead. "Your friend has been given a new name," he told me. "She is now known as Amaryllis."

"I kind of liked Leyla," I said.

"You must learn to give up control," said Tree. "Surely, as a clergyman, you know that the key to peace is relinquishment."

"That's true, in a way," I said, "but relinquishment to Whom?"

Tree just smiled. "You will learn, eventually. We all do."

I realized we were no longer talking about when I was going to see Leyla. "Tell you what," I said. "How about you relinquish your control over Leyla's initiation period, and let me talk with her?"

He smiled again, gently. "I have told you, Pastor Borden, there is no longer anyone here by the name of Leyla."

"Then let me see —" I paused. "What did you say her name was now?"

"Amaryllis."

"So let me see her."

He shook his head. "I do not think it would be wise at this point."

"Give up control," I said. "Relinquishment is the key to peace." I smiled with beatific satisfaction and said, "Practice what you preach."

Once more there was a faint but ephemeral flicker of irritation behind those deep, brown eyes. Immediately, Tree smothered it with a smile. "You are young, Pastor Borden. Eventually you will learn."

"I would guess I am about five years younger than you," I said to him. "But I think I have already learned enough about this place."

Tree waited, his hands folded quietly in his lap, looking at me with his intense, warm gaze. It was hard to stay angry at him.

"Look," I said. "I am not here to make trouble for you. We live in a pluralistic society. You have your beliefs, and I have mine. I accept that, and I'm not here to change you. I just want to see Leyla."

"And yet, you do not accept that someone close to you also shares my beliefs."

I opened my mouth, and then snapped it shut. I had almost blurted out that Leyla certainly did not share those beliefs. But if I said that, her cover would be blown. It could even get ugly if Tree knew she was a reporter. I certainly didn't want to endanger Leyla in any way.

"It would help me accept it, if you would allow me to speak with her," I said at last.

Tree leaned back and made his fingers into a steeple. "The Forest Way is all about opening up like a new plant, relinquishing and growing with nature and with each other. We are one. In the beginning, a new initiate is very much like a young sapling. She needs to be sheltered, nurtured, guarded from the elements until she takes root and grows strong. Seeing you right now would be like uprooting a little tree."

I wanted to uproot his face. But I decided it wasn't something a good pastor would do.

Tree leaned forward, gazing at me with those deep, deep eyes. "Why don't you join us, Pastor Borden? See what the love and joy is all about? After your own initiation period, you could see Leyla again. You could share in her love, like we all share in each other's love, but you would no longer feel the need to possess another."

The intensity was startling. For a moment, all I could see was his eyes. I hardly heard what he was saying; it was just that his voice was so wonderful to listen to. He kept on talking and I kept on listening. At last, he stopped. With an effort, I shook myself mentally. "If you don't possess her, why can't I see her?" I asked.

He sighed and leaned back again. "I have tried," he said.

"I have not yet begun to try," I said, my head clearing rapidly. "I have friends in law enforcement. Unless you allow me to see Leyla, things are going to get very uncomfortable for you."

Tree looked down at his lap, as if considering something. I noticed that there were two men standing at the edge of the room, just outside the hallway that led to the back of the lodge. I didn't remember seeing them arrive. Finally, he looked up.

"I will allow you to see her," he said. "But not today."

"Today," I said.

"Two days," said Tree firmly. "If I get any calls from the police, I will inform them that you already have an appointment to see her." He twisted and nodded at the two men standing near the hallway. "My friends heard me make the appointment, and they will corroborate the story. Besides that, I am certain you would not lie to the police. Come back in two days." He nodded at the men again and they walked forward and stood in front of me, a little closer than was socially acceptable.

"Please make sure that Pastor Borden gets safely to his car," said Tree. He stood, and without another word or glance, left the room.

I looked up at the two men. I have a certain amount of experience in martial arts, including a black belt and, unfortunately, two or three fights where my life was on the line. I could have taken them down, maybe. Then again, maybe not – nothing in life is certain. But taking them down would not show me where Leyla was.

The shorter of the two men saw me considering the situation. He was wearing a winter Parka over that same, vaguely Indian clothing. He looked about forty years old, with thick, black hair, a dark five o' clock shadow on his cheeks and startling, cold, blue eyes. He was maybe five-nine and heavy in a muscular kind of way. He pulled his parka back to show me a gun in a shoulder holster.

I nodded, and stood up. "I appreciate the input," I said. He nodded back at me. They accompanied me all the way back to my car and watched with tender solicitude as I drove off through the darkening winter afternoon.

CHAPTER TEN

Alex Chan and I were in Jensen's office for a war meeting. As chief of Police, Jensen had an office that boasted a view of the lake, if you pushed a chair into a corner, stood on it, and craned your neck. Other than the view, the room boasted a desk, phone, computer, two chairs and three steel filing cabinets. The privileges of rank.

"First things first," I said. "Why don't I get us some coffee?"

"I'm the chief," said Jensen. "I've got people for that." He pushed a few buttons on the phone, and another voice echoed from the speaker.

"Yeah?"

"Hey Sorenson, bring us three coffees. One black, one with two creams, no sugar and —" he broke off and looked at Chan.

"None for me," said Chan. "We Orientals drink tea."

"Yeah, but only when it's iced and packed with sugar," I said.

"Make it two coffees and an iced tea," Jensen said to the speaker.

There was a slight pause. "What do you think this is, room service?" said Sorenson's voice, dripping with acid. The connection ended. There was a brief, embarrassed silence.

"Hard to find good help these days," said Chan.

Jensen punched the phone again, with a little more force than necessary. This time he didn't put it on speaker, but spoke quietly and forcefully into the handset.

Chan craned his neck to see the lake. I carefully examined a commendation that Jensen had hanging on his wall. After a minute, the chief hung up.

"Be just a minute," he said, like nothing had happened. He looked at Chan. "No offense, but you're a lawyer. I kind of think of you as the opposition."

"Come on, Dan," I said, "Alex is a good guy."

"No, it's all right, Jonah," said Alex. "I am committed first to upholding the law. After that, my next commitment is to the best interests of my client. Justice only comes third, and doesn't always help my client. If I can get my client off the hook, while still upholding the letter of the law, I do it, even if he's guilty. That means sometimes I work at cross-purposes with the police."

Jensen grunted. "At least you're honest."

"I wouldn't get carried away," said Chan with a smile.

"Who's your client here?" asked Jensen.

"Jonah," said Alex promptly.

Jensen thought for a minute. "I guess that makes it all right with me, then. I just don't want you suddenly suing one of us on behalf of the Forest Way."

"Not going to happen," said Alex.

The chief considered this for a bit longer. "Okay then, Jonah, why don't you get us up to speed?"

"Okay," I said. "I told you both on the phone yesterday that I tried to see Leyla, and they wouldn't let me – not until tomorrow. You both told me that the best thing was to wait until then. But I want some kind of game plan for going in. I think we need to take her out of there right then, if she won't come."

"Why wouldn't she come?" asked Chan.

"This cult leader is crazy good at influencing people. If I had his voice or charisma, I could double the size of Harbor Lutheran."

"You might be able to double the size of Harbor Lutheran if you had *any* voice or charisma," muttered Chan.

"Nice," said Jensen. Chan shot him a grin.

"Thanks guys," I said. "It's nice to know I'm supported." Actually, I knew that the reason they were joking around was precisely because this was such a big deal. In a twisted, macho way, it was their way of saying they felt bad, and that they had my back.

"Anyway," I said, "I've been doing some reading. Cults often deprive people of foods that help the brain function normally. Sometimes they drug the food that is given to members. They engage in group exercises and hypnosis and all kinds of activities to break down mental resistance. I don't know if Leyla is herself or not."

There was an awkward, serious silence.

"I say, let's just go in and when she comes to talk with you, we just take her," said Jensen. "I'll go with you. They won't call the cops, because I *am* the cops. Besides, what's one member to them? It will be an easy choice for them to just let her go with us."

"Thanks, Dan," I said. I felt a slight lessening of the tension that had been with me for twenty-four hours.

There was a knock at the door and an officer appeared, holding two cups of coffee and a bottle of iced-tea. His face looked a little sour. The name-plate on his uniform read "Sorenson."

"Here you go, Chief," he said neutrally, handing the drinks out. Without a word he turned and left.

"Any problems with Dan's plan?" I asked Alex.

"Well, *I* won't sue you," said Alex. "But that won't stop another attorney from representing Forest Way in a suit if they feel some kind of damage has been done."

"We aren't going to shoot up the place, Chan," said Jensen. "We're just going to get Leyla and go home."

"You asked if there were any potential issues," said Alex.

"*He* did," said Jensen, jerking his thumb at me.

"Do we need a warrant?" I asked.

Jensen shook his head. "We won't get one."

"I agree," said Chan. "No judge is going to issue any kind of warrant based on what we have. We go as private citizens."

"That means Dan can't use his authority."

"No, but if they get difficult, I can bully and bluff them a little. A lot of folks don't know the limits placed on the police. A bunch of weak-minded tree-huggers won't give us any crap." Jensen turned and looked at Alex. "If you ever bring that up, I will deny I ever said such a thing."

Chan spread his hands, looking innocent. "Hey, I didn't say anything."

"I don't know what to think, Dan," I said. "One guy I met was definitely a little soft around the frontal lobe, but the leader, and two other guys I met, seemed like people to be reckoned with. One of them was carrying a gun."

Jensen frowned. "You still couldn't get a warrant," said Chan. "It's not illegal to own a gun, and not illegal to carry it on private property."

"I don't like it," said Jensen. "It makes me think of the Branch Davidians, down in Waco Texas. They had guns too."

"So let's get Leyla out of there," I said.

They both nodded. "I think we all agree on that," said Chan. "Let's just do this."

~

"Friendly bunch," said Jensen, looking at all the "no trespassing" signs as we drove down the Forest Way entry road.

"At least they left the gate open for us," I said as we drove through it.

As we drove up, the front door of the main lodge opened, and two people in winter parkas came and stood outside. They looked like the same two men who had escorted me off the premises, two days ago.

As Jensen and Alex Chan got out of the car with me, the shorter man with dark hair and the five 'o clock shadow frowned. "Who are these people?" he asked.

"My friends," I said. "They are here for moral support."

"We didn't invite your friends."

"It doesn't matter who you invited," said Jensen. "We're here."

He walked toward the door. The dark haired man moved to step in his way. Jensen is a pretty big man, with ice-blue eyes that could out-stare a dead fish. He let the shorter man have the benefit of that stare for a minute. "I wouldn't," he said in a neutral tone of voice.

The dark-haired man thought about it. "We'll let Brown, uh, Tree, sort it out," he said.

We all traipsed into the lobby area of the lodge, stamping our boots to clear most of the snow. Five o' clock Shadow moved quickly to where Tree waited in one of the chairs. He stood and they had a hurried conversation. We waited. After exchanging more words with the shorter man, Tree strode over to us. "Hello Jonah," he boomed, and threw his arms open and hugged me like he had before, ending with the head rub.

"Hello, Tree," I said, fighting not to be calmed by that remarkable voice. "This is Dan Jensen, and Alex Chan."

"Welcome!" cried Tree, and flung his arms around Chan, rubbing his head also. When he stepped back, Alex's carefully styled hair stood out slightly on one side.

"Dan!" said the great voice, throbbing with vibrancy and passion. He embraced a shocked Jensen, who stood like a two-by-four until it was over.

We all stood there, feeling a little foolish, except Tree, who seemed perfectly at ease.

"What can I do for you, my friends?" asked Tree, gazing intently at each of us.

"We are interested in the welfare of Leyla Bennett," said Jensen. Chan nodded. His eyes still looked a little dazed after the hug.

"I see," said Tree. "Well, I promised Jonah he could see the one you call Leyla today. But I didn't promise that to anyone else." He nodded at the departing back of the man with the five 'o clock shadow. "Rock has gone to set up the meeting place. In a minute, I will take Pastor Borden to see Amaryllis. You two will wait here with Birch and Chestnut."

Birch was apparently the man who had been with Rock earlier. Chestnut was a short, wide man who strode into the room and leaned against a wall near the bookcase. The wall looked flimsy next to him. As before, everyone was dressed in that vaguely Indian or Pakistani style.

Jensen looked at me. His eyes were troubled. "We want to go with him," he said.

Tree placed a strong brown hand on Jensen's shoulder. Jensen looked at the hand, but Tree didn't appear to notice, and left it there. "I understand you are troubled, my friend. I assure you, your mind will be put at ease before you go." He squeezed Jensen's shoulder and smiled, and then turned to me. "Come, Jonah. They should be ready soon."

Tree led me down a passageway toward the back of the lodge. We passed through a sitting area with patio windows. In the summer, there might have been a patio outside the windows, but now it was only snow. Next to the sitting area, one of the glass doors opened onto a walkway that had been cleared. Tree opened the door, and ushered me back into the cold. We walked between high snow banks to another building. It was built of logs and looked recently renovated, but it was smaller than the main lodge. We stamped off our boots in a small foyer, and then passed through into a plain hallway that apparently ran the length of the building. Tree guided me to the left and paused before the first door on the left. He put his hand on my arm.

"We need to go over some ground-rules," he said.

I didn't like the sound of that.

"First," he said, "you must not touch her."

"Are you crazy?" I said. "I love Leyla. She's my fiancée. I haven't seen her in a week. Of course I'm going to give her a hug."

"No touching," said Tree, like a firm parent. "We're doing this as a courtesy to you. We don't have to do it at all."

"What are you saying?"

"I am saying these rules are not negotiable. You can agree to them, or you can leave right now."

"What happened to all that warmth and love?" I asked.

Tree smiled gently. But to me, at last, it looked completely fake. Even so, his words were spoken in a kind tone. "In time, you will understand, and even accept. But for now, these are my rules."

I took a breath through my nose, and let it out slowly through my lips. "Okay," what else?"

"I will be in the room with you."

"This is a private meeting."

"I'm sorry, Jonah," he said. "It is not." I started wondering when he began to call me Jonah. I thought I had told him to call me Pastor Borden. I was less tempted to like him now than ever before.

"I will be there to make sure you do not break your word about not touching, and that you don't lie. I am here to protect Leyla."

I felt a sudden rush of blood and pure rage pouring into my brain. For a moment, I think I actually wanted to kill him. I didn't say anything, but Tree abruptly stepped away from me and then put his hand on the doorknob. It looked to me like something in my expression had scared him. Good.

"So do you agree?" he asked.

I didn't really have a choice. I had to see Leyla. And I doubted they'd stop us if we just got up and walked out. Holding Leyla against her will would be kidnapping, after all, and I didn't think they would do that unless they kidnapped me too, and I'm sure they knew I would be problematic for them, not to mention that the chief of police was sitting in their reception area. Rules or not, Leyla and I would walk out of there to freedom in just a matter of minutes.

"Okay," I said.

The room was plain, with painted white walls and gray industrial carpet. There was a wide table in the middle with two chairs on opposite sides. One wall held a mirror. That was it.

"Sit down, Jonah," said Tree, gesturing at the table and chairs. I chose the chair that faced the door. Tree stepped back out into the corridor for a moment, and then came back in. A few seconds later, Leyla came through the door.

She wore the same Indian-style pants and top that everyone seemed to have. She had no makeup on, and her hair lacked its normal shine, and looked a little disheveled. There were circles under her eyes, and her eyes themselves looked red and dull.

She was the most beautiful thing I'd ever seen.

"Leyla!" I almost yelled. I stood up. Her eyes flickered and she took a half step toward me. But Tree took her arm, raised his other hand palm up towards me, and seated Leyla in the chair opposite mine. I subsided back into my own chair.

"Hands on the table," said Tree. Leyla glanced at the mirror on the wall, and then obediently placed her hands on the table. So did I. The table was too long for us to touch fingers.

"Leyla," I said, trying to ignore Tree, "it's time to come home."

She opened her mouth to speak, but no sound seemed to come. She cleared her throat and spoke in a voice that was hardly more than a whisper. "I can't, Jonah." She wasn't looking at me.

Tree cleared his own throat, as some people do sympathetically when a speaker has a problem.

"No, Jonah," said Leyla in a louder voice. "I belong here now." She still didn't look at me.

I was struck by a sense of unreality. I couldn't have heard her right. For a moment I didn't know what to say, and there was perfect silence in the little room. After a few seconds, I found some words again. I put out my hand toward her.

"They won't stop us, Leyla. Let's just go now. We'll walk right out of here."

Her face contorted as if in some kind of painful spasm. Then she smoothed it out again. Tears began to roll out of her eyes.

"No, Jonah," she said. She looked at the mirror, and the wall, but not at me.

"Leyla," I said. "This is getting serious. Trust me. Listen, remember what we talked about before you came here. I've learned some things. You really need to come with me right now."

"No, Jonah," she said. "I belong here now." She started to cry in earnest. She looked up at the mirror, still avoiding my eyes, and whispered, "I hate you." Her weeping got harder.

I caught her eye in the mirror. "What did you say?" I asked.

Suddenly she whirled to me, and pushed her chair back. Tears were flowing freely down her cheeks. But she met my eyes for the first time. Finally I could see there was life there, intensity. She said, looking directly at me, crying all the time: "I hate you Jonah Borden. Do you understand me? I *hate* you. I don't want you to rescue me. I hate you, Jonah." Her voice rose to a scream. "I hate you!" she collapsed on the table sobbing uncontrollably. "I hate you, she murmured once more through the sobs.

Tree stepped forward and took her elbow. "I think that's enough of this," he said, and Leyla obediently stood, still weeping uncontrollably, and went to the door. It opened, and the man whom

Tree had called "Rock" was there. He took her by the arm, and led her outside into the hallway.

I stood up, stunned, staring sightlessly at the mirror for almost an entire minute. Finally, Tree came toward me. "Come, Jonah. I realize that this must be hard for you." He put his hand on my right elbow.

I twisted to my right, flinging off his hand, and with all the force of my turning body, I smashed the heel of my left hand into his nose. I felt a distinct crunch as it broke. Later, I might look at it differently, but at the time it seemed to be the most satisfying feeling in the world.

He staggered back, crashing into the wall and sliding down hard onto his rear-end. Bright blood spurted out of his face. I took one step toward him and lifted my right foot to smash his face into pulp while he sat there, and then the door crashed open and Rock was there, a big chrome revolver leveled at my chest. His eyes widened as I swiveled in mid-kick, but his mind couldn't seem to register that I wasn't going to stop. My right foot caught his hand, and sent the gun flying. I followed my right foot, stepping down, and spinning all the way around, I smashed my left elbow into the side of his head.

And then suddenly there were two more men in the room. One of them was built like a mountain, and he bull-rushed me, pushing me up against the wall with his forearm on my neck. I slammed my shin into his groin as hard as I could, and he slowly slid off me onto his knees and began to retch. But the other man stood back out of range, two hands on his gun, which was pointed at my chest. He looked like he knew what he was doing. Out of the corner of my eye, I could see a flicker of light from the mirror.

We stood like that for what seemed like a long time, the gunman staring at me unwinking, while I stared back, unmoving. Various groans issued from the three men on the floor.

"Don't shoot him, don't hurt him," Rock croaked at last from the floor where he lay. He slowly got to his feet and braced himself with his hands on the table. He shook his head, as if to clear it. He looked at me and shook his head again and swore. He looked like he wanted to say something to me, but after a moment he just said, "Take him back to the lodge and make sure all of them leave. Don't hurt them."

Slowly the other man I had kicked stood up. It seemed like he was getting up for a long time, partly because he was still recovering from the kick, but also because there was so much of him to get off the floor. He was about six-foot five, and built like an NFL defensive end. The look he gave me was not kind.

"Easy," said Rock. "Just make sure he leaves."

The man with the gun jerked his head at me, and he and his massive friend fell in behind.

I looked at Tree as I left the room. He had covered his face with his hands, blood staining his fingers, and he rocked back and forth in pain. I didn't know what to say, so I turned and left.

When I stepped out the door, I almost ran into the little, balding man named Twig in the hallway.

"Hmm," he said. "Well."

"Out of the way, Twig," said the gunman from behind me. He said the little man's name like it was an insult.

"Hmm. Well, OK, sorry," mumbled Twig, and scooted out of the way, following us with his eyes as the other two hustled me outside, and along the path to the main lodge. One of them still had his gun leveled at me.

"There's a cop in the lodge," said the other one, the one built like a mountain. "Better put that away."

"I don't want him pulling that karate crap on us," said the gunman.

"Make him go ahead," said the big guy.

The gunman spoke to me. "Hey preacher, listen up." We all stopped.

"What?" I asked.

"We'd just as soon waste you, but we don't want to clean up your brains," said the cultist holding the gun. "Cliff, here doesn't like to get blood on his clothes."

"Cliff as in the name, or as in the steep part of a mountain?" I asked. "Because it's confusing with all these Forest names."

"Shut up," said Cliff.

"Good point," I said. "So you don't want to shoot me. What then?"

"So, you walk ahead of us and play nice. Look ahead, and don't turn around. You turn around, we'll shoot you and let one of these soft-headed granolas clean it up, maybe even your girlfriend. You just go on, get your friends and go home. You try anything else, we'll waste your friends too. Do it in front of your girlfriend."

At the mention of Leyla, I almost lost it again. But I pulled it together and took a deep breath.

"Okay," I said.

"Walk," said the gunman.

I walked. After I had taken three or four steps, I could hear the crunch of their footsteps through the snow as they followed me again. I didn't turn and look.

We went into the main lodge without incident. For a brief moment I considered trying something while I was inside and they were not, but I remembered Birch and Chestnut waiting with Dan and Alex. We couldn't take them all on, not the three of us.

I came out of the hallway into the foyer and walked to where Jensen and Alex were sitting in front of the fire.

"Let's go," I said.

"Where's Leyla?" asked Jensen.

"Tell you in the car," I said.

"We're leaving without her?" asked Alex.

Birch and Chestnut were consulting with the other two who had followed me back.

"We don't have any choice," I said.

"Go back in there," said Alex. "Let's get Leyla, and then we can go."

Jensen was looking at the four men who had turned toward us and spread out just a little bit. They didn't say anything.

"Jonah's right," he said. "It's time to go now."

Chan tried to protest again.

"Shut up, Alex," said Dan. "Let's go."

They got up and we walked out the door to my car. I pulled the keys from my pocket and tossed them to Jensen. "You drive," I said. I got into the passenger seat.

The others got in, and Jensen started the car. As we pulled out of the driveway, my hands began to shake uncontrollably.

CHAPTER ELEVEN

Jensen drove a hundred yards down the main road, and pulled over, tight against the high snow bank that had been formed by the plows on the shoulder of the road.

"What happened?" he asked.

I shook my head and took a few deep breaths. I looked into the dirty gray snow bank.

"Take your time," he said.

"Leyla -" Another breath. "Leyla said she wanted to stay."

There was silence in the car.

"What about those guys?" asked Jensen. "They looked ready for a fight."

I shook my head again. Breathed for a little bit. "I don't know what they have done to her. She said – she said something hurtful. After she left I was pretty upset. Tree came over like he was going to give me comfort."

They waited in silence.

"I broke Tree's nose, and roughed up that other guy, the one they call Rock. The two that you saw came in. I put the big one down and then the other one pulled a gun and stopped me. I think they were worried I'd go ballistic again."

Jensen swore softly.

"Was she drugged?" asked Chan suddenly from the back seat.

"What?"

"Do you think they drugged her up for your interview, made her say what she said?"

Sudden hope flashed into my mind. But when I thought back to the encounter with Leyla, hope faded.

"No," I said after a while. "She seemed maybe sad, and definitely upset, but I don't think she was under the influence of anything. I mean, I could tell something was wrong, but it wasn't that."

"Are you sure?" asked Jensen.

"Dan, I'm a pastor in Grand Lake, and I'm the police chaplain. You know that I know what drunk looks like, what high looks like."

"Yeah, I guess you're right," he said reluctantly.

"But *shouldn't* she have been under the influence?" asked Chan.

"What do you mean?"

"I mean, our theory is, this cult does a little bit of brainwashing. If Leyla was brainwashed, she should have seemed – I don't know, different, zoned out, not all there like she used to be."

"She didn't seem like that either. She seemed like herself, but very upset."

"Is Alex right?" asked Jensen. "Do cultists come across that way?"

"I don't have much experience with active cult members," I said. "I've helped some folks deal with fallout after they leave a cult, but I've never had much contact with anyone who is actually in a cult while I'm with them."

"Could she have been warning you off?" asked Alex. "I mean, like she still wanted to pursue her investigative report?"

Hope blossomed and died again, all in a second. "I want that to be true, but it didn't seem like that either. I mean I think there are a lot of other ways she could have done that. And I told her pretty clearly that I wanted her to come home now. I think she would have trusted me."

There was silence.

"So what do we do?" asked Jensen.

"We can't really accuse them of wrongful imprisonment, if they let you see Leyla and she told you she was fine," said Alex.

"She didn't exactly say that. But she said she didn't want to come back with me, and I wasn't supposed to try to get her out."

Jensen grunted. "This isn't right."

"Agreed," said Alex. "But we aren't going to figure it out right here. And from what Jonah said, if we try to bust back in there right now, they'll be ready for us. Besides, you'd want someone other than just me to back you up, if we're talking physical confrontation. Let's go on home and give this some thought."

We drove back to town, to the police station, where Alex and Dan had their cars. I got out to move to the driver's side. Alex and Jensen kind of hung around.

"You'd be welcome to come over for some dinner, if you like," said Jensen to me. "I'm sure Janie wouldn't mind."

"Or, we could hang out," said Alex.

I looked at him, surprised.

"You know, like we could order pizza and play video games," he said after a moment.

"Thanks guys," I said. I meant it. "I think I'd like both of those things, but maybe not quite yet. I've got a lot to think about."

"Don't think too much," said Jensen. "Sometimes it's all right to just forget about it all for a little bit."

"Okay," I said. "I'll catch you guys later. Thanks again, for everything."

~

The snow began to fall as I turned out of the parking lot. As I headed south out of town, the great tilted mass of the snow covered ridges fell from my right toward the ice-bound shore on my left. The scene was filled with flying snow, dark lonely pines and indomitable basalt rock. And always, off to the left, farther away now because of the ice, heaved the massive bulk of Superior, gray and torpid under the darkening sky. It was a wild, brutal kind of beauty. I looked at it, and somewhere inside of me, I knew that come what may, all would be well. It wasn't a feeling. It wasn't based on my desperate wish for everything to turn out the way I wanted. But it was a certainty that I was immovably fixed in the love of the Creator of all of this rugged stunning landscape. *Faith is the reality of things hoped for, the conviction of things not seen.*

Minnesota's North Shore – which is what they call the Lake Superior Coastline – is, as I have said, a place of remote, unyielding beauty. As prosaic as ethnic Scandinavians usually are, even they have noticed this, and so there are occasional turn-outs and lookouts along highway sixty-one, which runs the length of the Shore. Just south of Grand Lake, the road climbs over a wave of land. At the top, is one such lookout. I pulled off into it and gazed across the ice toward the water pushing sullenly at its white chains.

I breathed in a little bit. Then I breathed out. I drank in the beauty and loneliness around me. I felt like maybe I should cry, but I couldn't seem to. If someone in my situation had come to me for pastoral counseling, I probably would have encouraged crying. I prayed. At least I still had that. Finally, I drove home.

The snow was beginning to clog up the road a little bit by the time I pulled into my garage. Another snowy night at home in my cabin, high above the lake. Another night alone. Alone wasn't bad before I met Leyla. It still wasn't entirely bad. But now, without her, it didn't feel quite right. It was missing some ingredient.

I thought about her, and the interview. I thought about the feeling when Tree's nose broke under my hand. I winced. And then I realized I had a phone call to make.

I stamped the snow off my boots, and put on my slippers. Going into the living room, I stoked up the fire. I made a pot of coffee, and filling my mug, went into my office, and sat down. I looked up a number, and punched it into my phone.

"This is Brad," said my handset. Brad Michaels was a member of my ministry association. We weren't authoritarian; we weren't even technically a denomination. We were just a group of pastors and churches, mostly Lutheran, who were committed to encouraging each other in faith, and staying in relationship with each other.

"Hi, Brad, this is Jonah," I said.

"Jonah!" said Michaels. "Good to hear your voice."

"You still the champion at Wii Frisbee golf?" I asked.

"You'd better believe it," he said.

We chatted a bit more, and then he said, "Well Jonah, what can I do for you?"

"You can listen to me, you can pray for me, and you can give me some counsel, if you have any."

"Sounds pretty much like what we do all the time," said Michaels.

"Yeah. But this time is pretty rough."

"What's up?"

I took a breath. "You know we've talked about my gift for martial arts. About what I've had to do sometimes."

"Yeah?"

"Today I did something with it that I didn't *have* to do."

"What do you mean?"

"I attacked someone. It wasn't self-defense. It wasn't to protect someone else. It was because I was angry."

"Did you..."

"I didn't kill anyone," I said, knowing what was on his mind. "I broke one guy's nose, and knocked another guy senseless for a minute."

"Wow," said Michaels.

"I guess I kicked a third guy in the family jewels, too," I added. "Anyway, I'm wondering if maybe I should, I don't know, step down from ministry or something, or get help of some kind."

"Why don't you tell me more about what happened?" said Brad.

So I told him. When I was done, he was quiet for a little bit. Then he spoke. "There's a lot going on there, Jonah. Let's break it down. First, I can tell even over the phone that you know what you did, even in those circumstances, was wrong; I can even tell you that feel remorseful about it. Am I right?"

"Of course it was wrong," I said. "That's why I'm calling you. I let my emotions control me, I gave in to rage and I physically hurt three people."

"Okay, well we agree on that. But we also agree on something else. As your brother pastor, I know we agree that even *that* sin was dealt with, by Jesus on the cross."

I was quiet for a bit. "Thank you," I said at last.

"Thank *Him*," he said. "Now, as far as you stepping down. I don't have the authority to make you do that, of course. But even if I did, I wouldn't recommend it, not now at any rate. You aren't hiding it; you are trying to deal with it openly. If it becomes a problem for your congregation, I'd be happy to visit with them about it." There was a pause. "This is not an excuse Jonah, but I have to say, you were exposed to extreme pressure in a highly unusual situation. I guess what I mean is, though what you did was wrong, I'm not certain that your actions today are a symptom of some deep unresolved inner problem. If you think you need counseling, by all means, get some. But I don't think this automatically means that."

"Okay," I said. "I appreciate your thoughts, Brad. On a different subject, do you know anything about the Forest Way?"

"I think I've seen some of their people in the Twin Cities, selling tea and wild blueberry jam at the mall," he said, "but I don't know anything about them. I'll tell you who might know, though. I have a buddy I went to college with, who has become some kind of expert on cults."

"Can you get me his name and contact info?" I asked.

"Sure thing, Jonah. I'll email it to you as soon as we hang up here."

We said a prayer together over the phone, and then broke the connection.

CHAPTER TWELVE

I got another mug of coffee, and went over to my stereo to put on some tunes. I paused. Somehow, even music right now seemed too shallow, too frivolous. I went into the kitchen, but I realized I wasn't really hungry. In fact, I felt kind of sick to my stomach. I sipped some coffee. Praise the Lord, that still tasted good. I drank some more and sat on my couch.

My mind played the interview with Leyla over and over again. I had no insight. I felt no better for the endless gnawing of my thoughts. At last I got up and walked over to the shelf by my television and considered my meager movie collection. *Cast Away* is a great show, but it was too close to home just then. Likewise some of the other dramas. My eyes fell on *Sky High* and I smiled. *Sky High* is about a High School of teenage superheroes – and their sidekicks. It was offbeat, funny and had no theme that remotely connected with my life right now. I slipped it into the DVD player, and went back to the kitchen while the disc loaded. Rooting around in my cupboard, I found some brandy. I made a cup of hot cocoa, dumped a generous splash of brandy into it, and settled down for the show.

Halfway through the movie, I paused it and made popcorn. I had two more brandy-laced hot cocoas. Slowly, I began to relax and forget about Leyla for a little while. After the credits rolled and the screen went dark, I sat in front of the fire, feeling mellow, thinking about nothing.

I thought I heard the faint sound of a snow machine. A minute later, there was a knock at my door.

I live up on a ridge that overlooks Lake Superior. I'm three or four miles from town, and not very close to any major highway. Mostly, when people came to see me, they called ahead to make sure I was home. I wasn't on anyone's way to anywhere. The point is, if visitors are coming, I usually know about it beforehand. In addition to all that, it was eleven o' clock at night.

I flipped on the outside light, and looked through the window at the side of the door. There were two women standing on the stoop. I could see that the snow was still coming down thickly. Several inches had accumulated since I got home.

I glanced around and didn't see anyone else. Most times, in a small town or rural area in Minnesota, it was silly to even lock your doors. Most times, of course, you hadn't beaten up three cult members of a group that carried guns.

I opened the door. One of the women had long, braided, dark-red hair, and was only wearing a polar fleece, sweater and jeans, which was grossly inadequate at that time of year. The other woman was blond. She had on a heavy, green parka, but on her legs were only black hose and high-heeled shoes. She had a big purse, almost like a shoulder bag, clutched to her chest.

"Can we come in?" asked the woman in the polar fleece. "We have kind of an emergency here."

I stepped back and motioned them inside. "Come on in."

The red-haired woman took the other's arm and led her inside. The blond woman in the parka and hose was shivering. Her lips looked bluish. I shut the door.

"I'm Daisy Painter," said the redhead, sticking out her hand in a business-like way. I'm with the Minnesota Department of Natural Resources."

I shook her hand. "Jonah Borden." The blond stood shivering and saying nothing.

"What can I do for you?" I asked.

"I was out doing my final check tonight, and I found this woman stranded in a car. She says her name is Heidi. She's hypothermic. We have to get her warm right away. Do you have a bathtub?"

I glanced from Daisy Painter to the blond named Heidi. It was a thick blizzard out there, no question. But who would be up in the hills at this hour, dressed in hose and high heels?

This was all very unusual. "I'm sorry, where did you say you found her?"

The woman called Heidi never stopped shivering. "I was going to a party. I sl-slid into the snow bank, and then my c-car wouldn't start." Her words were not only stuttered, but slightly slurred. "There's n-no cell service out here."

"Yours was the closest house I could find," said Daisy. She shook her head. "Look, we don't have time for this right now. We have to get her into a warm bath right away, or she's in serious trouble."

I was inclined to agree. Blue lips, slurred speech and uncontrollable shivering were all signs of hypothermia. If Heidi didn't get warmed up soon, her life could be in jeopardy. "Okay," I said. I led them down the hall to the guest bath. The redhead turned on the water in the bathtub immediately, and then turned to me. "I have to get her in the tub, get her warm. Do you have any clothes she could borrow?"

"Okay," I said.

I showed her the towels, and then left, closing the door behind me. I got out some shirts, and sweats and wool socks, and brought them to the door of the bathroom and knocked. Daisy answered, and I handed her the clothes. She took them, leaving the door ajar and put them on the counter next to the sink. In the mirror, I caught a glimpse of Heidi's naked body as she stood in the bathtub. I quickly averted my eyes. Daisy seemed not to notice, and she continued to stand in a position that allowed me to see Heidi in the mirror. I resisted the temptation to keep looking, but I didn't easily forget my involuntary glimpse. Heidi was a very shapely woman.

"Give me her wet clothes," I said, forcing myself to look only at Daisy. "I'll put them in the dryer." Only after I turned away did Daisy think to shut the door.

I was holding a little black dress, and some other, more private, garments that I thought it would be unhelpful to think about. In any case, these were definitely not the clothes to wear outside in the Minnesota winter. I took it all to my clothes-dryer and threw it in.

I went into the kitchen and made coffee. After a minute, the redhead, Daisy, came out. "I think maybe she's going to be okay. Thank you so much for helping her."

"No problem," I said. "What was I going to do, let her freeze to death?" I pointed to my mug. "Coffee?"

"Yes please," said Daisy. I handed her a fresh mug, and looked at her more carefully. She looked to be about forty, with striking green eyes to go with her hair. She was short, and a little stocky. She had freckles on her face, and a pleasant, down-to-earth attractiveness.

"What were you doing out there without a coat?" I asked.

"The parka is mine," she said. "This girl, Heidi, is the one with no coat. I found her about a hundred yards from the car, walking down the road in that ridiculous outfit. I gave her my coat, got her on my snow machine, and brought her to the first place I found. I'm glad you had your lights on. Do you mind if I see what the snow is doing out there?"

"Sure," I said. I went into the great-room, and raised the blinds, and snapped on the outside lights so she could see how hard the snow was coming down.

"Still coming thick and fast," she said.

"Sure is," I said, sipping some coffee. "So, you're with the DNR?"

Daisy nodded. "We're doing a nocturnal winter wildlife study right now, and I was out on the snow machine, checking my stations. I was just heading back when I came across her."

"Well, you did a good thing. With no heat, she was in big trouble, in or out of the car."

She nodded again, sipping her coffee and staring out at the falling snow.

"So what do we do now?" I asked.

"I'm sorry," said Daisy," but that's up to you." She walked over and turned off the outside lights, and then went back into the kitchen and put her mug in the sink. "I need to take the snow-machine back to the station, and record my results, and I'd better get my car out of there before I'm snowed in. I was hoping you could take care of Heidi from here. She's out of danger. Just give her some more time to warm up, and then you can do whatever you want with her." She laughed suddenly, as if she was embarrassed. "That came out wrong. I meant..."

"I know what you meant," I said, smiling. "It's fine. I can run her into town when she's ready."

"She *is* quite a looker though," said Daisy. "You know, it will be the just the two of you here on a lonely, snowy night. If she's grateful to you, you never know...." She gave a coarse little laugh that was not attractive at all.

"Thanks," I said, feeling a little prim, somehow. "I'll run her into town as soon as she's ready."

Daisy shrugged "Well, thanks for helping out. I have to run." She went back to the hall bathroom and spoke to Heidi for a minute, and then came out, pulling on the green parka.

"Be good now," she said, as I opened the door for her, "but not *too* good." She gave another coarse chuckle as she walked down the steps. A few moments later I heard the roar of the snowmobile and then it faded off into the night.

I got myself another cup of coffee and sat down in front of the fire. In the bathroom, I heard a blow-dryer start up. That was odd. I didn't own a hair dryer. Heidi must have had one in the big purse or shoulder bag that she had brought with her. It seemed like a strange thing to carry into a snowstorm when you left your car, looking for help, but then, the feminine mind has always been mysterious to me.

After a while I heard the door open. I got up and turned around. Heidi was walking down the hall toward me. She was wearing one of my cotton button up shirts, and a thick pair of wool socks. She had a kind of sway to her steps that seemed a little provocative, somehow. The shirt hung down to mid-thigh, and she wasn't wearing anything on her legs. They were very nice legs, too, well worth showing off. But they weren't mine to look at, so to speak, and so I looked up at her face. Her eyes were big and blue, and her blond hair was dry with a windblown look. She had a little bit of light make-up on her eyes and lips, expertly applied. I thought about what Daisy said about us being alone together, and something indefinable nudged at the back of my mind somewhere.

Heidi came to me, and touched my shoulder, and then stood in front of the fire. She glanced out the window.

"Thank you so much, Jonah," she said, turning back and meeting my eyes. "You really saved me."

"I think that was Daisy," I said. "All I did was answer the door."

"But now, it's you," she said. "Just you. And me."

"I'd better get you into town," I said. "Why don't you put on those sweats I gave you, and we can get going?"

"Can I wait for my clothes to dry?" she asked in a small voice.

I felt stupid. "Oh. Of course." I tried to recover. "Do you want some coffee?" I asked.

"Yes, thank you," she said, staring out at the black window again.

I brought a mug to where she stood by the fire. She took it and sipped for a minute.

"Aren't you cold?" I asked, nodding briefly down at her smooth bare legs, but trying not to really look at them.

"The bath warmed me up wonderfully," she said. "And the fire is perfect. I'm fine, thank you. Jonah." She put down her mug and turned to me. She gently took my coffee mug from my hand and put it next to hers. Then she turned back to me, slid her arms around my neck and whispered, "And now let me warm *you* up."

She kissed me. My body began to respond, and clamor for more. But my heart and my soul quietly whispered something else. I listened to the whisper.

The little nudge in my mind pushed harder.

I gently disengaged her arms, and stepped away. Her hands went to the buttons on her shirt, and she began to undo the top one.

"Heidi," I said, "stop it."

She paused, leaving her hands on the button. "What's wrong?"

"Everything here is wrong," I said. And then the nudge in my mind exploded into insight. For the first time that night, my brain started functioning. I knew now what was happening.

"This is a set up," I said out loud. "It's too much like a fantasy to be real."

"So you're saying I'm your fantasy?" asked Heidi with a giggle. "I like that." The first button came undone and her hands moved to the next one.

"Cut it out," I said. "You and I both know this isn't real. You might as well drop the charade."

"I don't know what you mean." She pouted her lips.

"Yes, you do. You were brought here to put me in a compromising situation. Daisy conveniently just had to leave, letting us be alone together, and here you are coming on to me, and you barely know me."

"Don't sell yourself short," she said. "You're a hot guy."

"Knock it off," I said.

"Fine," she said, cocking her hips and putting a hand on one of them. "You want the truth? It's true. You've been set up. But it's too late. They've been out there taking video and pictures since I walked into the room. They've got me wearing nothing but your shirt, and us kissing." She took a step toward me and her voice softened. "We might as well go ahead and have some fun, if we're going to be blamed for it, right? I wasn't lying about you being attractive."

I took a step backward. "For me, it's not about being caught. It's about what I actually do or don't do. And I won't do this. I wouldn't do it, even if I knew I would never be caught."

"Don't you find me desirable?" she asked.

"Of course I do," I said, "but that's irrelevant. Some things are more important to me than what I might want in a particular moment."

I turned to the black window and stared out into nothingness for a moment, glaring at unseen lenses. Then I shut the shades, and stalked down the hall, and into the bathroom. I grabbed the pair of sweatpants that was still sitting next to the sink, and a Seahawks sweatshirt that I had offered her with the other clothes as well. I came back out and shoved them at her. "Go put these on," I said roughly, "and please keep them on."

She took the clothes wordlessly and went back into the bathroom. She was in there for some time, and at last she came out, wearing the sweats and the jersey. She sat down on the couch, seeming very subdued.

"Who sent you?" I asked. She drew her knees up onto the couch and shook her head.

"Just some people I know."

"Who?"

"It doesn't matter. I don't know much about them, and I don't know why they wanted to set you up."

I was quiet, staring at the fire, thinking.

"You have a wife, don't you?" she asked dully after a little while.

"Fiancée," I said.

"Tell me about her," she said.

"Leyla? She's beautiful. She has a laugh like a little creek, bubbling over stones. She's smart and insightful. She's open, always willing to give me a chance, always willing to give a new adventure a chance. She's very loyal. Once you are her friend, she's on your side, for life."

I stopped, thinking about earlier in the day again. I got up and got myself some more coffee. Heidi took some too.

"Is she going to believe you didn't go through with this?"

I was silent for a minute. "We'll work it out," I said at last. "But even if there was no Leyla, I still would have said no."

"You don't have to spell it out," she said, sounding bitter. "A girl knows when a guy isn't into her. She knows when she isn't attractive."

"You've got to be kidding," I said. "You are drop-dead gorgeous. It's got nothing to do with you at all."

"So what then?"

"There's someone else too. Someone even more important to me than Leyla."

"What do you mean?" she asked, meeting my eyes.

So I told her what Jesus means to me. I kept it short and simple, as I usually do, because frankly, most people aren't that interested. But Heidi surprised me. She seemed genuinely interested, and even asked a bunch of questions. It turned into a good conversation, and since it was about a subject that I have a lot of passion for, it was some time before I remembered that she had been sent here originally to set me up. When I did, the thought, jarred me.

"Listen," I said, when there was a lull in the conversation. "This is good stuff. I hope you're really as interested in all this as you seem to be. But you can't stay here any longer. Call in your friends. It's time to go home."

She shook her head and looked away. "They aren't really my friends."

"Regardless, you have to go."

She shook her head again. "They won't come for me. I'm on my own."

"You're serious."

She shrugged. "I don't even have a phone number to reach them."

"Are they still out there?"

"I doubt it. The show's over. Besides, they probably already got what they wanted."

"Are you from Grand Lake? Can I take you home?"

She shook her head. "Duluth."

I sighed. "Your clothes are probably dry. Why don't you go get them, and then I'll take you to town. You can stay in a hotel or something tonight."

Heidi made no further objections. We drove into town, and then turned south on highway sixty-one. As we passed the southern edge of Grand Lake, Heidi turned in her seat, and looked at the receding lights.

"Where are you going?"

"I'm taking you home. Duluth, you said."

She twisted back and stared at me. "No," she said. "No, Jonah. You can't. We're in the middle of a blizzard here."

"The roads aren't that bad," I said. "Looks like they've had snowplows through here recently. And this car does pretty well on bad roads."

She shook her head. "It's not that. It's..." she shook her head again, and then began to cry. "I don't deserve this," she said through her tears.

"I've received an awful lot that I don't deserve as well," I said.

We were silent for the next two hours or so. The going was slower than normal, and it required most of my concentration just to drive. Heidi was content to be silent, and I think she even fell asleep for a while. In spite of my confidence, it was a pretty dicey thing, and I breathed a sigh of relief when we finally reached well-plowed roads south of Two Harbors. When we got to the northern edge of Duluth, I roused Heidi, and she gave me directions to an apartment building south of downtown. It wasn't a very nice neighborhood.

When we stopped, she sat in the front seat for a minute, looking at the wall of the building. I turned and grabbed her shoulder bag from the back seat, quickly slipping a hundred dollars cash into it as I did. When a girl is willing to do what Heidi had tried to do, she was probably pretty hard up for money.

"Do you need anything else?" I asked, handing her the bag.

"Why did you do this for me?" she asked. "After what I did to you? I may have ruined your relationship with your fiancée."

"I think Leyla knows what kind of man I really am," I said.

She unclipped her seatbelt, leaned over and kissed me gently on the cheek.

"I don't know how to thank you. I don't deserve this."

"Forget about it. Do something nice for someone else sometime. You know, pay it forward."

Something in her eyes gleamed. "I will. I will do that, Jonah Borden. Thank you." She brushed at her eyes, and then quickly got out of the car, clutching her bag. She walked up to the door with a little bit of spring in her step, and a little bit of sway too.

I blew out a big breath of air, and drove back to the north side of the city, got a hotel, and went to sleep.

CHAPTER THIRTEEN

I drove home the next morning. Later, at the office, Julie beeped me. "Phone call. Your future mother-in-law."

I had put off talking to Leyla's family, mostly because I had no idea what to say. "Put her through," I said.

"Jonah," said Leyla's mother. "What's going on? I can't get ahold of Leyla. She was supposed to be back from that assignment on Sunday. We need to make a decision on the flowers, and her dress still needs altering, and did you guys ever decide about the cake?"

Victoria Bennett was a wonderful lady, and I was looking forward to being part of her family. But she was in full mother-of-the-bride stress-mode, and that was going to make this situation even harder.

"Tori," I said. "I need to tell you something."

"Well, go ahead. By the way, have you decided on the food for the reception?"

"Tori, I need you to forget about the wedding for a minute. Leyla has –" I stopped. I didn't know how to go on.

"Jonah?" said Tori. "What happened? What did she do? Because, for the record, I can't imagine a better person for her than you, and if she's messed this up –"

"I think she's joined the cult," I said, interrupting her.

There was a vast silence on the other end.

"The cult she went to investigate?"

"Yes," I said. "The Forest Way. I went to get her yesterday, and she didn't want to come home."

"Are you sure she just didn't want to do more investigating?"

"She said her home was with the cult now. She said she hated me."

"That can't be," said Leyla's mother.

"I couldn't believe it either," I said. "But that's what happened."

"So she's still up there?"

"Yes."

"We'll come in and talk some sense to her."

"I don't think that will work," I said. "I went there with the Police Chief and a lawyer, and after Leyla told us to go away, the cult kicked us out. They don't like visitors."

"What are you going to do?"

"I'm going to get her back, Tori," I said. "I promise.

Work was a little tough the rest of that day. I had to do some sermon preparation. You put your heart and soul into a sermon. Not only that, but most of the bible, when you get down to it, is really about your heart and soul. And mine were bruised, torn and fragile. Those things make it hard to prepare and preach a good message when your feelings are so raw.

I hammered away at it for a while, and finally sought solace in another cup of coffee.

"Hey, Boss," said Julie as I stopped by the coffee machine. "Isn't Leyla supposed to be back sometime soon?"

I was quiet for a little bit.

"What's going on, Chief?" Julie's tone was part anxious, part ready-to-be-angry.

"I don't know," I said.

"What do you mean, you don't know? What did you do?"

"I went to get her at the Forest Way," I said. "She didn't want to come."

Julie stared at me. I looked at her with interest. I'd never seen her at a loss for words.

"Seriously," she said at last. "What's up?"

"I *am* serious," I said. "I don't understand it either."

She opened her mouth, but I held up my hand. "But I'm not letting it go, Julie. I'm just not sure what to do next."

Julie looked out the window. The sun was shining brilliantly in a perfectly blue sky. The snow was dazzling. She turned back to me. "Whatever you need, Boss, we've got your back. Not just me. I know the whole church will feel the same."

"Thank you, Julie," I said. "I believe you. If you don't mind, however, I'm not quite ready for the whole church to know. I mean, it might be kind of embarrassing for Leyla, if she eventually comes back."

"*When* she comes back," said Julie firmly. "Good thinking."

I felt a tiny bit of tension ease off me as I went back to my office. The coffee helped, but I think it was from Julie's response, too.

I had an email from Brad Michaels. He gave me the contact information for his friend, Jackson Brandt, who was some kind of professor, and an expert on cults in North America. I looked at it for a minute. Then I dialed his number.

"History department." The female voice was professional, but obviously Southern.

"Hi, my name is Jonah Borden. I'm a pastor in Minnesota, and I am trying to reach Dr. Brandt. A friend of his told me to call him."

"Just hold on a second, Sweetie," said the voice. I smiled slowly. It felt good to be called "Sweetie" by a perfect stranger.

"This is Dr. Brandt," said another voice. This one was male, and he too, had an easy Southern drawl. It didn't make him sound uneducated. In fact, it gave his voice a kind of authority, especially once he started talking about his area of expertise.

"Hi, Dr. Brandt," I said. "My name is Jonah Borden, and I'm calling you from Minnesota. I got your name from Brad Michaels."

"How is Brad these days?" asked Brandt. "I hadn't heard from him in almost a year, until he emailed me about you."

"I think he's well," I said. We exchanged a little bit of small talk until there was a pause.

"What can I do for you, Pastor Borden?" he asked.

"I'm in the middle of something with a cult up here," I said. "I think I need a little help."

"Brad told me that you are dealing with the Forest Way?"

"That's right."

"I wasn't familiar with them, so I did a little research earlier today," said Brandt.

"What can you tell me?" I asked.

"Well, they certainly fit my definition of a cult. They are pretty secretive, which is normal, so I don't have as much detail as I would like. But apparently they do engage in ritual practices."

"What does that mean?"

"I guess you could say a ritual practice is a form of worship. You know, chanting things, saying prayers, meditating, that sort of thing."

I thought about Leyla worshipping anything besides the God she had come to know and love. I felt a little sick. "What are these rituals about?"

"As far as I can tell, they are for the worship and praise of nature, and perhaps also their leader, who styles himself as nature's prophet or something like that."

"Tree," I said.

"Herman Brown," said Brandt. "But we'll get to him in a minute. Another characteristic of cults – at least by my definition – is a measure of control and isolation of the members. Forest Way definitely qualifies here. Members generally live communally at their compound in Minnesota. They do not have much contact with outsiders, and their leaders keep it that way."

"So tell me about Tree."

"Tree's real name is Herman Brown," said Brandt.

"I can see why he changed it," I said.

Brandt chuckled politely. "Anyway," he said, "Brown actually has a PhD in sociology from the University of Minnesota. Apparently, while he was at the University, he formed some kind of political/environmental group. It sort of morphed into a pseudo-religious thing, and by the time he earned his degree, he had a little following." I sipped some coffee while I listened to Brandt. Another good reason to listen more than I talk.

"Brown called his group 'The Forest Way,' so it's held the same name throughout its history. They remained pretty small for several years, picking up a few of the usual types, you know, lost souls. They were based in Minneapolis."

"The Twin Cities is nice, but it isn't exactly the Forest," I said.

"Maybe there was a little hypocrisy there," said Brandt. "Out in the woods, there is no one to convert, and no money."

"But they are out in the woods now."

"True," said Brandt. "Something changed about two years ago. All of a sudden, both their numbers and their influence exploded. They paid cash for that place up by you."

"No loan?"

"No loan."

"That property is prime real-estate. Most of the land around here is National Forest. Private land like that would go for millions of dollars."

"I didn't know that," said Brandt. "That makes this even more interesting. Anyway, they paid cash for it, and then they renovated it, and moved in. And they grew very rapidly. Now they have satellite groups in Minneapolis, Duluth, and Eau Claire, Wisconsin, as well as Thunder Bay, Canada. But their main headquarters is up there by you."

"What do the satellite groups do?"

"Well, as I said, it's all very secretive. In the amount of time I had, I was only able to do a little bit of research, but with the university library, I can dig a little deeper; you know, access old newspaper articles and government documents. My best guess is that they rotate people in and out of the satellite groups to sell their products to fund the organization."

"What do they sell? I think I've heard it's blueberry jam, and tea."

"I think they also sell some soap and lotion and a few things like walking sticks; maybe a little wild honey. They claim it's all hand-made, hand gathered, in harmony with the forest."

"Doesn't seem like they could make enough to fund themselves that way."

"No, it doesn't," said Brandt. "But often times, cult leaders get their members to transfer their life-savings to them. My guess is that two years ago, Brown hit the jackpot by recruiting a very wealthy member."

"Do you hear anything about brain-washing?" I asked.

"The usual," said Brandt. "They do group 'exercises,' which is really a way of saying they control the environment and use peer-pressure to make people conform. They usually deprive members of protein, which is essential to proper brain function and higher cognition. They certainly control the flow of outside information to their members. They probably engage in hypnosis, but I can't verify that from the small amount of research I've done."

"It sounds to me like you have done a lot of research."

I could almost hear the shrug. "I'm a university professor. Research is my thing. And cults are my thing. I'm pretty good at what I do."

"Thank you so much," I said.

"May I ask, what is your particular interest?"

The raw place inside me opened up. And somehow, it was easy to talk to this stranger on the phone with his laid-back Southern accent. After all, his secretary had called me "Sweetie."

"I have a loved one – my fiancée, actually – who joined."

"Oh my goodness, I'm so sorry."

"She doesn't want to come home."

There was a silence on the other end. At last he spoke.

"I study cults. I don't usually get involved. But there are people who do. We call them 'cult-busters.' They go in to the cult and rescue members who are believed to be brainwashed. They 'de-program' them. They usually do it for families of cult members, for a fee."

"Is that legal?"

"Some of them walk a fine-line. Usually, the deprogrammed member does not press charges, but occasionally, people really don't want to be rescued. Some cult-busters get sued. But I don't know of any of them who have faced criminal charges."

"Where would I find a cult buster?"

"As it happens, one of the most active cult-busters in the country is based in Minneapolis, Minnesota. I could give you his name."

For the first time in twenty-four hours, hope forced its way back into my heart. It was a small, hard, cold little thing, but it was hope, nonetheless.

"Please do," I said.

CHAPTER FOURTEEN

Darkness comes early in the winter in the North, drawing a thick curtain across the ridges, dimming the lights on the lake, smothering the sun in cold and cloud. I came home when the light seemed a distant memory. I parked in the garage and then walked the quarter-mile back down my driveway to the mailbox.

Back in my kitchen, I threw most of the mail away. It was a waste, but junk mail still kept a lot of Minnesota pulp-loggers in business. Every cloud has a silver lining. I looked at the stiff eight-by-ten envelope that had come along with the other mail. There was no return address, nor postage, just my name, hand-written on the front.

I slit it open, and pulled out some large glossy photographs in between pieces of cardboard backing. The first photo showed Heidi, in just my shirt, walking down the hall. The second was her kissing me. A third showed her unbuttoning the shirt. A fourth picture was of the two of us talking and drinking coffee. The photos were a little grainy, but they were plenty clear enough. My face was recognizable, I guessed. Anyone who knew my cabin would identify it as the location.

I looked through the envelope again, and found a single note, obviously printed from a computer. It said:

Leyla has already seen these pictures. She never wants to see your face again. Let her go, and move on.

I felt something like a violent jolt stab through my stomach. It felt like real physical pain. I ran to the sink and retched twice. Shaking, I sat down on one of my kitchen barstools. The story that the pictures told was clear. Anyone else looking at them would come to the inevitable conclusion.

I got up, still a little shaky, and made coffee. The horrible thing was that the camera had recorded things that actually happened. The pictures didn't tell the whole story, to be sure, but they captured little moments that were true. Lies mixed with truth were the most powerful lies of all.

I built up the fire, and then took my coffee to the couch. After a few sips, the shakiness went away, replaced by a cold, towering anger, and a sense of diamond-hard resolve.

Leyla had been told lies, kept isolated, maybe even brainwashed. I wanted her to still love me when it was all over, but that wasn't the most important thing. What mattered most was what was best for her, and there was no way that it was best for her to remain with the Forest Way. Of course I wanted to get back to where we had been before she left, but the most important thing was that she should once more be happy and safe and free. These photographs proved to me that at the very least, the Forest Way was dealing with her dishonestly.

~

The next morning I met Dan Jensen and Alex Chan at Lorraine's. Just to be different, I had an omelet and waffles, instead of my usual Superior Skillet.

"Is the world coming to an end?" asked Lorraine as she herself delivered the food.

"Desperate times call for desperate measures," I said, trying to remain cryptic.

Lorraine set a pot of coffee down between Jensen and me.

"That should last five minutes between you two," she said. "I'll be back with more."

"I need to tell you guys something," I said. "But it has to remain confidential."

"No problem," said Chan. "I'm your attorney. But I'm not sure it's a good idea to divulge confidential information to a policeman."

Jensen grimaced. "Lawyers," he muttered.

"You are both here as my friends," I said. "I want to explain something to both of you, speaking as friends."

"Okay," said Jensen. "But I hate to tell you, Alex is probably right. If you disclose something pertinent to an investigation, I may have to inform others."

"Can I just talk to you as friends, and then, as friends, you can advise me whether I should speak with the police?"

"Did you commit a crime?" asked Jensen.

"Don't answer that," said Chan quickly.

"You guys should do a routine. You're a real scream," I said. "Of course I didn't commit a crime."

Chan opened his mouth. "Why don't you two just shut up and let me talk," I said. "I'm trusting you."

They both nodded, and Jensen sipped some coffee.

I took some coffee as well, to fortify myself, and then told them about Heidi, and the photographs.

"You sure you didn't sleep with her?" asked Chan, when I was done.

"Don't be an idiot," I said. "I know you don't share my belief system, but you know that it's a big deal for *me*. I'm not immune to temptation, but you guys ought to know that if I did screw up big time like that, I'd own up to it. Especially if there are pictures."

Jensen nodded. "I know it, and I believe you. But if it gets out, who else will believe you?"

I waved my hand in dismissal. "The real point is," I said, "I know for sure now that they are tricking Leyla. They are withholding information, feeding her disinformation and lies. Can't we get them with that?"

Both of them were shaking their heads. "There's nothing here that we could turn into a warrant," said Jensen. "It isn't illegal to lie to people, if you aren't using the lies to defraud them."

"Besides," said Chan, "how are you going to prove they are lying to her? What you said about those photos sounds pretty damning. It will be only your word against this Heidi's that you didn't sleep together. I think most people will believe Heidi, especially if she's as good looking as you say."

"This just isn't enough evidence to take any kind of legal action," said Jensen.

"I agree," said Alex.

"So you are saying there's nothing we can do?"

"Right now, no," said Chan.

"I'm still working on the murdered John Doe," said Jensen. "If we can connect him to the cult somehow, we'll be able to go in with warrants. We'll get those SOB's, Jonah, just be patient."

I nodded, and had some more waffle. I drank some coffee.

"Well," I said after a moment, "I'd better get to the office."

"I've been wondering about that," said Chan. "What do you do all day, anyway?" Jensen was shaking his head in warning, but I saw him. I glared at both of them.

"Don't you read the newspapers, or the internet, or watch TV? Pastors only work for an hour a week, on Sunday mornings," I said. "So the rest of the time, we spend working out new ways to spend all the money we fleece from gullible church members. When we're not doing that, we have to work hard to make sure that gay people know how much we hate them, and to ensure that scientists know how ignorant we are. When we feel *really* energetic, and the mood strikes us, we may go out and oppress some minorities and women."

Chan looked at me expressionlessly. "Feeling a little tetchy today, are we?"

"Sorry," I said. "Some people have a hobby of pastor-bashing, and once in a while it gets to me. It's been a bad week, anyway."

"It was an honest question," said Chan mildly. "I was just curious."

I sipped some coffee. "I study the bible extensively, and try to find ways to communicate timeless truth in a relevant way. I pray a lot. I meet with people and develop leaders in the congregation, and support them as they lead various groups and programs. I visit people at the hospital, and in prison. I get involved in the community. I try to help people make valuable connections with each other. I work as the police chaplain," I nodded at Jensen.

Chan nodded, and ate some more oatmeal. "Interesting," he said. He took one more bite. "Since you help people make valuable connections, do you think you could introduce me to this Heidi?"

CHAPTER FIFTEEN

I met Nick Vargas at the Culver's at the edge of town. Restaurant chains weren't really my thing, especially not when I was at home in Grand Lake. But I knew too many people at Lorraine's and Dylan's. I didn't want the whole town asking me who I was meeting with, and why.

Vargas was a little under medium height, wide, muscular and hirsute. His hair was black and thick, almost as thick as his eyebrows. He had bright blue eyes that were startling in the midst of all that dark hair. His grip was firm.

We ordered, I paid, and we took our numbers to a table by the window. As we sat down, I pulled an envelope from my coat and pushed it across the table.

"I've reserved a two room cabin for you, at Norstad's Northwoods Cabins, just north of town. The place belongs to a member of my church. He won't bother you, or worry about what's going on down there. You have it for a week. This time of year, it should be pretty private, like you asked. Here's half the money, like we talked about."

"The cabin sounds good," he said. He looked at the envelope, and then pushed it back toward me. "I want you to understand me, before I take your money."

"You've already driven all the way up here," I said.

"Just listen," he said.

I thought that would give me time to drink more coffee, so I said I would.

"I was raised in California," said Vargas. "Near San Francisco."

As a beginning, it wasn't very promising. This sounded like it was going to be a long story. I began to look around for more coffee.

"My parents got divorced right after I went to college." I nodded. I thought I was hiring Vargas to help me, but it seemed like I was doing the pastoral thing for him instead. Oh well, part of my call means I need to be more ready to serve than to be served.

"The reason for the divorce was because my mother joined a cult." I perked up a little at that.

"The cult was called Paradise Gate," said Vargas.

"Wait," I said. "*The* Paradise Gate?"

Vargas nodded emphatically. "Forty-three people offed themselves for a freaking UFO, and one of them was my mother."

I stared at him. "Your mother was one of those?"

His blue eyes bored steadily into mine. "Black shirt, Nikes, the whole freaking nine yards."

"Wow," I said.

"Yeah," he said.

I waited. I was pretty sure he was making a point.

"I was twenty-five. I got my calling the day my mom drank that phenobarbital cocktail. My life's mission is to prevent that from ever happening to anyone else. I can't save everyone, I know that. But I can help the ones who ask for it."

I sipped some more coffee, still listening.

"I just thought my mom was kind of loopy, you know. I didn't worry about it much, until it was too late."

"It's an amazing story," I said. "I'm glad you told me. But I get the feeling there's a reason you told me all this."

He leaned back and pointed at me, just as our food arrived. I had a cheeseburger, fries and a malt. I burn a lot of righteous calories cross-country skiing in the winter time.

Vargas took a bite of his own sandwich, and then spoke again. "I told you about my mother, because you need to know I'm deadly serious about this. Sometimes, things get a little rough. I don't apologize for that, because I've experienced the alternative."

"Okay," I said.

"Not okay," he said. "When I get your fiancée out, I may have to break a few trespassing laws. I may have to break a few heads. When I've got her, I'll take her to the cabin. She will be isolated for twenty-four to forty-eight hours. I may have to scream at her, maybe douse her in cold water. I might play loud music in her face, force her to stay awake for long periods. I'll almost certainly be holding her against her will for some of that time. She might be locked in a room alone for hours at first. I'm comfortable with all that. Are you?"

I leaned back a little. "How physical will you get with her?"

"I won't beat her, or do anything sexual," he said. "Think, maybe a little like Marine Corps boot camp. I'm every bit as in your face and mean as the drill instructor."

I ate thoughtfully. Malts were really a summertime food, but to me they tasted good anytime, especially with a cheeseburger.

"I just can't leave her there," I said.

Vargas was quiet, eating his own food rapidly and efficiently.

"Okay," I said. "I'm in."

He nodded in satisfaction. "All right then. Now, I'll take your money."

After he had tucked the envelope away, he said, "Do you know of anyone in this area that could give me a hand?"

"What do you mean?" I was puzzled.

"I mean a guy, or possibly a gal, who is tough, knows how to handle himself, and knows the area. Someone to help me scope out the place, someone to watch my back when we snatch your fiancée."

"Why not me?" I asked him. "I know the area, and I know how to handle myself."

Vargas looked at me skeptically. "When I say, handle yourself, I mean –"

"I broke the cult leader's nose two days ago," I interrupted. "Disarmed his right hand man and put him down."

Vargas stopped and stared at me. "And where did you learn how to do that?"

"I've been in martial arts since I was a kid. My parents got me into it to channel my energy and aggression. I've got several brownbelts in different disciplines, and a black belt in Tae Kwon Do. I was a junior Olympian."

"Junior Olympian? That's impressive."

"I disqualified myself. Another kid accidentally popped me on the nose hard enough to make it bleed. I got a little crazy inside, and went after him like it was a real fight. The judges had to pull me off."

"A pastor who breaks heads," said Vargas. "That's new."

"Well, I don't break as many heads as I'd really like to," I said. "As a pastor, I meet a lot of stubborn people who do stupid things to screw up their lives, and the lives of others."

Vargas looked at me speculatively. "If you're my wingman, I can't have you crusading. You're pretty emotionally involved in all this. Honestly, I'd rather have you totally out of the picture until your fiancée is completely deprogrammed."

"You said it yourself. I would just be there to provide support and have your back. Once we get her, I'll leave her with you until the deprogramming is complete."

Vargas thought a little more. "All right, let's do this. You tell me everything you know about the cult, and give me the layout, and your impressions of the people you met. I'll put off my decision about back-up for a little while."

We cleared our baskets and napkins from the table, though I continued to sip at my malt. Vargas got some paper, and I sketched a rough map of the cult compound. After that, I told him everything I could think of. When I was done, he asked several incisive questions that helped me to remember other things I hadn't thought to tell him.

Finally, after about ninety minutes, Vargas pushed his chair back.

"You'll do, Borden. You can be my back-up man. But you have to do exactly what I say, when I say it, understand? I want to run this thing like a military operation. You obey my orders, and save any questioning for later. Got it?"

"I can do that," I said.

Vargas thrust his chair back with energy, and stood. So did I. We shook hands.

"I need to do some more research. I'll be in touch in a day or two. We'll get her out, Borden, don't you worry."

I shook his hand and he left. I got myself another cup of coffee, and sat, drinking it, watching as the snow began to fall again. Hope grew in my heart just a little more.

CHAPTER SIXTEEN

Somehow, I pulled off my sermon on Sunday. The positive thing about Scandinavian Lutherans is that when you do a poor job preaching, they react exactly the same as when you do a good job. I often marvel at the fact that these people are the descendants of the dreaded, fearsome Viking pillagers. Maybe what happened is that they repressed their emotions for generation after generation, until the pent up energy of an entire race was released in several centuries of conquest and bloodshed. I wondered how many generations it would be before it happened again. As far as I could tell, it didn't look imminent, but maybe that's what the Anglo-Saxons had said, right before the first longboats came storming across the North Sea.

At any rate, no one attempted to conquer me, or even pillage me, after the church service, and I made it home unscathed.

In my kitchen, I cut up some squash and zucchini and sautéed them with bell peppers, garlic and onion. I seasoned the whole thing Mexican style with lots of cumin and some coriander and red pepper. With a splash of creativity I was quite proud of, I even added a little cinnamon. After the veggies cooked down a little, I added grape tomatoes and kidney beans, and then almost a cup of evaporated milk. Garnished with cilantro, and served with tortilla chips, it was a hearty, Mexican-veggie winter stew.

Melanchthon came bounding into the kitchen. I had known him long enough to know he wouldn't eat veggie stew, so I opened a can of tuna for him, and put it on the floor.

Football season was in full swing. I watched the football Vikings, who seemed to bear little resemblance to the ancient marauders. As usual, the guys in purple were stringing their fans along. They looked like they might either win a Super bowl, or maybe end up with the number one draft pick, depending on which week you watched.

The Seattle Seahawks had recently become contenders again, so I was able to watch my favorite team for the late game. As it turned out they were playing the San Diego Chargers, rivals from before the Seahawks' switch to the NFC. It was a good game, and I almost forgot about Leyla while the guys in green just barely edged out San Diego with a last minute field goal.

The phone rang, and the real world came crashing back through my football bubble. It was Leyla's mother, Tori.

"Jonah," she said. "Has there been any change?" We've talked to some lawyers, but they don't think there's anything we can do."

"That's what my lawyer says too," I said. I'm working on another approach. Probably the less I say about it, the better. Just know that I will not give up on her."

"You're a good man, Jonah. She doesn't deserve you."

"I don't know about that," I said. "These cults use brainwashing techniques. I think she's just confused right now."

"Jonah," she said, "What do you want to do about the flowers and the cake? We need to make some decisions soon."

"I honestly don't know what to do," I said. "Can you hold them off for a week?"

"That's cutting it pretty close, can you just make some of these decisions?"" she said.

"I don't know what else to tell you, Tori. Just hold them off."

We talked for a little longer, and then hung up. What I had been unable to bring myself to say was that I did not know if we were even going to have a wedding.

~

The next day was Monday, my day off, and it was the day Vargas had arranged for us to scope out the Forest Way compound. I met him in Grand Lake, and we drove up into the hills from there. We passed the entrance road, and pulled into a snowmobile parking area about three quarters of a mile further on.

"We'll have to hoof it from here," said Vargas. We pulled on waterproof outer trousers. Each of us had a small backpack with assorted items. Mine held two quart-size thermos bottles full of hot coffee. You can never be too prepared.

"I'll get the snowshoes," I said, moving to the trunk.

"I've never used snowshoes before," said Vargas.

"These are nothing like the old birch and sinew shoes," I said, showing him. "Aluminum and nylon, and a binding that rotates with the movement of your foot. If you can walk, you can snowshoe in these babies." I handed him a pair. "Those are Leyla's," I said.

He glanced at me.

"I bought them for her last winter, but our last trip out, she left them at my place." I showed him how to fasten the bindings, and I pulled four adjustable poles out of the trunk.

"We use these like ski poles?" asked Vargas.

"They aren't really necessary," I said. "But you can use them to balance if you need to. For your first time out, it will give you a little confidence."

Vargas produced two white-pattern camouflage ponchos to put on over our clothes and packs. "No sense sticking out," he said.

With the snowshoes on, we set out. Our feet sank maybe six or eight inches into the snow. Without the snowshoes, we would have been struggling through drifts ranging from knee-deep to thigh-high.

After about half a mile, we slowed down. The trees were thick, mostly a mix of pine, birch, maple and alder. There was a little rise in front of us. We approached cautiously, and then finally, Vargas said we should crawl.

Crawling didn't work very well. Leaning over from the platform of my snowshoes, my arms plunged into the cold powder up to the shoulders, and my face was engulfed. I thrashed around until I was sitting with my legs out to the side. I looked at Vargas, who was dealing with similar trouble.

"Any better ideas?" he said, catching my look.

"Let's take the shoes off anyway," I said. We did, and then kind of swam through the snow to the top of the little ridge. We had to sort of pack the snow down in order to lay on it and see what was beyond the ridge.

The Forest Way compound was in a little hollow directly below us. The last building was only a hundred yards away, directly in front of us. Three other buildings moved away in a line to our right; the structure at the right end of the line was the main lodge where I had first met Tree.

"What's that road?" asked Vargas in a low tone, pointing to a snow covered drive that went into the woods past the last outbuilding.

"I don't know," I said. "I never noticed it before. But from my experiences of camps and retreat centers around here, I'd say it probably goes to a machine-shed or something like that.

"Okay," he said. He pointed to our right. "We can get a little farther along this ridge, so we're looking down almost on the middle of the compound. Let's do it."

We backed off the ridge, and proceeded along it toward the lodge. Before long however, it dropped away on that side. We swarmed through the snow again. We were now about seventy yards further in the direction of the main lodge, but still about a hundred from the nearest building, which was now the second one from the lodge.

"This will do," said Vargas softly.

As it turns out, stake-outs are boring. And cold. Very, very cold. After about half an hour, I slid below the ridgeline for the first dip into the black gold I carried in my pack. Vargas glanced down. I raised the cup toward him, and he shook his head.

Afterwards, I clambered back up, and practiced being cold some more. The sensible people in the Forest Way were all snug inside their buildings. From the smoke and the smell, they were enjoying crackling wood fires. Eventually my toes and fingers started to get numb. I slid back down, and opened my pack, digging for some chemical hand-warmers. I put one in each of my boots, and then one in each of my gloves. The last glove was awkward, but I'd lived in Minnesota long enough to manage it okay.

Vargas was looking down at me. "Me too, after you get back up here."

I slithered up beside him, and then he dropped back to do the same thing. Occasionally someone would come out of one of the buildings and walk to one of the other ones. There didn't seem to be any real pattern to it. Once I thought I saw the slim accountant-guy, Twig, going from the first building to the lodge. Several times, smokers emerged from one or another of the buildings to get their fix.

Two hours, and a full thermos of coffee later, a fair number of people came out of the fourth building, the one farthest from the lodge, with a smattering of people from the second and third. There were probably forty people altogether, with several children and possibly some teenagers among them. We lifted our binoculars and scanned the groups.

"Do you see her?"

"I don't know," I said. "It's hard to tell with everyone wearing parkas and hats. Almost all of the parkas are the same color, too." I looked some more. "That could be her, in that little group going between the second building and the lodge right now." I felt a queer twist in my stomach, thinking of Leyla walking and talking with these people I didn't know; rejecting me to be with them.

Slowly everyone filed into the main lodge. My stomach twisted some more as I watched young children and babies being carried along.

"Lunch time, probably," said Vargas.

"That was probably her then," I said, still feeling funny.

Lunch was long. It was two hours before people began leaving the lodge.

"That's a long lunch," I said. I had already had mine. Leftover Mexican veggie stew doesn't taste quite the same when it's almost frozen.

"It's typical for cults to have group exercises at times throughout the day, to maintain and strengthen the bonds of their members. They probably had lunch, and then had a group session."

"There's Leyla!" I said.

"Quieter," hissed Vargas. "Where? Point her out to me." We were both looking through binoculars.

"Over there, the group that just passed the second building. She's next to the tall guy in the green parka.

"So she was the one you saw earlier too," said Vargas, looking. "Okay, I'll be able to identify her later."

A few of the cult members went back into one or the other of the two buildings nearest the lodge, but most returned to the third building from the lodge, which was the fourth and last one overall in the compound.

About ten minutes later, Vargas stiffened. "Hello," he said.

A group of five people was filing down the road that led past the fourth building, back into the woods. We looked at them through the field glasses. There were three men and two women, all bundled against the cold. But something seemed different about this group. They walked with more swagger, and joked around a little bit. Two of them were smoking cigarettes. Each one of them carried a knapsack. They too went to the main lodge. Their lunch, if that's what it was, was shorter, maybe a half an hour or so. They strode briskly out of the lodge, past the three other buildings, and down the forest road.

"I think we should check that out," said Vargas.

"Why?" I said. "Leyla wasn't part of that group. She's in the fourth building right now."

Vargas grunted. "Good point, Borden. Eyes on the prize, Vargas." He seemed miffed at himself that he hadn't stayed focused.

We switched out our warmers again, but the cold felt like it had seeped into my bones. It was hard to talk, because I couldn't feel my lips. I pulled my scarf up to my eyes.

"So what are we looking at?" I asked.

"Probably, they have some kind of daily work routine. The buildings need to be cleaned and maintained. The bedding needs to be washed. People need to cook and clean up afterward. I would guess that fourth building is either a place where they hold sessions or maybe it's where they make the crafts that they sell, or probably both. Besides the lodge, the other two buildings are probably sleeping quarters. We just watched everyone take a break from work, have lunch, clean up and then probably a group session at the lodge. Now they're back to work."

We waited some more. I passed the time by trying to figure out which would kill me first, cold or boredom. Finally, it began to grow dark.

"We should go," I said.

"No, this is exactly the most useful time to be here," said Vargas. "The rest of the day has just been preliminary to this."

I looked at him sourly. "Why didn't we just wait until now to come out here then?"

He shifted to an elbow and looked at me. "Look Borden, do you have people coming along and telling you how to do your job?"

"All the time," I said, smirking in satisfaction, since it was perfectly true. Everyone thought they knew what a pastor should do, and how he should do it. Then I realized he couldn't see the smirk, under my scarf.

"Whatever," he said. "I'm the expert here, so shut up."

"Nicely argued," I said, but I left him alone.

The darkness grew thicker. Lights came on in the cult buildings. By five, all traces of the sun had been erased from the warmth-deprived sky. At five-thirty rectangular bars of light stabbed onto the snow when doors were opened and people began to file out of the fourth building. It was too dark to pick out Leyla from the others. Many of them went into the second and third buildings, and reappeared in small groups maybe fifteen minutes later, heading for the lodge.

"Suppertime," said Vargas.

About an hour after that, a faint but deep thudding began to emanate from the main lodge.

"Dinner and a movie?" I asked.

"Dinner and a session," said Vargas. "They're probably hammering on a drum for some ceremony or other."

I felt sick again, thinking of Leyla in the middle of all that, falling for it, participating willingly in it.

Now it began to get seriously cold. The stars above were gorgeous and bright, spread out against the shining blanket of the Milky Way. It was lovely, but mostly, it was cold. To the north a little green began to flicker against the dome of the sky. It flared out, and then streaked red and faded back. The lights leaped and stained the sky and moved and slid back into darkness.

Vargas nudged me. "Aurora," he said.

"Yeah," I said. The northern lights. They were pretty. But mostly, it was cold.

It was somewhere around ten o'clock before the lodge began to empty. We had used up our last warmers. Vargas had a set of night vision goggles, but I didn't. He watched as the Forest Way people walked back to their quarters. After everyone was back inside, it stayed quiet. No one came out. They were smart enough to stay indoors where it was warm.

At almost midnight, Vargas nudged me.

"Okay," he said. He checked the ground with his night vision equipment to make sure we hadn't left anything.

"If they come up here, they'll be able to tell someone was here," I said.

"I know," said Vargas. "But at least we won't leave them any clues about who or when."

He led the way through the trees for the first hundred yards or so, and then slipped off the night vision goggles. "I think we can use flashlights now," he said, and we did.

Back at the parking area, after we had stripped off our snow suits and parkas, we got into the car, where I had the heater going full blast. My hands and nose began to sting as they warmed up. My feet, however, remained cold until I went home and took a hot bath.

CHAPTER SEVENTEEN

I went back to work the next day, but late that afternoon I rejoined Nick Vargas in the snow-machine parking area near the Forest Way.

"I've been watching all day," he told me. "Seems pretty much the same as yesterday."

We made our way in the failing light back to our observation post. It was still cold. The Forest Way people did the same things they had done the night before. The only difference, as far as I could tell, is that there were no Northern lights in the cloud-covered sky. We were back with our cars a little after midnight.

"See you tomorrow night," said Vargas. "Same time, same station."

"Tomorrow's Wednesday," I said. "I have committee meetings, choir, youth and ten other things."

Vargas stared at me a minute. "And you'll do all that, instead of being here for your girl?"

"Are we going to grab her tomorrow night?" I asked.

"No, we need one more night of observation," he said.

"So observe. I'm telling you Vargas, I'd almost rather freeze my butt off than sit in a committee meeting. But I can't get out of it without people asking some very pointed questions, which may lead them to this whole scheme."

"Fine," he said. "Thursday's the dress rehearsal then, and we'll do it on Friday."

~

Throughout most of Wednesday evening, I thought fondly about lying, half frozen in the snow, watching cultists go about their mundane business. An average church committee meeting takes about as much time as the Byzantine Empire, and is more boring than watching grass grow. I'm convinced that most clergy suicides are the direct result of committee meetings.

You do sometimes get time to think during such meetings. For instance, just then I was thinking, who was Robert, and why do we have to follow *his* rules to have order? I fantasized about the day that Borden's Book of Bored Meetings would be the new standard in church governance. Forrest Gump said, *sometimes there just aren't enough rocks*. I say, *sometimes, there just isn't enough coffee*.

"Pastor?" It was Mike Slade. I realized that everyone had fallen silent. I had no idea what we were currently talking about. It could have been a resolution to hire a new carpet cleaning company. It might have been a motion to pay the youth group to clean out the church freezer. Or maybe it was a vote to send my entire salary to orphans in Albania.

"Could you repeat the question?" I said. I felt like I was being interrogated by congress. Twelve people looked down the table at me. Slade cleared his throat.

"I said we were out of coffee. Should we make some more?"

Now it was my turn to stare. "You had to ask?"

"Sorry," said Slade. Someone went out to start another pot, and then the meeting resumed.

Eventually the meeting ended, because people started dying of old age. At least, that's how it felt. Leaving the church building, I stepped outside and breathed in a deep gulp of pure night air. Immediately I started coughing, because generally, breathing deeply outside in December in Northern Minnesota sends a thousand tiny needles of pain into your lungs. Karma is a bear. I was glad Jesus had rescued me from it, but it still seemed like every now and again, I got bitten by it.

CHAPTER EIGHTEEN

On Thursday night, Vargas walked us through what he called the "dress rehearsal." We started at our usual observation post, and worked our way slowly to the right, closer to the main lodge. The county road was only a hundred yards through the trees behind us. At this point, the trees were only eighty feet or so from the path between the main lodge and the other buildings. In the parking lot by the lodge, there was a sulfur streetlight. It was on the other side of the lodge from us, and the big building cast a deep shadow over our new position. During the day, the new spot under the leafless winter trees would not give us enough shelter from being seen, but at night, the trees cast confusing shadows, and the whole area was protected by the dark shadow of the main lodge. We watched while the cultists went into their evening meeting.

"Okay," said Vargas in a soft voice. "At this point tomorrow, I sneak over and wait against the side of the building. You wait here with the grenades."

"Where did you get those, anyway?" I asked.

"Better you don't know," he said. "Will you use them?"

"If I have to."

"Okay, can you see me over there?"

He wanted to play pretend. I was too cold to argue.

"Sure."

"Night vision goggles on."

I slipped on the pair he had loaned to me. The world no longer looked as full of shadows. Everything had a kind of greenish tint to it. I found I could see some distance in the dark, but it was a little grainy.

We waited, and in the cold, I almost thought fondly of the committee meeting. I'm fickle that way. When the cult meeting finally broke up, Vargas leaned over and whispered in my ear. His breath was warm, and not very pleasant.

"OK, I'm in position by the corner of the lodge." He paused while we watched the people walking by on the path, less than thirty yards away. "There she is," he whispered. I wasn't sure how he could tell, but he had more experience with the night vision equipment than I did.

"Now I'm approaching. Now I have her and we're moving back. Wait, we've been noticed, people are calling out, asking questions."

I wasn't enjoying the fake drama, but I had agreed to do everything his way. "Okay. I throw a grenade."

"Which one?"

"The one on my right, the smoke grenade."

"Okay," he said, still whispering in my ear as the people passed by. "That doesn't stop them. People start pursuing."

"I take off the goggles, blow the whistle and throw the flash-bang."

"Good," said Vargas. We waited until the last of the cultists were gone. "Now let's trace the path."

"And she'll just come with you?" I said.

"I know how to deal with cultists," he said. "I know how to use their own tricks against them. She'll obey me, just like she obeys the cult leaders."

That was not a pleasant thought for me, and I dropped the issue.

~

On Friday, it began to snow in the late afternoon. As the shadows drew in, the snow got thicker. I met Vargas down at his rented resort cabin. We left my car there, and drove up into the hills.

"You ready?" he asked.

"I guess so," I said.

"Let's go over it again," he said, and so we did.

"This snow is going to help us," he said. "It will be that much more confusing." Vargas seemed keyed up, but not nervous. Excited might be a better word to describe it, like a professional athlete before a big event.

"Is this legal, what we're doing?" I asked.

"Hell, no," he said. "We talked about this at the very beginning. You aren't backing out on me now, are you?" He looked at me for a second in the light of the glowing dashboard. I wished he would keep his eyes on the road.

"No, I'm not backing out. I'm just nervous, is all."

"Look, Borden, these people are not going to go running to the cops, trust me. I've done this type of thing before. The last thing this sort of cult wants is a police investigation."

"Okay," I said.

He reached over and slapped me on the shoulder. "We'll get her, Borden. Don't you worry."

We got in position early, and settled down to wait. As usual, the cult-members went trooping into the main lodge for their evening meal and subsequent group session. Fifteen minutes after the last one went in, Vargas slipped out of the trees and up to the wall of the main lodge. I pulled on my night vision goggles. In the greenish light, he was clearly visible, and looked horribly exposed. I pulled the goggles off, and couldn't place him in the deep shadows. I put them back on again. He gave me a thumbs up.

I settled down to wait. I heard the drum beat. There was some muffled shouting from inside the lodge that sounded like it was a part of some kind of ceremony. I waited some more. I tried to remember a time when I had ever felt warm, and I couldn't. I got a hand warmer from my pocket, activated it, and stuck it into my right mitten. Finally, at least part of me was a little bit warm. The snow thickened, and even with the night vision goggles, it was getting hard to see Vargas.

I went through another warmer before the cultists began to file out of the lodge again. My heart began to thud loudly in my chest. I pulled a grenade from my right hand pocket, and peered through the driving snow. Vargas moved, suddenly. He seemed to put his arm around someone, though it was hard to see through the snowfall. I heard a soft rat-tat-tat sound, almost like a distant woodpecker.

Vargas turned abruptly off the path, leading the other person into the deep shadow of the lodge building, though through my goggles I didn't really notice the shadow. However, even with the goggles, they were hard to see through the falling snow.

The other cultists did not seem to notice. They were all hunched over against the snow, hurrying to get back to their sleeping quarters. Now Vargas was ten yards off the path. Now fifteen. He and Leyla seemed to be going very slowly. He stopped and hoisted her up in a fireman's lift, and came trundling through the snow at a slow jog. Now he was almost back to my position. I thrust the grenade back into my pocket.

"What's wrong? I asked in a hoarse whisper as he reached me. "Let me help you."

"Not now. No time. Let's go. Go!" he replied.

We hustled through the trees. Tonight we had parked directly on the county highway and we had only a hundred yards to cover. I brought up the rear, expecting some sort of shout of discovery from behind us, but it never came. We broke through the snow bank at the edge of the road. I pulled out the keys. Vargas bundled Leyla into the back seat, and climbed in after her. I jumped behind the wheel, shaking, and started the engine. I couldn't believe it as I pulled the car away and sped toward Grand Lake. We had gotten Leyla, and everything had gone off without a hitch.

"We got her Borden," said Vargas. "I told you we'd do it."

"Thank you, Nick," I said. "I don't know how to thank you."

"That snow was incredible. It kept everyone's head down, it hid us quickly. They probably haven't even missed her yet. Couldn't have gone better."

"Thank you," I said again. I could feel a tremendous sense of relief lifting a huge weight off me.

"For me, this is just the beginning," said Vargas. "The deprogramming is rough. But the hardest part is done."

I heard a groan and a mumble from beside him.

"What happened to her?" I asked. "Why couldn't she walk?"

"I tased her," said Vargas.

"You *what?*"

"I used a police-issue Taser on her," he said calmly. "It was the only way to get her to come quietly. I didn't tell you before-hand that I was going to do it, because I knew you'd throw a fit."

"Darn right," I said.

"Before you go off on me, let me say my piece," said Vargas. "I told you in the beginning that I play rough, and you know why I do. I know the stakes in this game, far better than you do. She'll be groggy for a few more minutes, and then she'll be just fine. In fact, she'll be a lot better than she would if she were still back there."

I didn't say anything, and we drove in silence the rest of the distance back to Grand Lake.

"Okay," I said, as we pulled into the quiet little lakeside resort. "You did what you had to. I still would have wanted to know ahead of time."

"Maybe, maybe not," said Vargas. "Help me get her inside."

The two of us supported her, and brought her into the cabin. She mumbled incoherently, and her voice seemed kind of hoarse. We fumbled around in the dark, and Vargas led us to a couch, where I laid her gently down. Vargas flipped on the overhead light. I moved the hood of the parka back from her face, and stared down into the eyes of a stranger.

The woman we had rescued was not Leyla.

CHAPTER NINETEEN

The whole world seemed to shift. I straightened up.

"This isn't Leyla," I said. The woman had dark hair, and dark eyes, like Leyla. She was about Leyla's height, and though Leyla was not overweight in any way, this woman was considerably thinner. She looked maybe five years older or so, with a few light scars on her cheeks.

"What?" asked Vargas, walking across the room towards us.

"You got the wrong person," I said. My voice seemed a little harsh in my own ears. "You screwed it up, Vargas, and now they'll be watching out for us."

"What are you talking about?" he said.

The woman was trying to mumble something.

I glared at Vargas, and pointed my finger at the woman on the couch. "This – is – not – Leyla!" I said, spacing out the words and spitting them as I said them.

"What's going on?"

Both of us turned back to the woman.

"Relax," said Vargas. "Let me get you a drink of water, and some aspirin." The living room and kitchen were connected. He went over to the sink, got some water, and returned with two pills. The woman took the pills and drank the water.

"What's your name?" I asked.

"Amaryllis," she said. I felt a cold wash of fear.

"What did you say?" I asked. "What did you say your name was?"

"Amaryllis."

"That was supposed to be Leyla's cult name," I said.

Amaryllis shook her head. "It has been my name since I learned the Forest Way."

"Do two people sometimes take the same forest-name?" I asked.

"No," she said. She didn't seem inclined to sit up yet. "I am the only Amaryllis."

Questions piled up in my head like a traffic jam. I turned back to Vargas.

"Was this deliberate?" I asked him. "Are you working for Tree?"

"Don't be an ass, Borden," said Vargas. "I screwed up. It was dark and snowing, and I was sure it was her."

I was quiet. There was a superficial resemblance.

"Herman Brown told me that Leyla's forest-name was Amaryllis."

Amaryllis spoke up. "Tree thought you might try to take Orchid by force. He wanted to confuse you, so he called her by my name, since I look like her."

"So you were a decoy?" said Vargas.

Amaryllis sat up and nodded.

"How do you feel about being expendable?" said Vargas. "That means that Tree wanted to keep Leyla, more than he wanted to keep you."

A flicker of pain and confusion crossed her face, but she shook her head and smiled. "Everyone has a place to serve. It is my honor to serve the Forest in this way."

"So Leyla's forest name is Orchid?" I asked.

Amaryllis nodded.

"Why is he so intent on keeping your girl?" Vargas asked me.

"Leyla is a very beautiful woman," said Amaryllis. "Tree always says he must spread his seed, and the more beautiful, the better it is for the Forest."

She was basically saying that Tree used many women for sex, and he wanted to use Leyla for the same purpose. My face grew hot, but my stomach grew sour. I suddenly wished that I had done more than break his nose.

Amaryllis began to nod as if she were sleepy. "I'm very tired," she said.

"Help me get her into bed," said Vargas.

She seemed to need a lot of help. We took her into one of the two bedrooms in the little cabin. We helped her out of her coat and boots and sweater, and tucked her in, wearing her Indian outfit, which looked comfortable enough as pajamas. Vargas laid out a clean pair of women's jeans, underwear, and a blouse.

"They should fit," he said. "Change into them when you wake up."

Amaryllis' eyes could barely stay open. We left the room, closing the door.

"Why is she so tired?" I asked. "Did the Taser mess her up, somehow?"

He shook his head. "I sedated her with those pills," he said. "It's all part of the process."

"What process?" I said. "You got the wrong person."

"I know," he said. "And I feel rotten about that. But I'm not going to throw this Amaryllis person back to the wolves. We've got her now, and she deserves a chance at freedom. I'll de-program her."

"I'm paying you to de-program Leyla Bennett," I said. "That is not Leyla Bennett."

"Look," he said, "if we try to take her back right now, all kinds of bad things could happen. She's sedated. Unless we walk her right up to the door of the Forest Way, and make sure they take her in, she'll just collapse outside and freeze to death. And I don't know about you, but I don't think it's such a good idea to walk up to those nuts and say, 'Hey, we tried to kidnap one of your people, but we got the wrong one. Can we give her back, and get the right one now?'"

"Okay, so we can't take her back just yet. But I'm in this for Leyla. This is not a personal crusade against cults."

"I understand that you're angry, Borden," said Vargas. "And I'd be mad as a bee-stung bear if I were you. But I'm still going to get Leyla out too, believe me. My life's mission is to save anyone I can. I didn't try to get the wrong woman, but now that I've got her, I'm not going to turn my back on her."

"Can you even do two at once? Won't the deprogramming keep you here, instead of going back to get Leyla?"

"The first twenty –four hours is a little bit low-key. Mostly, I just feed them a lot of protein, and let them settle into being away from the cult. I can lock her up and go out."

It still made me uncomfortable to hear his methods: tasing, drugging, imprisoning. But I believed him when he told me it was his life's work. His heart was good, even if his hands were a little rough.

"Want some coffee?" asked Vargas.

"Now you're just bribing me."

He grinned, and went into the kitchen. After it was brewed and we had filled our cups, we sat down in the living room.

"I hated what she said about Tree wanting to keep the beautiful women," I said. I felt like I was pretty calm, considering that it made me want to find some dynamite, and blow Tree into sawdust.

"I hear you," said Vargas, "but something isn't right here. Even if he is a womanizer, it still doesn't make sense. Those types of cult leaders have all the booty they can handle. They aren't desperate, if you know what I mean, and it seems a little strange to get hung up on one particular woman when you can have fifteen others."

"*I'm* pretty hung up on her," I said.

"Yeah, but you aren't a twisted, screwed up megalomaniac, sleeping with a different woman every night. He's got to know that you will make trouble, and it shouldn't be worth it to him to keep Leyla. The easiest thing for him, and the safest for the cult, would be to just let you take Leyla home. He's risking a lot to keep her."

"But Leyla herself doesn't want to come home," I said miserably.

"Hey," he said, catching my eyes. "That wasn't her, saying that, not really. That was the cult. I know you don't think she was drugged or brainwashed, but I'm not sure you know what brainwashed looks like. I'm telling you, Herman Brown ought to have let her go. This doesn't set up right."

"Yeah, but he's a narcissistic, power-drunk egomaniac. Maybe logic isn't his strong suit."

Vargas shook his head. "I don't know. Something doesn't smell right here. I've put my teeth into a lot of cults over the years. I haven't figured it out yet, but something here is off."

"So what's the plan?"

He got up and went into the other bedroom of the cabin. Coming back to the living room, he tossed an envelope to me. It was the money I had paid him. "For starters, I won't take anything until Leyla is out, safe and sound."

I tapped the envelope against my cheek. "I want to be all noble and say that isn't necessary," I said. "But the truth is, I want you as motivated as can be to get her out, and soon. So, I'll keep it. Thanks."

"It's only fair," he said.

"But I look forward to paying you again," I said, "and soon."

"I hear you, man. I know you just want her out. So do I. Can you come sit with this Amaryllis while I go back to the Forest Way tomorrow, and see the situation, now that we've done this?"

"What do I have to do?"

"Make sure she's OK. Feed her meat and eggs. Don't let her go out. She'll probably sleep a lot."

"I can come for a few hours, but not all day."

"Okay. Come by about nine."

We finished our coffee, and I drove home.

CHAPTER TWENTY

It was late when I got home, but I couldn't go straight to bed. I was upset and wound up tight. I wandered from room to room, ending up in my office. Something on my desk caught my eye. It was the last note Leyla had written me. I picked it up and looked at it, as if somehow those five terse words could explain everything to me about why Leyla would throw away our love and the life she had known and had zest for.

Everything is fine.

Love,

L

It wasn't much of a note. She had written it after I had told her that I was concerned about the cult, and concerned for her safety. Leyla was a writer, and it wasn't like her to be so brief.

Something tweaked in my subconscious. I looked at the note again. It was on thin, white paper, like that was all she could find quickly to write on.

The tweak became a distant alarm bell. The note before this one had been brief also. I looked around for that one. It wasn't on my desk, or in any of my drawers. I sat down on my chair and thought. I had picked up the second-to-last note on a Sunday. I pictured myself, out in the woods, looking at it. I had shoved it into the inside pocket of my parka. Jumping up, I went to the back hall where my coats hung, and dug around in the parka. My hands touched paper, and I pulled out a grocery list. I felt around some more, and came out again with the second-to-last note from Leyla.

Bringing the second note back into the office, I flipped on my desk lamp and spread out the paper beneath it. The first line said: *I've got to be quick. I'll write more later.*

Underneath that, it said *Everything is fine.*

This was followed by *Love,*

And below that was *L.*

It was written on lined yellow paper. She had written me two notes prior to this one. They were a little longer. She had said she missed me, that she was excited about starting our life together soon, and she was so grateful that I supported her decision to do the undercover report.

I looked at this one again. It was reasonable, I supposed. Sometimes, especially in her situation, I could imagine she was in a hurry. Then I looked at the last note. It seemed exactly the same, except the first line was missing.

It seemed exactly the same. My heart began to pound. I put the last note under the light, next to the second-to-last. Then I tilted the lamp to shine upwards. I put the last note over the top of the other one, and held them up against the light. I adjusted the papers a little bit, and looked carefully. They *were* exactly the same. The last one could have been traced from the one before it.

I took the notes out into my garage, to my fly-tying bench. I flipped on the bright working light and held the last note under the big magnifying glass that was clamped in place to help me when I made flies for fishing. The paper was thin, but under the magnifying glass, I could see that the pen marks were deeply impressed upon it, like the person who wrote was pushing down hard.

I switched to the previous note, the one on yellow, lined paper. I turned the page obliquely. In a few places I could see the marks of impressions on the paper right next to, but not quite on, the lines made by the pen. Like someone had written there with a pen that didn't work. Or, as if someone had traced the writing on this paper.

I flipped off the light and brought the notes back into my office, sitting down at my desk. I leaned back, thinking.

Why would Leyla trace her own note? Obviously, she wouldn't. Therefore, I could assume she hadn't. Someone else had done it, someone who wanted me to recognize Leyla's handwriting. And that person had to have done it before Leyla's note on yellow paper was put into the drop box. I paused. No, that wasn't quite right. Someone could have followed Leyla, removed the note from the box, traced part of it, and then replaced it.

Why?

To keep me from coming to get Leyla. But I had come anyway. And when I did find her, Leyla told me that she hated me.

Hated.

The little distant alarm began ringing again. In the time since it had happened, I had tried not to think about my last conversation with Leyla. It was astonishingly painful, and I still felt shame over my unprovoked attack upon Tree and Rock and Cliff. However, now I forced myself to think about every detail. Leyla, not meeting my eyes. Telling me she belongs with the cult, in a dull, flat voice. Staring at the big mirror, whispering, "I hate you." Then turning to me with new energy, with a look – a look as if she has just had an idea. Looking me in the eyes now. Saying, screaming, "I hate you, Jonah. Do you understand? I hate you."

She hates me. Do I understand?

No, I don't understand. I tried to be dispassionate. I could understand her being deceived by the cult. I could understand her, brainwashed, under Tree's influence, telling me that she was staying with the Forest Way. I could understand her saying that she was sorry, that's just how it had to be. But why would she *hate* me?

Maybe she had seen the pictures of Heidi, almost-naked, wearing nothing but a shirt that belonged to me, in my great room. But no, that had not been until after the interview. Hate didn't belong in that moment. And when she said it, she wept like her heart was breaking. I winced away from the memory, but quickly brought my focus back.

Hate was over the top. It didn't make sense, it didn't fit in. Removing all the emotion of the moment, it was almost a silly thing to say. Yet, in spite of the weeping, she seemed lucid when she said it. That's what had convinced me. But I didn't understand.

I got up and went into the kitchen and put on some coffee, and then stoked up the fire, letting my mind idle for a moment while I went about these routine tasks. When the coffee was done, I poured a cup, blew across it, and took a sip.

Ah, blessed black elixir! And then I had it. I didn't understand because it was not understandable. Hate was too over the top, too – I stopped. Too unreal. Too fake. Leyla would not hate me. I knew her very well. We loved each other very much. Even if something came between us, I couldn't believe that she would actually hate me.

She was sending me a message. By telling me that she hated me, she was saying, "This isn't real. Do you understand? Don't believe me!"

She had been asking for help.

CHAPTER TWENTY-ONE

I looked at my clock. It was twenty minutes after two in the morning. Jensen, Chan and Vargas would all be asleep, and there wasn't much anyone could do until morning anyway. I went to bed, but I didn't sleep much.

I got up before the sun, which is easy to do in the far North in the wintertime. I made pancakes and drank coffee, and drove down to the Shore to the cabin where Vargas was staying. I got there half an hour early. I opened the screen door to the porch, and stamped across to the door. There was a piece of paper stuck between the door and the jamb. I pulled it out. It was a note, written in a messy, sprawling style.

Borden,

I'm going out early to do more recon on Leyla. I'm going to investigate that area down the little road, at the edge of the compound. Something seems fishy there.

Amaryllis will be fine until you get here. I should be back by 1, or 2 at the latest. Eggs, milk and meat are in the fridge. She'll eat them when she gets hungry enough. I've got her coat, mittens, scarf and boots, so hopefully, she won't try to run away.

There's a file in my bedroom with some info on the Forest Way and Herman Brown. Browse at your leisure.

Don't worry about Leyla. We'll save her, I give you my word.

Key is under the mat.

Nick V.

I looked under the doormat and found the key. I opened the cabin door. The living room was empty. One lamp was on, in a corner by an overstuffed chair. I locked the door behind me, and hung my coat on a coatrack. I took off my shoes and padded in my thick wool socks past the kitchen to the small hallway that held the two bedrooms and the bathroom. One of the bedrooms was opened. The bed was neatly made. I glanced in, flipping on the light. There was male clothing in the closet. Vargas' room. Going out, I knocked gently on the other door. There was no response. I opened it quietly, just enough to see inside. There was someone in the bed with long dark hair. She seemed to be asleep. I closed the door and went back into the kitchen. The fridge was stocked with steak, eggs, bacon, turkey sausage and milk. Bacon. Good man, Vargas. There were also some English muffins that said "now, with more protein" on the label, as well as butter and some Swiss cheese. The freezer held a can of Folgers coffee.

The dining table was opposite the kitchen area, and was really just one end of the sitting room. There was a Minneapolis Star-Tribune on the table, and a brown manila folder, which turned out to be Vargas' file on the Forest Way and its leader, Herman Brown.

I hunted down a medium sized saucepan and filled it with more than a quart of water and put it on to boil. Then I mixed some coffee with water and two eggs, and crumbled the eggshells in, too. Once the water boiled, I dumped in the egg-coffee mixture and made Swedish egg coffee. Even the coffee would be full of protein this morning.

While I boiled off the foam, I put some bacon on to fry slowly. I turned the coffee off and let it settle, tending to the meat. Cooking is a fun way to kill time. Once I had a mug of coffee in hand, the only thing missing was some music. I could have maybe sung some songs myself, but that seemed too cruel to do to someone just rescued from a cult.

The smell of bacon is irresistible. I had it on good authority from Jewish friends who had fallen off the kosher-wagon on occasion, that at times they craved bacon like an ex-smoker craves cigarettes.

Sure enough, it had the effect I intended. The bedroom door opened and Amaryllis came out. She was about five foot seven, like Leyla. Her hair was dark, and about the same length. At the moment, said hair was kind of messy. There were dark circles under her brown eyes. Her face was more round than Leyla's, and in the cold light of morning, she didn't look that much like her.

"What's that smell?" she asked, shambling to the dining table and sitting down.

"Bacon," I said. "It'll be done in a minute." I broke a couple of eggs into the pan with the meat.

"Want some coffee?" I asked.

She looked disoriented. "What happened? Where are we?"

I brought her some coffee, though she hadn't responded to my question. Who wouldn't want coffee? She sipped it, almost as if she didn't realize what she was doing.

"You are someplace safe."

"You kidnapped me," she said. "I remember, last night. You came and took me away."

"We thought you were my fiancée, Leyla Bennett."

"So Tree was right. He always is."

I let that pass, and put some bacon and eggs on a plate and brought it to her. She shook her head and pushed the plate away.

"I don't eat meat. It is not the Forest way."

"What do you mean?"

"We are one with the Forest. We are creatures of the Forest. We don't eat meat. It isn't natural."

"Wolves eat meat. They are creatures of the forest. I've seen a few not far from here."

She shook her head. "But most forest creatures do not. And wolves are not common."

"Coyotes, then."

"They're like wolves. You are naming the exceptions."

"I can name a dozen forest animals that all live in this area and eat meat," I said. "Foxes eat meat. Mountain lions, too. Sometimes even black bears eat meat. Bobcats and lynx. Mink, weasels, fishers, pine-martens, wolverines, skunks, possums and raccoons. There, that's thirteen counting the wolves and coyotes, and I haven't even really had to think about it."

She was quiet.

"Oh," I said, "and otters, eagles, hawks, falcons, owls, and vultures. Almost every species of fish eat other fish. Are you saying none of these animals and birds is natural?"

"I'm confused," she said.

"That's OK," I said. "In fact it isn't surprising. You need protein to think straight. Have breakfast." I pushed the plate back in front of her. It smelled good, even to me, and I wasn't hungry.

"Tree says it is wrong."

"Why is it wrong?"

"It exploits animals."

"So, all those animals I named are exploiting other animals?"

She shook her head in irritation. "Tree explained it better than I can."

"How about eggs?" I asked.

"It exploits the fowl who lay them."

"Chickens lay eggs, whether or not we eat them."

She looked confused again. "No, we make them lay eggs."

I laughed. "No, we certainly do not. It's like a woman's menstruation. It happens naturally. Chickens lay eggs because they are chickens. No one can make them, or stop them."

"But the eggs would turn into chicks if we didn't eat them. It's like we are eating unborn babies."

I smiled again. "Even if that were true, it would only be so if the eggs are fertilized, and then also incubated. But chickens lay eggs, whether or not they are fertilized, whether or not there is a chick inside. It takes a rooster to fertilize them. No rooster, and the egg will stay the same until it rots. Even if an egg is fertilized, it will never develop into a chick unless it is also incubated. And these days, it is virtually impossible to go to a store and find a single egg that has even been fertilized. There are no chicks in there, and there wouldn't be, even if you incubated the eggs."

She looked at me quizzically. "Really?"

"Really."

Hesitantly, she reached over and drew the plate toward her. Slowly, she picked up the fork and cut off a piece of egg and put it in her mouth. I could tell from her expression that it tasted good. It didn't hurt that there was probably some bacon grease on the egg. After a while, she began to eat steadily. When she had finished the eggs, she looked at the bacon.

"I don't know what to do," she said.

"I'd eat the bacon," I said. "But if you like, I'll make you some more eggs."

"Thank you, that would be nice," she said.

I fried two more eggs and put them on her plate. I snagged a piece of the bacon that was still in the frying pan, and began to nibble at it, sans plate and fork. I sipped my coffee in between bites.

She watched that for a minute, and then broke a tiny piece of her own bacon and ate it.

"Wow, that's really good," she said, closing her eyes.

We ate in silence for a minute, and afterwards, she finished the rest of the bacon that I had cooked up.

"Now what?" she asked, when she was done.

"I don't really know," I said. "Let's clean up."

We cleaned the kitchen without saying anything. It wasn't as awkward as it sounds. In fact, it felt comfortable and domestic. Afterwards, I took a cup of coffee and sat down in the living room. She followed me and in stood in front of me.

"Sit down," I said. She ignored me.

"What was your name before Amaryllis?" I asked her.

"It doesn't matter," she said.

"It matters to me," I said.

She looked puzzled again. "Ann," she said, after a moment.

"I like that," I said. "Ann."

"That's not my name anymore," she said.

"I like it," I said again. "I'd like to call you Ann."

"I am not her, anymore."

"Was Ann such a bad person to be?" I asked. I had no idea what I was doing. I did have some practice bringing truth and light into lies and darkness, but I had never dealt with an active cult member in this way. It just seemed like something to ask.

She was quiet for a long time. "I don't know. I wasn't at peace when I was Ann. I had no direction. When I joined the Forest Way, I had direction and purpose. I had peace."

"What is your direction and purpose?" I asked.

"To serve Tree and Forest," she replied promptly.

"You mean your leader, Tree," I said.

"Yes."

"That's an awful lot to expect of another human being – to give you purpose and peace."

"Tree is not just another human being. He is the physical manifestation of the Forest Spirit."

I wondered how much bacon I would have to feed her before she realized how strange she sounded.

"If he is the manifestation of the Forest Spirit, then why doesn't he want you to eat meat, the way so many creatures in the *real* forest do?"

"I don't know," she said.

I decided to let it rest for a while.

"I want to go home," said Ann.

"You mean home, or back to the Forest Way compound?"

"The Forest Way is my home."

"I'm sorry," I said. "That isn't possible. I think you can help us find Leyla. Maybe you can give us information that will help us rescue her."

"I will not help you to thwart the will of the Forest."

"Okay," I said. "We'll talk about it later. You can watch TV, or read the newspaper, or we can talk some more about other things."

"I'm tired," she said. "I might like to go back to bed."

"Go ahead," I said, waving my coffee cup.

CHAPTER TWENTY-TWO

After Ann went back to bed, I pulled out my phone and called Alex Chan.

"Do you know what time it is?" he asked. He sounded groggy.

"I don't know, maybe 10 o'clock," I said. "Why?"

"Oh," he said. "Never mind. What's going on?"

"I think Leyla is being held prisoner against her will. I don't think she's been brainwashed at all."

"Okay," he said carefully. "What makes you think that?"

I told him about the notes, and my thoughts about her saying she hated me. I didn't mention Ann, or our escapades of the past week.

"All right," he said. "That makes a certain kind of sense. But if that's true, it's also very bad for Leyla."

"I know."

"I still don't know that you have enough to get a warrant. But it is serious enough that maybe judge Hamilton would go for it. Let me make some calls. We'll have to bring in someone from the Sheriff's department. I'll call Dan too, and see if he's willing to help."

"Thanks, Alex."

"I'm not engaged to her, but she's my friend too, Jonah."

"I know. I appreciate it."

"Okay. I'll call you in a bit."

I opened the file on Herman Brown, mostly to keep my mind occupied while I waited.

The folder was a mix of printed notes, financial statements, copies of official records, and some handwritten observations and thoughts. I flipped through it all, and found that there was one printed document that basically summarized all the information in the file. Vargas had scribbled some notes here and there on the printed pages.

Brown was forty years old. He claimed to have been born in Blue Earth, Minnesota. Actually, according to the file, he was born at Fairview Hospital in Minneapolis, and raised in Wayzata, which was a wealthy suburb west of the Twin Cities. Apparently, he used his claimed birthplace in Blue Earth as a sign of his destiny to restore unity between Human and Forest. I thought that was a little ironic. Blue Earth was a great environmental-sounding name, but there wasn't much actual forest near that farm-town out on the prairie.

After High School, Brown attended Carlton College in Northfield, an exclusive private school. He did graduate work at the University of Minnesota, ending up with a PhD in sociology. As Dr. Jackson Brandt had told me, while still in graduate school, Brown started gathering some radical environmentalists and having meetings. The Forest Way grew out of that. There wasn't any known record of violence from the group. Brown had apparently benefited financially from his followers. There were several bequeaths and asset transfers to Brown from those who joined the Forest Way. Five years ago, he had a net worth totaling about half a million dollars. And then, just a few years later, the Forest Way paid cash for the property near Grand Lake. According to Vargas' file, the value of the property was around five million, or, ten times Brown's last known net worth. There was no explanation in the file for how that became possible.

Although Brown was clearly the leader of Forest Way, Vargas noted that in recent years, a man known only as "Rock" had risen to become a kind of lieutenant to Brown. Vargas had scribbled a star next to his name, and a note that said "joined three years ago."

It had never been a large organization, but a few members had left the cult over the years. Vargas had apparently found one of them. The person in question had not said much that was useful. She described the cult as 'bogus,' and called herself stupid for ever being a part of it. Brown had used brainwashing and mind control techniques, but there was no evidence that he had ever kidnapped anyone or held them against their will. Vargas had located a few people who had been around the fringes of the cult and attended some meetings. They did not like what they saw, but they had not been coerced into joining.

After forty-five minutes, I was getting very antsy. Ann was still sleeping and I had not heard from Chan. Finally, after almost an hour, my phone buzzed.

"Borden," I said, answering.

"Jonah," said Alex. "It's all set up. You and I will meet with Judge Hamilton, Dan Jensen and Jack Jaeger in an hour at the courthouse."

I thought about Ann. Vargas might not be back by then. "Alex," I said, "what if I can't make it?"

"Are you insane, Jonah? You've got to be there, and bring those notes. The judge is going to make a decision mostly on your testimony."

"It's just that I have a situation here. I'm not sure how to get away without causing a problem."

"What are you up to Jonah?"

"Don't sound so suspicious," I said.

"I know how intensely you want to get Leyla out of there," said Chan. "Have you done something illegal?"

"No!" I said. "Of course not." I paused. "I don't think so, anyway."

There was a stern silence from Chan.

"Maybe," I admitted. "I guess I don't know."

"Don't tell me where you are or what you are doing, not yet anyway," said Alex. "Just meet me at the courthouse in an hour."

I hung up. If Ann really wanted to, she could just get up and leave. It was bitterly cold out, almost twenty below zero, and only a fool would go outside for any length of time without a coat, mittens or shoes. Frostbite and hypothermia would begin in a half-hour, or less. On the other hand, we weren't far from Highway sixty-one. If I were gone, Ann might try to run up there and flag someone down. I needed someone to sit with her.

When I thought about it, there was really only one option. I called Julie.

"Can you come up to Norstad's Cabins for a few hours?" I asked her.

"What are you talking about?" She sounded suspicious.

"It's difficult to explain," I said. "I need you to sit with someone for a while."

"You also need me to finish the church bulletin," she said.

"You can bring the laptop."

"What kind of person am I sitting with? Is this a baby, or an Alzheimer's patient? An insane person? Do you want me to babysit an axe-murderer?"

I drew breath to answer.

"I won't change any adult diapers," she said firmly.

"Okay, okay," I said. There was no point in dissembling with Julie. "I am with a member of the Forest Way. She may be able to help us get Leyla back. But I'm afraid if we leave her alone, she'll run away, and she might freeze to death."

"This is to help Leyla? To help her get out of the cult?"

"Yes."

"Why didn't you just say so?" asked Julie. "I'll be right there."

"Julie," I said quickly, before she could hang up.

"What?"

"I'm not sure how, well, *legal* this is."

"You really think she can help us figure out how to get Leyla back?"

"Yes."

"Do I have to stop this woman from leaving if she really wants to?"

I thought for a minute. "No. But maybe you don't have to take her anywhere she wants to go, either."

"Don't tell me any more about it. I'll be right over," said Julie again.

"Thank you. I mean it."

"Add it to the long list of things you owe me for," said Julie, and hung up.

Ann came out of the bedroom as I put down the phone.

"I want to go home," she said.

I didn't know Vargas' plan, but he wasn't here. I decided to wing it.

"Ann, I think you can help us figure out how to get Leyla back. Once you do that, you're free to go wherever you want."

"I will not thwart my Leader," she said. "Besides, Leyla would not want to leave him either."

That stopped me cold. Was I wrong in my belief that Leyla was being held against her will? Nothing in the file on the Forest Way gave credence to my theory. It might just be wishful thinking, and Ann might be able to tell me the truth, right now. "Have you talked to Leyla? Do you know she wants to stay?" My heart began to pound as I waited for the answer.

Ann looked proud. "I haven't seen her for a week or more. But *everyone* wants to stay. We belong in the Forest. We belong to Tree."

"But what if she did not? If it isn't right for us to keep you here, how can it be right for Tree to keep her there?"

She looked puzzled again, but she said, "Your friend would not want to leave. Not after seeing who Tree really is."

I thought no one would *stay* if they saw who Tree really was, but I held my peace.

"But just suppose she did want to leave? You would not want to force her to stay, would you?"

"No one need be forced. Once your eyes are opened, you don't want to leave."

"But what if your eyes are never opened?" I asked, trying to help her see it. "What if you remained ignorant? Shouldn't someone like that be allowed to leave?"

Ann looked troubled. "I suppose someone who could not see the truth should be allowed to leave. But it would be better for them to stay, and learn the truth."

"I believe she wants to leave," I said. "And I believe she is being held there against her will."

"Tree would not do anything wrong," insisted Ann. "Besides, I have not seen your friend for more than a week. I don't think she is even there anymore."

I grew cold at the thought. Tires crunched in the snow outside, and I saw Julie's car pull up next to mine.

"A friend is coming to sit with you for a while," I said. "Later, Nick will come back."

"Nick?"

"The man who brought you here last night."

I pulled on my coat and stepped outside to meet Julie. I explained about the food, and emphasized the need to keep Ann there.

"She's still under the influence of the cult," I said. "They use group exercises, peer pressure, hypnosis and other brainwashing techniques."

"Huh," said Julie, waving her hand dismissively. "I'll straighten her out for you."

"Julie," I said, "the human brain is very complex. I think deprogramming someone from a cult is kind of complicated. Just sit with her, make sure she's safe, and feed her as much protein as you can."

"Sure thing, Boss."

I glared at her, but she returned my look with innocence.

"Okay, then."

We went back in to the cabin, and I introduced Julie to Ann. As soon as Julie seemed settled, I picked up the folder on Herman Brown, and left.

CHAPTER TWENTY-THREE

As is so common the day after a big snow, the sky was brilliant and cloudless. The sun blazed in the sky, and sent bright echoes off a million angles of spotless white snow. The lake had already retreated several hundred yards and more off the shoreline, but out there the water was brilliantly blue, and the endless horizon throbbed with light and color. The plows had gone through, and the roads were fine. I took a deep breath. The North Shore changes and breathes with each new day, sometimes maudlin, sometimes mysterious, often gaudy in beauty, but never boring.

Judge Hamilton looked to be in her early sixties, with blond hair that was gradually turning white. We were in her chambers at the Superior Justice Center. The complex was relatively new, and Hamilton's space was open, carpeted in a tasteful burgundy Berber, with wide windows that looked toward the lake. The other walls were paneled in expensive looking dark wood, with matching wood bookcases that held rows of books that were all the same height. I was disappointed to see a computer on her desk. It seemed so prosaic and un-judge-like.

The Judge sat behind her desk and stared at Leyla's notes through a pair of red reading glasses. Chan, Jaeger, Jensen and I sat in a row of chairs, facing her across the big desk. I felt like we were naughty boys, called into the principal's office. After a moment, she put the papers down and looked at us over the top of her glasses. It reinforced the principal's office atmosphere.

"Is this all, gentlemen?" she asked.

"Go ahead," said Chan to me.

"When I went to see her, Leyla acted very strangely," I said. "At first she seemed drained, like she was emotionally exhausted. But then, she came alive, and began screaming that she hated me. It was completely uncharacteristic of her. It made no sense. It was only later that I realized it was *supposed* to make no sense. She was sending me a message that something was wrong, but she was not able to speak plainly. Then, when I looked closely at the notes, I realized she was being held against her will."

"That *is* uncharacteristic of her, your honor," put in Jensen. "I hardly believed it, when Jonah told us."

Judge Hamilton sighed. "Thank you, Chief. You weren't in the room at the time?"

"No," said Jensen. "We've explained all that."

"Precisely," said Hamilton. "Therefore, the only eye-witness is Pastor Borden."

"Yes."

"And you want a search warrant for this?"

"Yes."

"What are you searching for? You already know that the woman Leyla Bennett is there."

"Evidence of a crime. Kidnapping."

She sighed again, and looked at Jaeger, then Jensen, and then Chan. "Surely, you knew better than this."

Jaeger stared ahead with clear grey eyes. "I don't know anything, your honor. But if there is going to be a warrant issued, I will execute it."

"Dan?" asked the Judge.

"I know it's a long shot, your honor," said Jensen. "But there is something wrong up there. I have a dead body that I suspect was moved from the vicinity of the Forest Way. I don't know who else could be responsible."

"Exactly, Chief," said Hamilton. "You suspect. You don't know. And your evidence is the testimony of this man," she pointed at me, "who has an openly admitted reason for extreme bias against the cult. That's why I brought you all in here. Your probable cause is the unverified statements of a private citizen who has an axe to grind. A defense lawyer would eat this up. I will not authorize a fishing expedition based on his testimony alone."

"But they *are* holding Leyla," I objected. "That's not opinion. That's fact."

"So you tell me," she said. "But you also tell me that you spoke with her and, according to your own words, she told you that she hated you. She told you to go away and leave her alone. This isn't probable cause."

I opened my mouth, but she held up her hand.

"Pastor Borden, people have the right of free association. According to your own testimony, we know where Leyla Bennett is. According to that same testimony, she said she wants to stay there. It is not in my power to force people to fix their relationships."

I felt a slow burn in my cheeks. "This isn't a relationship problem. This is a cult problem."

"If I were you," said Hamilton, "I would not want any judge or government official to be eager to get involved in violating religious freedom. If they want to worship acorns, that's their business. In spite of the federal government's approach in recent years, I will not lightly violate personal, religious, privacy or property rights. As a pastor, I think you should be glad of that fact. If I can order a warrant because the Forest Way people act strange according to our standards, who's to say that Lutherans aren't just as strange? That is a slippery slope I will not set foot upon."

I looked at Chan. His face was expressionless. I looked at Jaeger, sitting on the other side of me, next to Dan. He could have been thinking about baseball. He looked bored. Dan's eyebrows looked a little tight, but he didn't say anything.

Judge Hamilton's face softened. She took off her reading glasses and looked me in the eyes. Hers were bright blue.

"Look, Pastor Borden, I'm sorry, I really am. Honestly, I'm inclined to believe you. But I have to uphold the law. And the law that protects you and Harbor Lutheran Church also protects Leyla Bennett and the Forest Way. If you can find me some solid reason to believe that Leyla Bennett is being held against her will, have Lieutenant Jaeger call me any time of day or night, and I will issue the warrant. But until then, I can't do it."

Chan had been silent the whole time. He nodded. "We're sorry for wasting your time, your honor. Thank you for meeting us on a Saturday."

Hamilton smiled. "Don't try to placate me, Alex, it won't work."

"It never crossed my mind your honor," he said with an entirely expressionless face. "Everyone knows you are the most impartial judge in Minnesota.'

Her whole face lit up with a grin, and she waved her hands in dismissal. "Oh, Alex, you are incorrigible!"

Chan's face was transformed by his own bright and sudden smile. "Yes I am. Thank you."

We rose and shook hands and left her chambers. She was still smiling and shaking her head when I closed the door.

"Does she try a lot of your cases?" I asked Chan as we started back toward the lobby.

"Quite a few," he said.

"You are one smooth, yellow devil."

He grinned again. "Just be glad I'm on your side, pale-face."

My own smile faded quickly as I considered the result of the meeting. "So what do we do now?"

"We keep working," said Jensen. "I think you're right. I think the note, the circumstances, and what Leyla said, add up to a clear message. She was trying to ask for help, without tipping them off. Honestly, I'm a little surprised Hamilton didn't go for it. What do you think, Alex?"

"I don't usually see this side of things," said Alex. "I'm usually coping with the results of a warrant, not asking for one. I've never seen it go down from this side."

Jaeger grunted. "I'm with Dan. I expected her to give us a break here. I mean, we aren't talking about an arrest here. Just authorization to look around and talk to people."

We reached the lobby, which was empty on this Saturday morning. We all stopped.

"What about what she said about religious freedom?" asked Chan.

"Crap," said Jaeger. "It isn't about that at all. We have eye-witness evidence that a murder vic was moved from the vicinity of that nuthouse. We have a note that was clearly forged. I say, she should have given us the warrant."

"It all comes back to me, though, doesn't it?" I said. "I'm the eye-witness that says John Doe was killed near the Forest Way. I'm the one who presented the notes, the one who saw Leyla. There is nothing but my word for all these things."

"That's probably it," said Chan. "You aren't an officer conducting a lawful investigation. She's treating everything as hearsay, because it all comes back to you, and you might be just pursuing some personal feud with Leyla."

"I'm not," I said.

"We know that, Jonah," said Dan. "But she's worried about appearing biased, or unduly influenced by one private citizen."

Jaeger grunted. His left cheek was working, as if he was chewing something. "What if she is?" he asked.

"What do you mean?" asked Chan.

"Judges get elected. They need campaign contributions. What if the Forest Way contributes to Hamilton?"

"That's a nasty thought, Jack," said Jensen.

"Yes, it is," said Jaeger. "Doesn't mean it couldn't happen."

"So now what?" I asked again.

"We're on this," said Jensen. "We'll keep poking at it until we get something that Hamilton has to pay attention to, and then we'll go in and get Leyla."

"You're on it with my permission," said Jaeger, looking at Jensen. "The county is my jurisdiction. But for once, I think Borden is probably right. Something's not right with those nutcases. My people will be keeping a sharper eye on them, and you go ahead and poke around, Dan."

"Thank you," I said.

"I'm not doing it for you," said Jaeger. "I'm doing it 'cause it's my job."

I opened my mouth, but Jensen glared at me, and I let it pass. A pastor, taking lessons from a cop in tact and diplomacy. I guess I needed all the help I could get.

CHAPTER TWENTY-FOUR

"I've got something for you guys," I said. "Wait here just a minute." I went out to my car, and got the folder on Herman Brown. Back in the lobby, I held it up.

"I have some information on the cult leader, Herman Brown," I said.

"I see why he changed his name to Tree," murmured Chan. I grinned at him.

"Anyway," I said, "I need this folder, but if you guys wanted, you could get copies right now."

Jaeger took the folder. "I'll take it up to my office and make copies." We walked with Jaeger to the wing where the Sheriff's offices were housed.

"Where did you get this stuff?" asked Jaeger, flipping through the folder as we walked.

"I've been talking to cult-experts," I said, skirting the whole truth. "One of them, a guy named Nick Vargas, put this together for me."

Chan glanced at me but said nothing. Jaeger just grunted.

Jaeger made three copies, and gave one to Jensen, one to Chan, and kept the third. He returned the original to me. We left Jaeger in his domain, and walked back to the front lobby. Jensen put his hand on my shoulder. "Hang in there Jonah," he said.

"Thanks."

After he left, Chan, pointed to a sitting area in the deserted lobby. "Okay, Jonah. You had better tell me what's going on."

I was quiet, trying to think how to begin.

"I'm your attorney, Jonah. This is all in confidence. But I can help you better if I know everything that's going on. You said you weren't sure about something you were doing. Tell me about that."

"This Vargas guy, the one who put together the folder, he's a cult-buster. I hired him to get Leyla out."

"Back up," said Chan. "What's a cult-buster?"

I told him about Vargas and his background. He grunted with interest when I explained about Vargas' mother.

"Anyway," I said, "we spent a lot of last week doing surveillance. Last night we went up there to snatch Leyla. We got the wrong person."

"What?" Chan fairly shouted the word. He glanced around the empty lobby, and then said in a quieter voice, "What do you mean?"

"It was dark, and snowing heavily. He grabbed the wrong woman."

"So you took someone by force from the Forest Way."

"Yeah, I guess so. I mean, I just drove the car, but yes, I helped. We thought it was Leyla."

"Where is this person now?"

"Hold on," I said. "Vargas wants to deprogram her too. He's a real crusader. He believes in his work. Plus, he says, maybe she'll give some information that will help us get Leyla. Already she told us that Tree deliberately allowed us to think this Ann was Leyla. He's going to great lengths to keep Leyla there."

Chan rubbed his face. "This is a mess, Jonah."

"I know," I said. "I'm sorry Alex."

He waved his hand. "Don't tell me any more right now. I need to think about this for a little bit. I would say, however, the faster she gets deprogrammed, the better. If she comes out of this still wanting to be part of the Forest Way, she'll probably press charges against both you and Vargas. Honestly, as your attorney, I need to tell you to let her go, right away."

"Okay, Alex," I said. "I understand."

It was after noon when I left the Superior Justice Center. I was hoping Vargas was back to the cabin already. I had no idea how to deprogram a cult member, and besides, I still had preparation to do for the next day, which was Sunday.

Pulling up to the cabin, I saw only Julie's car. I parked, and pulled out my cell phone, dialing Vargas. Reception was pretty spotty back in the hills off the Shore, and even if he had reception, if Vargas was still watching the compound, his phone would be off. As I expected, it rang direct to voicemail.

"Vargas," I said to the recording, "I'm getting a little nervous, plus I have to get to work today. Call me as soon as you get this."

I hung up and exited the car, and went to the cabin. Julie answered my knock. I stomped the snow off my boots and stepped inside.

"No word from Nick Vargas?" I asked. She shook her head. Ann was sitting at the table. There were playing cards spread out around her.

"You just interrupted a game of Gin," said Julie. She went back to her seat, and picked up her hand, without another word to me. I stood there and watched them play for a minute. Julie uttered a mild profanity when Ann said "Gin!" and laid down the rest of her cards.

"Your deal," said Julie, and got up and came back to where I stood. Ann got up and went into the bathroom.

"I think I'm making progress," said Julie. "I'll call you, if I need you."

"What kind of progress?" I asked. "You about to win a game of Gin?"

"I told you I'd straighten her out, Jonah," she said. "And I will. I make a mean steak, just ask Alex."

I knew Alex had a crush on Julie. I hadn't known it had gone as far as home-cooked meat. I shook off the thought.

"I think," I said carefully, "there may be more to it than playing cards and eating steak."

"Just because your mind operates like a Rube-Goldberg device, doesn't mean that everyone else's does," said Julie. "I don't think it's so complicated. She just needs a good dose of common sense. I've got plenty of that."

"Indeed, you're full of," I paused, "common sense."

She gave me a hard look. "I'm telling you, I've got this, Boss. I'm going to help her, and she's going to help us get Leyla back."

Truthfully, I had a lot to do before the service the next day. It couldn't hurt to let Julie stay – after all, Vargas would be back soon.

She saw me wavering. "Why don't you go on and take care of your stuff? I've already talked to Dagmar. She's coming in to copy the bulletins. She'll answer the phone while she's there. She told me she's bringing a bag of Kona Coffee for the office when she comes in to do the bulletins."

"You play dirty," I said.

"You're welcome."

"Okay. Call me if you need anything," I said.

"Will do, Chief," she said, saluting.

CHAPTER TWENTY-FIVE

I didn't hear from Vargas the rest of that day. I kind of hoped that he had returned with Leyla, and was planning to surprise me after church. I felt like a kid, waiting for Christmas.

On Sunday, I preached on Job. The last two weeks, I felt like I had been kind of phoning it in, but Job was real. He was a man who seemingly, had everything going for him, including faith. And then, in the space of days, he lost his children, his livelihood, all his possessions and his health. His wife suggested that he curse God for it. Instead, he said, "The Lord gives, and the Lord takes away. Blessed be the name of the Lord."

I felt like there was some "the Lord takes away," going on in my life. I hated it. I didn't want it. But Job challenged me to hold on with a faith that could say, anyway, "Blessed be the name of the Lord." I didn't care how many people fell asleep. That week's sermon was for me.

Afterwards, even though I was exhausted, as was usual every Sunday afternoon, I called Vargas. It went straight to voicemail. I went home, ate something, and stretched out on the couch. I figured maybe I should take a nap, as usual. If Vargas had got Leyla, I would probably need to be in good shape to help him. If he didn't, I'd need sleep to deal with the disappointment. The snow was falling again, frosting the pine trees outside my windows. The fire was warm and Melanchthon curled up with me on the couch, purring like a freight train.

When I finally woke up, I called Vargas again. Again it went to voicemail. I called Julie.

"Yo!" she said, answering the phone, sounding like her mouth was full.

"What time did Vargas get in yesterday?" I asked her. "Did he have Leyla?"

"I'm fine, thanks," she said. "And you?"

"Sorry," I said. "I'm a little tense. How is it going?"

"Just fine," she said. "Ann and I have switched to two-handed five-hundred, and she's beating my pants off." I heard a giggle in the background.

I opened my mouth, and then closed it again. "Did she just giggle?" I asked.

"Yep. We're having fun here."

"Is Vargas there? I can't reach him."

"He never came back," said Julie.

"What do you mean, 'never came back?'"

"It's simple English, Boss. Vargas never came back here."

"Did he call you? Send a message?"

"How would he have my phone number? I've never met the man."

Of course, she was right. "So you stayed overnight?"

"Sure. It was like a slumber party. We ran over to my place and got some clothes. We got some snacks on the way back. It's been great."

"How is Ann?"

"Why don't you come ask her for yourself?" said Julie.

"Okay," I said. I broke the connection. Melanchthon came and rubbed his orange, fluffy body against my legs. I scratched his ears.

"Okay, buddy," I said. "Sorry I'm not around much these days." I fed him some leftover pot-roast, and then left.

At Vargas' rented cabin, Julie opened the door just as I stamped my way onto the porch.

"Come on in, Chief," she said.

Ann was sitting on the couch. There was a picture frozen on the small TV. There was a woman in nineteenth century dress, talking to a man in a high, stiff collar, holding a horse.

"She's never seen *Pride and Prejudice*," said Julie. "Can you believe it?"

"Shocking," I said.

Ann was curled up, half-sitting on the couch, with her feet tucked sideways under her. If I had tried to sit like that, I'd be snapping tendons like old banjo strings.

"How're you doing Ann?" I asked.

She looked at me boldly. "I'm doing fine. This has been a really fun day."

I pulled off my coat and shoes, and went into the kitchen toward the coffee pot.

"It's fresh!" called Julie.

I poured a cup, and came back into the living room and sat on the recliner across from Ann. I wasn't sure how to begin.

"How are you feeling about the Forest Way now?" I asked her.

She wouldn't meet my eyes. She stared at the static picture for a long time without speaking. Finally she shrugged. "I guess I'm confused. These last two days seem surreal. Or maybe it's the last five years of my life that are surreal. I can't believe it's actually been five years, but Julie helped me work it out. I lost track of time, somehow. It's like this world has nothing to do with that one, and vice-versa."

"I would imagine confusion is pretty normal for someone in your situation."

"Of course it is!" said Julie sharply. I shot her a warning look, but without much hope. Most warning looks were lost on Julie.

Ann just nodded.

"Do you think you could tell us any more about Leyla?" I asked.

"I'm kind of confused about her, also," said Ann.

"What do you mean?"

"Well, at first I thought she was a novice, just like I was when I first joined. But then, I figured she must be a Guardian. Now, with what you've told me, I don't know what to think."

"I don't understand," I said. "What's a *Guardian*?"

"The Forest Way is made up of two sections," she said, shifting, and lifting her knees up to her chest, with her feet on the couch in front of her. My tendons twinged again at the sight. "Two thirds of us, or more, enter the Forest Way as novices. We learn from acolytes and elders, and of course, from Tree. We live in community, serving each other, and serving The Forest."

I remembered something Herman Brown had said when he introduced himself to me as Tree. "When you say 'The Forest,' do you mean 'Tree?'" I asked.

"The Forest is Tree; Tree is The Forest," said Ann. She said it like it was some kind of mantra. Then she looked confused, like she realized, at the edges of her awareness, how strange and robotic she sounded. "At least, that's what they taught us to say," she added, looking a little bit embarrassed.

"So, you said there was another section," I prompted.

"Yes. Tree is peace-loving, and he has taught us to love peace as we love him. But he knew that some people would not understand us. They would hate us, and seek to hurt us. He knew that the Forest would need protection. So he formed the Guardians. They are our protectors, Guardians of Tree and Forest and all of the Forest Way."

"So they are the same as the rest of you?"

"No. They don't go through the same initiation process as us. They have their own training, different from ours, because they must be prepared to use violence. There are fewer of them – they make up about a third of our community, or maybe only a quarter. They keep themselves somewhat separate from the rest of us. Tree says that is because they have a special calling. I think he likes us separate, because he doesn't want us to learn violence, and I suppose he doesn't want the Guardians to forget it."

It made a kind of sick sense. If most of your people are peace-lovers, what happens when you need protection? Tree had organized an answer to that question. But I didn't like the potential for a bad ending. It was hard to forget the Branch Davidians in Waco Texas or the craziness in Northern Idaho years before that.

"Walk softly, and train a bunch of thugs to protect you," I murmured.

"What?" asked Ann. Julie glared at me.

"Nothing," I said. "So what makes you think that Leyla was a Guardian?"

"Well, I don't know that she was," said Ann, staring off into space. "It seemed like she was a regular novice at first, but after seven days or so, she went off with Guardians. I haven't seen her very much since then, but a few times I saw her with them. I haven't seen her at all for the past few days."

"Can you tell me any more about the Guardians?"

"I don't know that much. Like I said, they keep somewhat to themselves. They also travel a lot. When we go out to sell our hand-crafted goods to the city-dwellers, there is always at least one Guardian for every one of us normal followers. Sometimes it's all Guardians who go to do the selling."

"You said the Guardians are trained to protect. Are there any women Guardians?"

"Oh yes. Not very many, but there are a few."

"Do they live communally with the rest of you?"

"Well, sort of. They have their living quarters in the main lodge. They are around, but they keep to themselves, and like I said, they are in and out a lot more than the rest of us."

"Why would Leyla join the Guardians?" I said.

"I don't know. It's strange too, because I really think she started out as a regular novice."

"You said that you knew Tree was using you as a decoy. Why would he need to protect a Guardian? I thought they were the protectors."

"I don't know," said Ann. "I'm confused about a lot of things right now."

I saw Julie giving me a meaningful look from my left, but I ignored it.

"Do you know why she was special to him? Why he would be willing to sacrifice you to keep her?"

She shook her head miserably. "I don't know that either. At first, I felt like it was an honor to help Tree by being a decoy for your friend. But now I know that means I am not as important to him as her." She dropped her face to her knees. "I'm so confused right now."

"Jonah," said Julie.

"Okay, okay," I said to Julie. I turned back to Ann. "I'm sorry, Ann. It must be very difficult right now."

She nodded, not lifting her head. Her shoulders shook a little bit, like she was crying. Julie brought her some tissue, which Ann accepted, raising her red-eyed face and blowing her nose with a loud, wet noise.

"Ann," I said. "You are safe here. You can take all the time you want to sort things out, and when you're ready, we'll take you where you want to go. Just take your time."

She nodded.

"Can I pray for you, Ann?" I asked. "You don't have to share my beliefs. It's just the best comfort I have to offer you right now."

"Yes," she said in a whisper. "Thank you."

Julie sat next to Ann on the couch with her arm around her shoulders. I put my hand on Ann's shoulder and said a prayer for her, out loud. Afterwards, as I was leaving, Julie walked out onto the porch with me, closing the door behind her.

"I guess you have *some* skills," she said, looking at me with narrowed eyes.

"Thanks for your confidence," I said. "What are we going to do about Vargas? I don't think it's a good idea for me to spend the night with Ann, or even a lot of time alone, for that measure. You know small towns. Word gets around, and it doesn't look good for a pastor."

"Are you asking for my help?"

"Julie," I said humbly, "will you stay with Ann another night?"

"Sure thing, Chief," she said. "Just remember you owe me another one. Chalk it up with all the other favors you owe me."

"I pay you for most of your work," I pointed out.

"Yes, but not enough."

I threw up my hands and left. There was never any point in trying to win with Julie.

CHAPTER TWENTY-SIX

It was late afternoon, and the sun had given up early. The snow continued to fall, not a blizzard, but a steady December snowfall. There would be a few extra inches on the ground tomorrow. I drove home through the falling dark, pondering the broken pieces of my love for Leyla.

I was worried about Vargas. The morning before, when he went out, had been bitterly cold, and temperatures had only climbed to ten above or so since then. If he had spent the night outside, he could be in real trouble, if not frozen to death. As far as I knew, I was the only one who had known his plans. I sighed. I was going to have to look for him.

Ann had given me more information, but I wasn't sure that it was helpful. I assumed the tough guys who had thrown me out, and probably Rock too, were Guardians. Leyla might have decided to focus her investigation on the Guardian arm of the Forest Way. It certainly seemed like most of those around when I met with Leyla had been Guardians. I didn't see how that information helped me get Leyla out. Judge Hamilton wasn't helping me get her out, either, which, in turn, meant that neither Chief Jensen nor Jack Jaeger could help me.

I didn't even know for sure *why* they were holding Leyla. I could only assume that they had discovered her real purpose for being there, and didn't want her to print the story. I tried to think like Herman Brown for a minute. If I was an egotistical, charismatic cult leader, and I discovered that an attractive reporter had infiltrated my organization, what would I try to do?

Without the Christian moral code to restrain me, my first impulse would be to seduce her. Heaven knows, I'd had trouble enough restraining myself until our wedding as it was. But the seduction could serve another purpose. If I was Brown, part of the seduction would be to win her over to my side. In fact, I'd try to start the brainwashing for real. The best way to squash the story would be to make a true believer of Leyla. Brown's personality was like a physical force. Even so, I didn't think he had succeeded yet, at the time I had last seen Leyla.

A new thought hit me like a fresh, cold snowball. If Leyla *was* being held against her will, and was sending me a message by saying she hated me, why hadn't she instead just walked out with me when I was with her? Surely the Forest Way people wouldn't have openly restrained her in front of me. If they had tried it, a legitimate charge of kidnapping could have been made. All she had to do was get up and come with me. *What made her stay?* Was I wrong? Had Tree already succeeded in winning her over by that point? If so, my entire interpretation of that interview was wrong. Nothing seemed to make sense any more.

I breathed in, and then out. It didn't seem to help, except to carry oxygen around my body, which, I supposed, had to be done. Well, at least I knew what my next step had to be. I had to find Vargas, and make sure he was okay. To spend thirty hours outside in Northern Minnesota in winter was extremely dicey. I couldn't wait until tomorrow. If Vargas was hurt somewhere, and stuck without shelter, another night would bring his chances of survival to almost nothing.

As I pulled into my garage, I dialed Vargas' number again. No point in getting cold for no reason. Once more, however, the connection went right to voicemail. I went inside and made coffee. Fending off Melanchthon's playful ambushes, I gathered some gear, a winter-rated sleeping bag and a small tarp with rope, and put it all into my external frame backpack. I added a few chunks of dry firewood to the load, and a hatchet. If I found Vargas, and he was hurt, we'd probably be stranded for the night. I filled a thermos with hot coffee, and stuffed it into the pack, along with my small bottle of brandy, and a spare freeze-dried meal that I had left-over from my last canoe trip of the fall.

When I opened my trunk to put my backpack in, I saw the gear that we had used the night we had snatched Ann from the cult. There were hand-warmers and the smoke grenades, as well as the flash-bang grenades. Without hesitation I stuffed them all into the outside pockets of my backpack. I noticed that Vargas had also left the night vision goggles in my trunk. I rammed them into my pack as well.

I went to my gun locker, removed my twelve-gauge shotgun, grabbing boxes of both shells and slugs. The forests around here are inhabited by wolves, bears and cougars. The bears should be asleep by this point in the season, but wolves and cougars hunt through the winter. Wolves in North America typically did not attack humans, but I'd rather have the shotgun just in case I had to put that to the test. And cougar attacks were well documented throughout the continent. In fact, I wondered if something like that had happened to Vargas, leaving him injured and unable to make his way back to his car. Even a bull moose could be real trouble. In fact, moose were more deadly to people than most predators. In any case, there was no way I was going into the woods by myself at night, unarmed.

I made sure I had two flashlights, in addition to the headlamp that I would strap to my head to leave my hands free. I clipped my snowshoes to the outside of the pack, and stowed my skis in the rack on my roof. I didn't know which ones I would use.

Once my gear was stowed, I went back in and suited up for a winter night outdoors. The bottom layer was thermal underwear, covering both legs and arms. Polypropylene socks went underneath my thick wool ones. Next came sweat pants and then waterproof nylon pants and on top, a wool sweater. I would wear my parka and a nylon-blend ski mask that would protect me from my neck to the top of my head, with openings for my eyes and mouth. On my hands I would have thin wool gloves underneath sheepskin mittens. Even with all that, I was going to be freezing within seconds of the time I stopped moving, but it was the best I could do.

I was in a hurry, and I thought I might be forgetting something. I probably should have paid attention to that feeling, but I didn't. I was only concerned about Vargas.

~

When I reached the snow-machine parking area near the Forest Way, I knew I was in for a long night. Vargas' car wasn't there. When we had looked at maps of the area before our stakeout, I had showed him the route to the drop-box I had used with Leyla. Vargas had decided against it, because at its closest, that trail passed a half-mile distant from the cult, and it was two miles from the nearest road at that point. I had chosen that as our drop-box location precisely because it was so unlikely to be noticed by Forest Way members, but it wasn't a very fast way to smuggle someone out of the cult compound. However, our snatching of Ann had put the cult on high alert, so probably Vargas had decided that after all, it was better to take that long, back way to avoid detection.

I sighed. The way to the trailhead by road was another half an hour at least, and the snow was thickening. At least I'd be warm for another thirty minutes.

It was closer to forty minutes by the time I reached the trailhead. Vargas' car was there. I tried the door, but it was locked or frozen; probably both. I brushed the snow off a window and looked inside with my headlamp. There was a crumpled fast food bag, and a cup in the holder. There were no notes or two way radios or anything useful like that. At least I knew he had come this way. It made me feel like a real detective, to think I had figured it out.

After a moment I also figured out that in terms of detective skill, it had been like deducing the fact that two plus two makes four. This was the only other place he *could* park and still be within five miles of the Forest Way. Oh well, I still had my day job.

I went back to my car, and stared longingly at my skis. They were by far the fastest way to travel, but I only had the one pair, and skis are awkward if you are trying to assist someone who is hurt. With a sigh, I stepped into my snowshoes instead. I snapped on my headlamp, and stared at a blinding wall of white reflected back from the snow in the air. That wasn't going to work, I couldn't see anything.

I flipped off the light. Snowfall at night often captures and reflects even the tiniest amounts of ambient light, making it seem lighter than it is. I thought I might be able to see OK without the headlamp.

After I walked into the first tree, I reevaluated. I pulled my arms out of my backpack straps, and rolled off my back onto my hands and knees. When the pounding pain in my head subsided to a dull ache, I remembered the night vision goggles. I put my headlamp on again while I rummaged in the pack for them.

I strapped them on, like I had two nights before. The eyepieces were like those on a pair of binoculars, except they were connected in the middle to something that looked like a small camera, and looked out of a single lens. Now, as before when I had worn them, I felt like some kind of cyborg with artificial eyes.

Combined with the ambient brightness captured by the snow, the goggles made the world almost as light as a bright, moonlit night, albeit a green, snowy one. I stood up and kicked the tree that had knocked me down.

"Hah!" I said. "I see you now, you stupid piece of lumber." Immediately I reached out and patted the trunk softly. "Sorry Lord," I muttered. "It's a very nice tree, I just wish you hadn't put it right there where I was going to walk into it."

I wondered if I was cracking up, and considered it likely. I decided I should find Vargas before I went completely mad.

Though it was twenty degrees below freezing, I stayed reasonably warm in my core. Snowshoeing through deep snow, carrying a forty-pound pack does keep a body toasty. But my fingers, ears and toes grew icy and numb fairly soon, as did my exposed lips. Every so often I reached up to press my ears against my head through the ski mask. I wiggled my fingers and toes, but it didn't help much.

A lot of people haven't been in snow shoes. The effort is a little bit like walking through dry sand at the beach. Each step takes just a little more work than normal, and you sink a little bit every time. Skiing the two miles to get near the Forest Way compound would have been a matter of fifteen minutes, less, if I wanted to make a race of it. Walking the trail in summer, with the pack, it might have taken forty minutes. In snowshoes, in the cold, with snow flying all over my green-tinted world, it took more than an hour.

I had told Vargas about the "hunting accident," and warned him to get off the trail before he got into the bottom of the little valley where I had kept the drop box with Leyla. So when I got through the cleft in the hills and started to descend, into that valley, I began to look for the remnants of tracks that Vargas might have left behind. After a few minutes, I realized this would be fruitless. It had snowed twice since Vargas left, and I had not seen any clear tracks on the trail so far. There were faint hollows, and the snow had clearly been disturbed at some time, but the flakes swirling through the air, and the several inches of new stuff on the ground, made it hard to follow any kind of trail.

Finally, I observed what might have been some disturbed snow, and turned toward my left, following the slope around toward the Forest Way grounds. Picking my way on the slope through the trees required a certain amount of care and attention, and I soon lost the trail, if it was a trail. I started scanning the trees.

"Vargas!" I shouted. "Nick, are you out here? It's Jonah."

Far off, a wolf howled. Alone in the woods at night, it was a wild, thrilling sound, and I felt a burst of adrenalin in my chest. But Vargas did not respond.

I stood still for a minute and tried to think. It was a move that made me cold very quickly. I hadn't seen any sign of Vargas on the main trail. If he was hurt, his injury had occurred somewhere nearby, because at this point I was probably only a half-mile from the Forest Way. In fact, since I was on a steep slope, the accident may have been very close indeed. Since I was from the Northwest, where we have real mountains, I couldn't really call the hills on the North Shore by that name, but there were many steep slopes and sudden drops, and even a few small cliffs, mostly between twenty and sixty feet high. Most of the cliffs bordered rivers and creeks, but those cut the land all throughout this area. And every so often you could find a small cliff in a hillside, apart from any waterway.

I moved again, much more cautiously now, straining to see the slope ahead of me through the trees and snowfall. After twenty minutes the slope had steepened considerably. I could reach out with my left hand and touch the ground on that side with hardly any bending. I was looking ahead and to the right when I took a step forward and my right foot slid out from under me.

I flailed my arms and slammed into the side of the hill on my left, landing on my back, careening down the slope, riding my pack like I was on a sled, yelling like an idiot the whole time. The world whirled green around me as I caught a glimpse of a place ahead where the snowflakes swirled in frightening emptiness. I grasped at branches as I jolted down the steep hill, but I only lost one of my mittens. A piece of brush snatched the night vision goggles from my face. And then I was swinging sickeningly over nothing, waiting agonizing moments for the violent slam of the ground. Only I didn't hit the ground. Instead, I did a slow bounce in the air, and then continued to swing in the emptiness. Just as I realized what had happened I swayed back and slammed into hard rock, and then bounced into open space again. I was hanging over a cliff of indeterminate height, my backpack caught in the branches of a young tree that creaked and groaned and shifted.

The straps of my pack were pulled up high, and my right arm began to slip out. I swung my left arm, trying to grab the branch or tree that was caught in my pack. I felt a few strands of fir needles, but nothing I could grasp. My movement caused a shift, and with a jolt I descended a foot, and then my pack held fast again. My right arm came out even farther, and now there was pressure on my left as well. I could see nothing in the dark and snow, without the night vision goggles. My right arm came all the way out, but I grabbed the strap with my hand, thankful that I had lost that mitten. I bounced in the air as the tree holding me responded to my flailing. My left arm was now high above my head, and I began to slide out of the pack altogether. I had a waist belt that should have prevented all this, but it must have come undone as I slid down the slope to the edge of the cliff.

I hung in midair, kicking my legs and trying desperately to reach the branch that was holding me.

"A little help here, Lord," I said. It was a short prayer, but it was succinct, and I'm sure he got the point.

My left arm came suddenly loose, and I held on with my right as my body swung out of the pack. The branch above me bounced once more, and then with a ripping sound the pack came loose and I plummeted into the darkness.

CHAPTER TWENTY-SEVEN

I plummeted all of two feet. I landed in soft snow, and automatically folded my legs and rolled over, coming up on my back. After a second, I began to laugh. Sometimes I do that in inappropriate moments. Of all the solutions I had thought God might come up with, I never expected a shorter cliff.

When I caught my breath, I realized I should have descended to the bottom of the valley in the first place. If Vargas had fallen, he would be at the bottom, as I now was, not up on the slope. Smart, Jonah. It only took a potentially life threatening fall to make you see it. Ah well, Divinity degrees did not often confer common sense.

I was a little bruised but nothing more. I might have been scratched too, but I couldn't feel the skin on my face or hands, so it didn't matter. I quickly put my right hand in my pocket to warm it. The most serious consequence of the fall was the loss of the night vision glasses. I rummaged in the pack and found a flashlight. I clicked it on. The falling snow reflected the light back at me so that I was standing in a bright bubble with a visibility of about ten feet. Everything beyond was white nothingness.

Like many backpacks, mine had a flap that came down over the top of the main compartment. The compartment could be mostly closed underneath the flap with a drawstring. I normally did that, and then put my rolled up tarp on top, holding it down with the flap pulled tight over it. The flap was held down by buckles, but one of the buckles had come undone, and the other was gone; the little strap had ripped from the pack. I cast about in the snow, and found my tarp lying near the base of the cliff. I shined the flashlight upward. I could just barely make out the top, about fifteen feet above me.

I secured the tarp with the remaining buckle, and some cord that I kept in one of the pockets of my pack. Then I shouldered my pack. Now that it was obvious to me that Vargas, if hurt, would be on the valley floor, I didn't know which way to go. I had already covered some distance on the upper slope, and I might have missed him. Should I go back, or continue?

I decided I should go on. It hadn't really become treacherous until I slipped. I moved forward again.

"Vargas?" I yelled. "Nick Vargas! It's Jonah. Where are you?" I paused, but heard nothing except the wind in the pines.

After about five minutes I realized it was useless to continue without the night vision goggles. My visibility was so limited by the white-out that I could easily walk within fifteen feet of an unconscious man, and never see him. I turned back, still calling out every so often. Eventually, the terrain began to drop in front of me, and I found myself on a slope once more. I stopped. Without the night vision goggles I felt almost blind. I really didn't want to fall off another cliff. Somewhere there was a scripture about not putting the Lord to the test.

I hesitated. The only other choice was to spend the night. I had come prepared to do that, if I found Vargas too injured to move, but winter-camping in Minnesota is more a measurement of stupidity and perseverance than it is an enjoyable form of recreation. I thought about the fall again, how it felt when I slid off the edge into nothingness.

With reluctance, I retraced my steps back to a fallen log I had recently passed. I began to scoop out a hollow, building a short, rough wall of snow about four feet from the log. When I had a depression about three feet deep, I unrolled the tarp, and secured it to the log with cord. I stretched it across the hollow in the snow, and then piled more snow on top of the other edge, packing it down to hold the tarp. I scoured the area and found some dead wood to help anchor it. Then I wriggled inside through a small opening I had left. Once inside, I pushed more snow up until my doorway was just a little hole to the outside world.

I was in an artificial snow cave. One wall was the deadfall, and the three others were snow banks; my roof was the tarp. Outside it was a few degrees below zero, but in here, after I breathed for a while, it would stay thirty degrees warmer, or, just below freezing. My sleeping bag had plenty of insulation to handle that. After I drank some coffee and ate a few nuts, I stripped off my boots, nylon pants and parka, and wriggled inside the bag.

I was warm enough, but I slept badly, having constant nightmares of falling. I finally slipped into a deeper sleep toward morning, cocooned in snow that molded to my body around the sleeping bag, thinking that I was closer to Leyla right now than I had been for many days.

~

I woke up to find my little snow cave luminous with the diffused light of the sun through my tarp and the snow around me. I was perfectly toasty until I crawled out of the sleeping bag. Thirty degrees was a lot warmer than it was outside, but it was still below freezing. I ate some more nuts, and tried to hydrate myself with coffee that had become slushy with frost overnight. Staying on my hands and knees, I pulled my pack together, knowing it would be much colder outside.

Rather than wriggling through the snow blocking my small opening, when I was ready, I simply stood up, pulling the tarp out of the snow-wall in front of me. I only got about two-quarts of snow down my back and on my face as it slid off the tarp. I blamed my lack of foresight on the cold coffee. Shaking the rest of the snow from the tarp, I rolled it up, fastened it to my pack, and stepped into my snowshoes.

It was bright and sunny, and cold. I didn't have a thermometer with me, but I guessed it was about zero. When the wind gusted it hurt my face, and I quickly pulled on my ski-mask. I had lost both the mitten and the cotton glove from my right hand, so I put the glove from my left onto my right and kept the mitten on my left. Both felt cold pretty quickly. I looked around. To my left, maybe a mile away, was a small ridge that I guessed led up to the compound of the Forest Way. To my right the ground fell away a little more, but not as steeply as the hill behind me, which held the precipitous slopes and the cliff that I had encountered the night before.

I was about to move to the right to look for Vargas when I saw a bright flash from the ridge to my left, from the direction of the Forest Way. I stood perfectly still, staring through the trees. I saw it again. It was a reflection of the morning sun, bouncing off of something up on the ridge. It wasn't steady, so something was moving the reflective surface.

It is an old trick to always carry a small mirror in wild country. I had one myself, in my pack. Not only can you look at your own face to facilitate talking to yourself, but a mirror is one of the best survival signaling devices. You can see the reflection of the sun on a mirror for miles, and it is very visible from the air. Perhaps Vargas had a mirror with him.

I started through the forest toward the flashing. Fairly quickly the ground dropped away and I was lower down, in thick trees and unable to see it anymore, but I had gotten a good look and knew the direction I needed to go.

It took me almost half an hour to get to the base of the ridge. I was about to start ascending when I caught the scent of cigarette smoke. I stopped, and then I heard voices above me, not far off.

"Those things will kill you, you know," said a light, quick, whining voice.

"Really? I never heard that." The second voice had a dead tone, but somehow managed to sound like suppressed violence at the same time.

"How long do we have to stand out here?" said the whiny one, "I can't feel my lips."

"With any luck, they'll freeze and fall off, and then you'll shut up," said the second voice.

"What's the point anyway? We can see the whole valley. It's just woods. There aren't even roads back there."

"There's a trail," said the dead voice. "People have used it before. They use it, but they never come back."

"Are you crazy?" said the whiny voice. "Rock just about tore your head off last time."

"We can't have people snooping around."

"It's a public trail, and it's almost a mile away. I'm not having any part of this," said the whiny voice, suddenly firm.

"I'm just messing with your head," said the dead voice. "Someone thought they heard shouting out there last night. We're supposed to see what we can see."

"So why the rifle and the scope?"

"You've got a pair of binoculars. I've got the scope. The rifle is for wolves."

"I thought wolves were protected."

"Shut up, you little twerp."

I heard a snort. "So we're just staying here, right? We don't have to go any closer to the trail," said the whiny voice. "If someone is snooping, we'll see him from here."

"We'll see 'em from here," agreed the dead voice. "I'm not going out there today. But I'll take a shot if I need to."

"Rock won't like that."

"Who'll tell him?" said the dead voice, with a dangerous edge to it.

"You'll bring the cops down on all of us. You can't just keep shooting people who wander within range."

The dead voice offered a forced laugh. "I'm talking about animals, twerp. Lots of them out here. I've already got a fox, a deer and a porcupine."

"You shot a porcupine with that thing?"

"Two hundred yards. It's a good scope."

They lapsed into silence. I waited, not daring to move. The slope at this point was very steep. I guessed that they were standing at some sort of lookout point, maybe fifty feet above me. The shoulder of the hill and some trees kept me from seeing them.

After a few more minutes of silence, the whiny voice spoke again. "Do you see anything?"

"Nah. Probably what they heard was wolves or coyotes making a kill."

"You got enough cancer to hold you for a while?"

"All right, fine, we can go inside. You wouldn't want to lose your nose, as well as your lips."

There was another sound, a bit of conversation I couldn't hear. Then I heard boots crunching away on a snowy path. After all sound ceased, I continued to wait. I grew very cold, and began to shiver, but just as I was about to move, I smelled cigarette smoke again. Someone was still up there.

I squeezed my hands and wriggled my toes, but it didn't really help. I waited. I had no doubt that it was the gunman, looking for one last chance to shoot something.

At last I heard a new set of footsteps up on the hill above me. A moment later I heard the murmur of voices, and then clearly, a new voice spoke.

"See anything?"

"No."

"All right, come on in then. And I don't want you out here by yourself again. I don't trust you anymore. I won't say it again. You are putting us all in danger, and I won't allow it."

"Fine," said the dead voice.

"Now," said the other. "After you."

"All right, all right," said the dead voice. "Just enjoying the view."

This time it seemed like there was more sound when they walked away. Again I waited, but heard nothing.

I was positive now that the flashing I had seen from afar was the sun reflecting from the binoculars and rifle scope. I hadn't been seen on my way to the ridge, so I retraced my own footprints back to where I had spent the night. From there, I skirted the bottom of the slope, and then, freezing and hungry, made my way back to the car, looking for signs of Vargas all along the way.

I didn't find him until the next day, and by then, I wished I hadn't.

CHAPTER TWENTY-EIGHT

The police don't look for missing adults until they've been gone for at least forty-eight hours. By the time I got home, that Monday morning, Vargas qualified. Just to make sure, I took a hot shower, and then ate two fried eggs with bacon, washing it down with a pot of coffee. No one was going to brainwash *me*.

My phone rang. It was Victoria, Leyla's mother.

"I tried to call you last night," she said. "But you didn't pick up."

"I'm sorry, I was out of cell-range," I said. "You know how reception is up here."

"The wedding is only two weeks away, Jonah," she said. "You have to make some decisions right away."

"Tori," I said, "I can't."

"Why not? You're a grown man. Leyla will just have to live with it. It's her fault for taking this stupid cult-investigation to such extremes."

Apparently, Leyla's family were comforting themselves in the belief that she was still there voluntarily, investigating the cult, neither brainwashed, nor held captive. "Tori," I said, "it's too much right now. I don't know what's happening with Leyla. I don't know if she'll get out in time for the wedding. I don't even know for sure that she *wants* a wedding anymore." Even to myself, I sounded miserable.

Tori was silent. At last she said, "There will be a wedding, Jonah. I don't say that just because I'm an over-eager mother-of-the-bride. I say it because I know Leyla, and I know she loves you. She

191

wouldn't change her mind like that. I've never seen her so full of joy as in this past year."

"I'm trying to believe that, Tori. Whether I believe it or not, I'm not giving up. I will make sure she's safe, and get her away from those people. But I can't make wedding plans right now."

There was another brief pause, and then she said softly, "Okay. I understand, Jonah. It will all be all right in the end. You'll see."

"Thanks," I said.

After I hung up with her, I called Dan Jensen. Technically, this would be the County's case, but I didn't always get along with Jack Jaeger, and it was a small town, and small county, population-wise. Dan would make sure the right people got on the case.

"Dan," I said, when I got through, "it's Jonah. I've got to report someone missing."

"Jonah," said Dan. "I know you're the police chaplain, but sometimes you are a lot of trouble too."

"I'm here to comfort the afflicted and afflict the comfortable," I said.

"What's that supposed to mean?"

"Never mind," I said.

"Okay. Who's missing?"

"A guy named Nick Vargas."

"Never heard of him. Is he new in town?"

"He was visiting," I said. "He went missing on Saturday." I was reluctant to tell Jensen about how I hired Vargas to kidnap Leyla back from the cult. And I really didn't want him to know about Ann.

Jensen blew into the phone. It was a habit he had when he was thinking. I doubt if he knew how annoying it was on the other end.

"If he was visiting, how do you know he didn't just decide to go back to wherever his home is without telling you?"

"Well," I said, "I guess I don't know for sure. But he left his car at the trailhead parking area, up off the Flintlock Trail. He left all of his stuff –" I paused. I didn't want Jensen poking around the cabin until Ann and Julie were out of it. "He left all his stuff where he was staying."

"Where was he staying?"

"I'll have to get back to you on that," I said.

"What do you mean, Jonah?" asked Jensen. "You must know where he was staying, or you wouldn't know he left his stuff there."

"It may be one of those confidential, pastor-things," I said. "You can start with his car, and by the time you're done there, I should be able to tell you where he was staying."

"Doesn't make sense to me," said Dan. "But then, you always were an odd one."

I said a silent prayer asking for forgiveness for the deceptive dissembling. But I didn't repent enough to tell Dan yet.

"All right," said Jensen, "How about a description?"

I described Vargas to him, and then we hung up. I called Julie.

"I couldn't find Vargas," I said, when she picked up.

"You could really use some social skills on the phone," she said. "Most people say, 'Hello, Julie, how are you? How was your date with Alex Chan? What's new for you these days?'"

"You had a date with Alex?" I blurted.

She sighed. "You are hopeless."

"I have only one Hope," I said. "But answer my question. You and Alex went out on an actual date?"

"Several, actually," said Julie. "How could you not know that, in a town this size?"

"I don't do gossip," I said. "Something about it in the bible. But I'm hurt that Alex didn't tell me."

"He was kind of worried about your reaction," she said, sounding uncharacteristically shy. "You can be a little protective of the people close to you."

"*He* is also one of those close to me," I said. "How does he know I wouldn't want to protect *him* from *you*?"

"Boss, I'm hurt."

"I'm not saying that's the case. I wish for both of you whatever is best. I just wish Alex trusted me more." I paused. "Anyway, I called about Nick Vargas. I couldn't find him last night or this morning. I've reported him officially missing. The police will be sniffing around the cabin soon, and it might be better if Ann were not there."

"No worries, Boss. Ann is cured."

Julie is not a subtle person. I was pretty sure that deprogramming someone from a cult was a tricky business that called for patience and subtlety, two things that Julie was not blessed with.

"Julie," I said carefully, "It may seem to you like Ann is cured, but that may just be how she seems on the surface. Cults do complex things to the human psyche, and I'm not sure that either you or I have enough expertise to know if she is better."

"Chief, I swear it's true. It surprised me too, let me tell you. I know I'm a very down to earth person, and I'm the last person I would expect to be able to help someone like Ann. But if you come talk to her, I think you'll see. I'm as surprised as anyone, but I guess maybe she needed exactly someone as straightforward as me."

I sighed. Monday was supposed to be my day off, and it was almost half-over already. "OK," I said. "I'll come down and talk to her."

Twenty minutes later I was in the little cabin, drinking coffee at the table. Ann sat across from me, her legs crossed Indian-style and pulled up on the chair. The woman apparently had no ligaments.

"I'm glad you came, Jonah," she said, looking at me directly with her brown eyes. "I want to thank you personally for what you did for me. I know it was kind of by accident, but you didn't have to help me afterwards." She seemed confident, and quite upbeat.

"It was Nick," I said, honesty compelling me not to take credit. "I wanted to let you go back, but he wouldn't hear of it."

"I really didn't interact with him much," she said. "As far as I'm concerned, it was you and Julie."

"Thank you," I said. "But it would not have happened without Nick."

"I'll have to thank him too then, when he gets back."

I looked at her closely. "What exactly are you thanking us for?"

"For saving me from the Forest Way, and from Tree. I can see now that I was totally deceived. I'm better, though. I'm over it all."

I sipped some more coffee, in case she wanted to keep talking. Just one more use for the black elixir.

Ann went on. "When I met Tree, my life was kind of messed up, and I was very lonely. It wasn't hard to think of him as some kind of savior, someone necessary to my life. You guys have shown me that I was wrong. The real world here feels lonely, and I feel kind of empty inside, like something is missing, but I don't want to go back."

"You're sure?" I asked. "Because honestly, I will take you back to the Forest Way right now, if that's really what you want."

"Boss!" said Julie.

"Really?" asked Ann, clearly surprised.

"No, Julie," I said. "We've given her a chance to see some truth. It's up to her now. We can't keep holding her against her will." I turned back to Ann. "Really. I will drive you myself."

"It's not against her will. She's been fine here."

"It's Okay, Julie," said Ann. "I don't feel like I was kept prisoner."

"So, if you want to go back," I said, "You can get your things, and I'll take you right now." I ignored Julie's glare.

Ann sat still for a moment, her eyes unseeing as she contemplated her choice. Then she shook her head and smiled.

"Thank you, Jonah," she said. "But I'm all done with that now. I'm totally over it."

I thought for a minute. She seemed entirely *too* cured. There was no ambiguity about her, no regret for leaving the cult behind. It seemed too simple. And yet, she had just clearly turned down an offer to go back to the cult. Maybe she was embarrassed about how totally she'd been duped, and that's why she was speaking in such absolute terms. I just didn't know enough about cult-busting to know. Even so, it was clear enough that she didn't want to go back to the Forest Way.

I nodded at Julie. "So now we know her choice is real. She's not just putting up a front."

"You didn't have to do that, Boss. I knew she was cured."

"It's okay," said Ann. "Actually, I didn't know for sure that I was free. But when Jonah gave me the choice, I could see what I really wanted. Now, I know for sure that I am done with the Forest Way. Jonah just helped me to see it was true."

I smiled beneficently. Ann smiled back.

"If I can talk to the police now," she said, "I might be able to help you. You know, I might remember more about Leyla and what's going on when they question me, because they're trained to ask probing questions."

"The police are going to look for Nick Vargas. We don't know what's happened to him," I said. "If I tell them Vargas was staying here, they'll come right to us. They'll ask us questions about him, but I'm sure we can arrange for them to ask you the other stuff too."

"Not too many questions," said Julie quickly. "And maybe she should have a lawyer, or someone here, who can make them stop."

"Okay," I said. "I'll call Mike Slade."

"Why not Alex?" said Julie.

"Alex is representing me," I said. "And I might need his help with this whole thing. It would be a conflict of interest for him to advise her."

"Okay," said Julie reluctantly.

Ann went into the bathroom while we talked about lawyers.

I called Alex, and explained the situation more fully than I had before.

"Jonah, you need a darn good lawyer," he said. "Lucky for you, I am one. I'll handle it with Slade."

"Thanks," I said.

"Don't thank me until you get the bill," he said.

We waited and drank coffee and played gin until Chan and Slade arrived. Ann seemed almost euphoric. Later, I wished I had paid more attention to her mood, but I was feeling pretty good too. It was a relief to be done with the awkward situation of keeping Ann away from both the cult and the authorities. When the lawyers had gone over the situation, I called Jensen.

"Okay," I said. "I've got it straightened out. Vargas was at Norstad's cabins, number five. There will be a couple other people there when you get there, and they'll be happy to answer your questions about Vargas."

"Thanks, Jonah," said Jensen. "I hope this won't screw up any confidential trust thing you had going."

I felt rotten for deceiving him. "Sure thing," I said.

Jensen got there in fifteen minutes. Jaeger was with him, and two uniformed sheriff's deputies. As they walked in the door, before anyone could say anything, Ann got up and ran over to them.

"Oh thank the Universe," she exclaimed. "Help me officers! These people kidnapped me and have been keeping me prisoner here!"

CHAPTER TWENTY-NINE

Julie said, "Ann?"

Chan, sitting beside me, went completely still.

Ann stepped behind one of the deputies, like she needed protection. "Arrest them!" She said, her voice ringing. "They kidnapped me!"

"What is this, Jonah?" asked Jensen, looking from Ann, to Julie, to Alex and back again to Ann. "Who is this person?"

"I'm a loyal member of the Forest Way," said Ann proudly, "and these people kidnapped me." Her voice had an edge to it, like she was almost hysterical. Jaeger started to move forward, towards me.

"Take it easy, Jack," said Dan, waving him off irritably. "We're in the city limits. Let me handle this." He looked at Ann. "Point to the people who kidnapped you."

She pointed at me. "He kidnapped me from my home in the Forest Way." She pointed at Julie. "She was my jail-keeper."

"And the other two?" asked Jensen.

"They just got here," said Ann. "I think they were cooking up some kind of plot to keep the first two out of jail."

Jensen nodded calmly. "Did they hurt you in any way?"

"They kept me tied up," said Ann. She looked around and realized everyone in the room was focused on her. "And they beat me," she said with a sob. It looked like maybe her eyes were tearing up.

"Dan," said Jaeger.

"Put a lid on it, Jack," said Jensen. Jaeger subsided. Jensen turned back to Ann. "Anything else?"

"Isn't that enough?" said Ann. She managed to sound indignant. "They kidnapped me!" Now the hysterical edge was clear.

"Okay," said Dan, mildly. He turned to the deputies. "Do you boys mind taking her out and keeping her safe in one of your squad cars?" They looked at Jaeger, who nodded. They took Ann by the arms, and speaking soothingly, led her out of the cabin, but as she left, she kept yelling back.

"Make sure they get what they deserve! They held me prisoner!"

While they guided her outside, Chan leaned over and whispered to Mike Slade.

When the door closed, Jensen walked into the open kitchen, found a mug and poured some coffee. He looked at Jaeger. "How about I take Borden, and you take Julie?"

"Just hold on a second now," said Alex. "You aren't going to give those accusations any credence, are you? You know Jonah, you know Julie. They aren't kidnappers."

"I've got to do my job, Alex," said Dan calmly, his face expressionless. "That woman came from somewhere, and she's making those accusations for some reason. I just want to find out what that reason is."

"Me too!" said Julie. There were tears on her face, which shocked me. Normally she was imperturbable. "I thought we were friends."

"Can we use the interview rooms, at least?" asked Jaeger. I want recordings, and I don't want these two to overhear each other."

"Steady," said Mike Slade. "Are you arresting them?"

"We just want to ask them some questions," said Jaeger. "It helps us out if we do that in a controlled environment."

Slade looked at Chan. Chan nodded. "Okay. We can go in for questioning. But I'll be present with Jonah, and Slade will go with Julie. If you don't like it, you'll have to go ahead and arrest them."

Jensen shrugged. "Suits me."

Fifteen minutes later I was seated in an interview room at the Superior Justice center. Alex Chan was next to me. The room had a floor of industrial carpet, a bare table, and a camera on a tripod in one corner. Alex and I sat on one side of a cheap, veneer-topped table. In the middle of the table was a little microphone, with a wire running away from it underneath the table. We waited for what seemed like a long time. During the car ride, we had gone over what I should say, though I hated the very idea of withholding anything more from Jensen.

"You're going to be fine, Jonah," said Alex. "I think you just barely managed to stay legal, although I'm not sure the same is true for Vargas."

"Why is Ann doing this?" I asked. "I thought she was fine with everything."

Alex shrugged. "You probably know more about cults than me. I assume the brainwashing was tougher than you thought, and she's still acting as a loyal member of the Forest Way."

Dan Jensen came into the room. He switched on the camera in the corner, and a red light glowed.

"That's video only," he said. "Audio is on the mic." He reached under the table, and then said, "We're recording."

Jensen cleared his throat. "Did you kidnap the woman known as Ann, or Amaryllis, the one who was in the cabin when we arrived?"

"What do you mean by 'kidnap?'" I asked. Chan shook his head and Jensen groaned.

"Jonah!"

"How about this?" I asked. "I did not intentionally take her by force from the Forest Way."

"Careful, Jonah," said Chan. "You too, Jensen, or I shut this down."

Jensen sighed. "Look, Jonah," he said. "I know you wouldn't kidnap a perfect stranger. I'm thinking you were trying to get Leyla out, but you got this woman by mistake."

Chan shook his head. "How about Jonah tells you what he and I went over beforehand, and then you ask some questions pertaining to that?"

"Fine," said Jensen. He sounded crabby. They both looked at me.

"I hired a man to help me save Leyla from the cult," I said. "His name is Nick Vargas."

"The guy you reported missing," said Dan. It was a statement, more than a question.

"Yes," I said. "Vargas did some things I didn't know he was going to do. We went to get Leyla on Friday night. He Tased her. Then afterwards, he gave her pills, claiming they were aspirin, but they were actually a sedative. I did not know about either of those things, until after Vargas did them. It was dark, and we didn't know that it was not Leyla until we got back to the cabin."

"So you thought you were saving Leyla Bennett, your fiancée, from the cult?" asked Jensen.

"Yes."

"So, why didn't you take this Ann back, once you realized you had the wrong person?"

"I wanted to. But Vargas had already sedated her. He convinced me that we couldn't leave her outside the compound in her sedated state, and we were both afraid for our physical safety if we made contact with the Forest Way people so soon after what we had done."

"So then what happened?"

"I went home. I came back in the morning, and Vargas was already gone. I stayed at the cabin and waited for Ann to wake up. When she did, I made breakfast and coffee for her, and we talked for a while. Then she went back to bed. Later, I called Julie, and she came and spent most of the rest of the time with her."

"Did you restrain Ann in any way?"

"No."

"You didn't tie her up?"

"No."

"You didn't lock her in?"

"No."

"So you're saying Ann stayed there of her own free will?"

"Vargas left me a note on Saturday morning. He said he had taken her coat and boots to discourage her from running away. I never found them. She told me that she wanted to go back to the Forest Way, but she never even asked me directly to take her there."

"I'll need to see that note," said Jensen.

"I hope I didn't throw it away," I said.

"You'd *better* hope. So you deny that you physically restrained her?"

"Absolutely."

"She didn't try to leave?"

"Not while I was around."

Jensen nodded. "So where did she get the drugs?"

"What?" The question caught me completely off balance.

"She was high as a kite back there, Jonah. If you were paying attention, I'm sure you would have seen it too. We're testing right now, to see what it was, but I'm guessing some kind of upper, like crack, or coke or meth. That's what had Jaeger's underwear all bunched up, back at the cabin. He thought I was missing it."

"You'll have to see if Julie ever left her alone. I have no clue," I said. But now that Jensen had pointed it out, it made sense: Ann's strange and irrational behavior today, the excitement, verging on hysteria.

"Did you instruct Julie to prevent Ann from leaving?"

"No," I said. I wanted to come completely clean, and tell him that I had told Julie not to take her anywhere, and that I myself had refused to drive her anyplace, until today. But Chan, as my lawyer, told me not to elaborate about all that unless I was directly asked.

"All right, let's get this straight. You didn't know what this Vargas was doing, until after the fact?"

"No."

"You yourself did not physically apprehend or restrain Ann in any way?""

"Absolutely not. I did not encourage her to leave, at first, but I never tried to stop her. She never even tried to walk out the door. In fact, Julie will corroborate that just before you guys got there, I offered to drive her back to Forest Way myself."

Jensen leaned forward and switched off the audio recorder. Then he leaned back in his chair and blew out a big, noisy breath.

"You're killing me, Jonah. I swear I'm aging faster because of you. But it all sounds okay to me. You came about as close to breaking the law as you could, without doing it."

I sighed, more quietly, and I felt Chan relax slightly, next to me. We left the interview room, and waited in the Superior Justice complex until Julie was done. When we compared notes, we found that Julie's interview had gone pretty much like mine. The one thing that Julie could add was that when they went out to buy snacks on the previous afternoon, Ann had wandered off in the grocery store to use the bathroom. It was possible that she had purchased drugs then, but none of us knew if she had been carrying any money, or not. We stepped outside into the bitterly cold, darkening air. Alex and Julie seemed to want to talk privately, so I got into my car and drove home to salvage the wreck of my day off.

CHAPTER THIRTY

On Tuesday afternoon, Dan called me again.

"Can you come down and clear up a few minor points for me?" he asked, once we had exchanged pleasantries.

"I don't see why not. Do I need Alex?"

"No," he said. "I promise you, this isn't about you."

"Okay," I said. I buzzed Julie, who was in on Tuesdays. "Hey, I've got to go back to the police station."

The sun was brilliant, and the hard, bright light bounced off snow and icicles, making it even brighter. I pulled out my sunglasses.

When I arrived at the station, I was ushered into Jensen's office. Jaeger was there occupying a chair in front of Jensen's desk.

"Jack," I said.

He nodded silently.

Dan gestured, and I sat in the other chair, facing him across the desk. He pushed a manila file folder across the surface toward me.

"Do you know this guy?" he asked.

I opened the folder. Stapled to the inside-back was a large picture of Nick Vargas. It was from the neck up. His chin was tilted up a little, and it looked like a straight-on mug shot, except that his eyes were closed.

"That's Vargas," I said. "The guy who is missing."

Jensen looked meaningfully at Jaeger.

I looked at the picture again, thinking of mug shots. My heart began to pound. They had done research on him – which I should have done myself, before I hired him – and found out that he had a criminal record.

"Is he in the system? Is he a criminal?" I hated the thought that Nick had played me. In spite of his gruffness, I kind of liked him.

"He's in the system now," said Jensen. "We're thinking homicide."

I felt sick to my stomach. "Who did he kill?"

"No, you idiot," snapped Jaeger. "He's dead. Someone killed *him*."

I felt a hollowness open up inside me. "He's dead?"

Jensen nodded. "We found him this morning, no ID, labels pulled off his clothes. Looked just like a hunting accident and a cover up again."

"The thing is," said Jaeger, they didn't do a very good job of it this time. He had bruises on him, several broken fingers, and a broken wrist."

"He could have fallen," said Jensen. "But of course, then he was shot."

"Are you saying he was *tortured*?"

Jensen just shrugged. Jaeger was glaring angrily out the window.

I was quiet for a minute, horrified at what Vargas' last hours might have been like. "He was a little rough around the edges," I said at last, "but he was a good man."

"The bullet was still in him. It was a .308. A lot of different guns fire that, but the bullet we took out of the tree up off the Gunflint was also probably a .308."

"Where'd you find him?" I asked.

"Down near county road seven," said Jaeger. Within a mile or two of the first John Doe."

I shook my head. "He had no business down there. He was scoping out the Forest Way for another try at Leyla. He left on Saturday. His car was up at the trailhead near the compound, miles and miles from county seven."

Jensen nodded. You sent us up there, and we found a car up there registered to Nick Vargas. Until now, we didn't have a positive ID on the dead man. He was looking like John Doe number two, until I remembered your description of Vargas."

"That's definitely Vargas," I said. "And we all know, because of the car, that he was up by the Forest Way. Plus, I may have overheard the man who shot him."

"What are you talking about?"

I told them about searching for Vargas, and overhearing the watchers on the ridge.

"This is enough for me," said Jaeger. "We've got to do something about those hippies."

"Hey, you might be insulting real hippies," I said. Jaeger paid no attention to me.

"Two men dead while believed to be near the Forest Way, both bodies clearly moved after death. One of them maybe tortured. We're going in. We've got to throw some bodies in the can."

I felt elated at the thought of something finally happening to free Leyla, and then I felt sad again as I thought of Vargas. He had said he would free her, if it was the last thing he did. His death might have done just that.

Jensen's voice cut in, and his words were like snow down my back. "Just who are you going to arrest Jack? Do you have a suspect?"

"Fine," said Jaeger. "A search warrant then."

"Maybe," said Jensen. "Maybe we get a warrant to search for the murder weapon. Suppose we find two or three rifles. Suppose one of them matched the bullet recovered from Vargas. If there's more than one set of prints on the gun, how do we prove who fired the gun? This long after, gunshot residue on the hands will be gone."

"We can't sit around and do nothing," said Jaeger. His tense, grating voice echoed my own frustration.

"No, we can't," said Jensen. "But we've got to be smart about this. Those people up there are plenty smart themselves. They may have ditched the gun already. I met their head honcho, Tree, or whatever. He's got plenty of self-confidence. I bet he's got so much confidence, he'll come on down here voluntarily and talk with us."

"You screw it up, you'll have nothing," growled Jaeger.

"I won't screw it up," said Dan.

~

Jensen didn't screw it up.

Later that day, to my amazement, I stood behind a one-way window and looked into an interview room where Jensen sat with Tree. He made Jaeger stay behind the glass where I was. We could see and hear them, but they couldn't see or hear us.

"I didn't think the guy would go for this," said Jaeger softly, shaking his head. "He came with no warrant, no lawyer."

"I'm surprised too," I said. "But Dan read it right. This guy has an ego."

"Mr. – ah – Tree," said Jensen. "I appreciate you coming down to help us out with our investigation. Frankly, we're stumped, and we need your input."

Jaeger shook his head. "Pouring it on a little thick, isn't he?"

"I don't know," I said. "Tree is probably used to his people treating him like this. Probably seems normal to him."

Tree laughed, a booming, hearty sound. His eyes twinkled and leaned toward Jensen. "You don't have to flatter me Dan," he said warmly. Not for the first time, I envied that magnificent voice. "I'm happy to help you guys. We're part of this community too, you know."

Jaeger swore. "This guy is good."

"Okay," said Dan, unperturbed. "Thanks. But it's true that we're kind of stuck."

"What's the problem?" asked Tree, leaning forward again, like he was the interviewer, and Dan the person who had to answer to him.

"Two men are dead," said Dan. His voice sounded harsh, after Tree's. "They both died quite near to the Forest Way compound. But both of their bodies were moved somewhere else after death. I'm afraid someone in your cult has gone rogue."

"You know this?" said Tree, acting surprised. To me, his surprise seemed too smooth.

"We have an eye-witness who found the first body, recently dead, near the compound. When he came back with help, it was gone. Later, it turned up many miles away. We are quite certain the second man was also near your property when he died. Even so, he too, turned up a long way away."

"Why is he telling him what we've got?" asked Jaeger. "I don't like it."

Tree leaned back, thinking. "So you don't have proof?" he said at last.

"Well, no," said Dan awkwardly. I looked at him closely. Something was up. "That's why we need your help. We think it is a Forest Way person, acting on his own."

"I'm sure it was not," said Tree. "There is a lot of wild land around us. Many people in the area hunt."

"Two bodies, both right next to your property," said Jensen.

"That does look bad," said Tree, frowning, still looking entirely comfortable. "Do you think someone is trying to frame us?"

I could feel Jaeger tense up beside me.

"I don't know," said Jensen, looking humble. "But it would sure help if I could come out there and interview your people, you know, eliminate them as suspects."

"And if I refuse?" asked Tree. "I'm sure that you haven't been able to get warrants or subpoenas for that, or you would have executed them already."

Jensen still looked almost tentative. "I know you want to help us. After all, you're part of this community too."

A small, slow grin tugged at the corner of Jaeger's mouth.

Tree was silent, thinking.

"Or were you just blowing smoke a minute ago?" asked Jensen, his voice getting a little harder. "Let me put it this way," he continued. "You have two choices. First, you can help us catch someone whose actions, I'm sure, you condemn anyway." He looked meaningfully at Tree. "Or, second, you can refuse to help. If you choose to do that, you and your people will know no peace until we catch the killer. People traveling to and from your property had better not speed, or have a broken taillight, or possibly have an under-inflated tire, because if so, they'll be stopped. The health inspector might need to visit your kitchens and examine them. I'm sure everything is shipshape, but it would be too bad if they had to shut you down. The Minnesota department of Agriculture might need to inspect the blueberry jam you sell. If you so much as sneeze, we'll have S.W.A.T. teams all over you. If we find you an accessory after the fact, heaven help you."

For the first time, Tree looked slightly irritated. "Are you threatening me, Chief Jensen?"

"I wouldn't do that," said Dan. "I'm just pointing out that you and I want the same thing: justice for the killer of these men."

"I certainly don't know who killed them. I highly doubt it was a member of the Forest Way. You would harass us on mere suspicion?"

"You wanted to cooperate," said Jensen. "Help us eliminate your people from the equation. Let us come in, and interview each one of them."

"Absolutely out of the question."

"So you are choosing option number two?"

"I didn't say, that," said Tree. "Give me some time to think about this. I could ask some questions myself. Maybe one of my people saw something."

"You have twenty-four hours," said Jensen. "After that, you default to option two."

Tree left, and we joined Jensen, walking with him to his office.

"Nice," said Jaeger. "You managed to be both good cop and bad cop."

Jensen grinned. "I think he'll play ball."

"You think he'll let you in?" I asked. My heart flared with hope for Leyla.

Jaeger shook his head. "I doubt it. But I think he'll give us the killer. It won't be worth it for Tree to keep sheltering him, now that we're focused on the Forest Way, and he knows it."

My heart fell. "Don't get me wrong, I'm glad you'll get the killer. But I kind of hoped you could get to the bottom of what's going on with Leyla. I still think she's there against her will."

"That's the beauty of this," said Dan, as Jaeger nodded. "He'll give us the shooter, to get us off his back. But once we have the killer, we'll sweat *him*, and offer him a reduced sentence if he'll turn around and give us something on Tree and the cult. Hopefully, he'll give us the lowdown on Leyla, and maybe there's more."

"You guys are devious. I'm glad you're on my side."

Jensen slapped my shoulder. "I told you we'd get her out Jonah. You just have to be patient."

"Thanks," I said, and I meant it. "Just watch your back. That's pretty much the last thing Vargas said to me."

CHAPTER THIRTY-ONE

I was at an area ministerium meeting in Silver Bay when my phone buzzed. A ministerium is a gathering of pastors. I don't know what other ministeriums do, but ours opened with a meal, then a devotion led by one of us, while the others sat quietly and probably thought out professional critiques on the devotion. Then we talked about ways we could work together. The North Shore Ministerium, as we called ours, wasn't so bad. Most of us were Lutherans, but we had three different kinds of Lutherans. We were diverse that way. Plus we had a Baptist, two Methodists and an Evangelical Free pastor.

That day, we had a devotion on Christmas, since it was less than a week away. I'm sure the other guys were probably trying to figure out if there was anything in it they could use for one of their three Christmas sermons. I was blissfully uncaring. One of the first things I had done when Leyla and I had set the date of New Year's Day for our wedding, was to arrange for the entire week off beforehand, which included, of course, Christmas. But I wondered, as I had often in the past week or so, about the wedding. I still had not done any planning or arranging in Leyla's absence.

After the devotion, we discussed the drug problem on the Shore. Meth use had grown over the past couple of years, and most of us had families in our congregations that were affected. Of course, it had grown all over the region, but that didn't make it easier. We were in the middle of sharing various resources we knew about for rehab when my phone buzzed. I checked the number, and saw it was Dan Jensen.

When the meeting was done, I got into my car, and dialed Jensen. Silver Bay had decked the Halls with boughs of holly, and Christmas lights and little banners on their street light poles. It looked like the North Pole.

"What's up, Dan?" I asked, when he answered.

"Where are you?" asked Dan.

"On my way home from Silver Bay," I said.

"Stop by the station on your way home," said Dan. "You'll be glad you did.

"Okay," I said.

"When can I expect you?"

The question surprised me. Jensen must really want me to show up. "I don't know. Four or five, I guess."

"All right," said Jensen. "Don't forget."

I hung up. When I came to a look-out area, I pulled off, pointing the nose of the car toward the lake. The water was frozen from the shore to about a half-mile out. It wasn't the smooth ice that you see on other Minnesota lakes in the winter. The wind and waves turned the Superior ice into a broken plain of jammed ice floes. It looked a little like pictures of the Arctic Ocean, although I understand the Arctic is not always so cold. Beyond the ice, the water was forcefully blue. A few pines stood in front of me, just to the left. The green, white, and blue were all intense in the bright sun. Score another one for the Creator of the universe.

I breathed in deeply. This kind of beauty was always alive at any given time, in different places all around the world, whether anyone noticed it or not. We could revel in it, find peace and joy in it, or ignore it and remain untouched by it. But it would go on, regardless of our attitude toward it. It was a little like the love of God, beautiful, passionate, powerful, deep, unchanging and yet possible to ignore. He loved me when Leyla was with me and we were preparing joyously for marriage. He loved me when she was trapped in a cult and our future was in doubt. My doubts and ignorance did not affect it. I just had to stop and look sometimes, and I would see it.

When I pulled into the police station, the snow was already looking blue in the fading daylight. Lights were on all over town. Not to be outdone by neighboring towns, Grand Lake was also decorated for Christmas. The streetlights were wrapped to look like giant candy canes. Christmas lights formed arches across the streets downtown. There was a large, live pine tree growing on the lawn in front of the old courthouse, which now held the city offices. It was decorated like a Christmas tree. In spite of all the *Christmas* decorations, however, the banners at either end of Main Street read, "Happy Holidays."

I pulled into a parking spot in front of the police station. The woman running the front desk recognized me, and waved me through to Jensen's office.

"Jonah!" said Dan. He was beaming.

He got up and poured me a cup of coffee, and then one for himself. It was bad, but it was better than none. Too many people feel that way about things other than coffee, like love.

I smiled back at Dan. "Got an early Christmas present?"

He kept grinning. "We all did. Tree's here."

I sipped some coffee. "What do you mean, 'here?'"

"He's here right now. In jail."

"In jail? Dan what's going on?" Jensen was smiling, but I wasn't sure.

"He came in this afternoon asking to talk to me again. We sat down, and he said he would give us the killers. He said he would even help us get Leyla out of the cult. But he wants some kind of immunity, because he's worried about convicting himself."

"He'll help us get Leyla back?"

"That's what he said. Right now, we're holding him as a material witness for the murders. He's got a lawyer coming up from the Twin Cities, tomorrow. They'll get together with a prosecutor, and go from there. But Jaeger will sit in on it, too. It won't be long now, Jonah."

"Why?" I said.

"What?"

"Why is Tree doing this? And why now? The first murder was three weeks ago. Do you really think he suddenly grew a conscience?"

"No," said Jensen slowly. "I don't know for sure. But if I had to guess, I'd say that something I said the other day scared him. There must be evidence somewhere that would make him an accessory after the fact, and he's hoping to turn over the shooter and get free of it all. But he wants to do it without getting convicted of anything himself. He knows we want to get Leyla out too, so he's using her as a bargaining chip."

It made sense. It was just so hard to believe that the ordeal was almost over. It seemed like the perfect Christmas present. It felt almost too good to be true.

I should have listened to that feeling.

CHAPTER THIRTY-TWO

The next morning, I was keyed up. I wasn't quite happy, because I was nervous, but I was also very excited. I could hardly believe that the ordeal was almost over. Tree was going to set Leyla free. I figured his lawyer wouldn't make it up here until after lunch; say, two o'clock. Then, because it was mostly a conversation between several lawyers, I supposed it would take them a few hours to hammer out the details of Tree's immunity deal. We could be driving out to the Forest Way to pick her up by six, and we could still have supper at my place at seven or so. I put a roast into my crock pot, so she'd have plenty of meat to eat.

As the day went on, I was continually distracted by thoughts of the coming reunion. Our wedding plans were in shambles. I wondered if maybe we could just elope. Maybe even tonight. After the ceremony, we could spend the night at a place I knew near Two Harbors. We could...I stopped that train of thought, which was fast becoming very un-pastorly.

I struggled through a few counseling appointments, and two visits with some house-bound members of the church. At five, I couldn't stand it anymore. I called Jensen.

He answered the phone with a swear word, which he repeated, involuntarily, it seemed. "I'm sorry Jonah," he said.

"It's not like I've never heard it before," I said. "My ears won't break."

"No, I mean," he stopped.

"You mean what?"

"Can you meet me in about an hour, at the WW?"

"I can," I said, "but I was hoping to be on my way to get Leyla by then."

"Meet me first," he said.

The WW was a popular bar in downtown Grand Lake. Technically, it was Wally's Walleye Bar and Grill, but for obvious reasons, most people called it "the WW." Dan and I often had breakfast together at another local spot, Lorraine's. Sometimes we would grab a lunch at Dylan's. I could not recall ever meeting him at the WW, though I myself went there two or three Fridays each month.

I was there at six. Ally, the petite, blond waitress, looked at me in surprise. "Jonah," she said. "It's Thursday, and it's only six." Usually, I came in on Fridays, around eight, and sat in the corner booth, where I did some informal counseling with people who wanted to talk. I was kind of the bar chaplain.

"I know," I said to Ally. "I'm meeting someone."

I ordered a coffee, and sat at the bar. Dan came in about fifteen minutes later. He walked up next to me and ordered a Brandy Old-fashioned. I looked at him.

"I thought you were a beer guy."

"Been a rough day," he said. His drink came, and he took two big swallows.

"What's up?" I said.

He took another swallow and then sighed. I pulled a bowl of peanuts toward me and had a few. Jensen looked at me, and then finished his drink in three more gulps. He gestured at the bar-tender for another. I began to get worried.

"Spit it out, Dan," I said. "While you still can." My heart began to pound in fear.

"Tree is dead."

CHAPTER THIRTY-THREE

"Tree is dead?" I asked. It is at times like this that my seminary training kicks in to give me insightful and helpful things to say.

Jensen nodded. His new drink came and he took a more moderate sip.

"How?"

"He was killed sometime early this morning in the jail. Someone stuck him with a shiv – a homemade knife. Got him in the neck and he bled out before anyone knew about it."

I couldn't put my finger on my own emotions. I had been afraid for Leyla. I wasn't exactly broken up to hear of Tree's death, but he'd been a constant part of my mental landscape for three weeks now. It was a strange feeling to think he was gone. It was the last thing I had expected to hear from Jensen today. I wondered irreverently how he was liking hell, and immediately felt bad about it. I took a big slug of my coffee.

"Wow," I said. I am a wordsmith. It shows.

"Yeah," said Jensen. "I've been dealing with the fallout all day. It's a mess when someone dies in custody." He sipped his drink again. At least the gulping was over.

A thought grew in my mind like a fast-approaching meteor. It was tactless, but I had to know.

"You said he died early this morning. So, did you get a deal or anything before it happened?"

Jensen started shaking his head even before I finished talking. "No, Jonah. It was like the middle of the night. He was in a cell with fifteen other guys. His lawyer hadn't even left the Twin Cities."

"So you don't have the killer."

Jensen shook his head.

"And you don't have Leyla."

He said nothing, and took a bigger sip of his drink.

Finally, he said, "I'm sorry, Jonah. I'm really sorry."

I drank some coffee and stared sightlessly at the back of the bar. I wasn't going to elope with Leyla tonight. I wasn't even going to have dinner with her. A strange and inconsequential thought popped into my head. I decided it was better to pursue that than my raging frustration.

"Dan," I said, "did you ever get an identity on the first guy, the John Doe?"

He looked up from his drink as if he was glad to think about something besides the disaster at the jail earlier. "We never did." He looked like he was thinking.

"Isn't that a little weird? I mean the guy must have had a life somewhere. Someone must be missing him."

"It's very weird, actually. So much has happened since then that we haven't been very focused on his identity. We're a small department here in town, and even the Sheriff's department isn't that big. We've been using our resources elsewhere."

"Maybe if we knew who he was, we might know something, like if he was killed for some reason, or just because they've got a crazy guy up there."

"Was there some reason to kill Vargas?"

I nodded. "He was poking around the Forest Way. Maybe he found something out. Maybe John Doe did also."

Dan sighed and looked back at his drink. "I guess we'll never know, now."

"So where does all this leave us with the Forest Way?"

He shook his head. "I don't know. I've spent the whole day dealing with this mess. I've hardly had a chance to figure that out." He sipped his drink. "My guess is, it's not good. Tree didn't actually tell us anything."

I tried to hold my disappointment in check. I felt sick to my stomach.

"Maybe," I said slowly, "maybe the cult will break up now. I mean, Tree was a seriously charismatic leader. I doubt that what they believe sounds good without him to say it. He was probably the glue that held them together."

Jensen turned to look at me and began to nod. He looked like a drowning man just noticing a life-preserver floating nearby. "That's true, isn't it?" he said. "I bet they'll break up. Even if they don't, Tree has no more reason to hold Leyla; he has no reasons for anything, anymore."

"You told someone at the Forest Way of his death?"

Jensen shook his head. He looked miserable. "We're trying to find next of kin, first. We haven't had much luck."

"I'm going up there," I said. "I'm not the police. I'm not bound by some obligation to tell next of kin first. I want Leyla out of there."

Jensen nodded, and looked at his glass. "I didn't hear you say that," he said. He took a sip. "Good luck."

CHAPTER THIRTY-FOUR

I went straight to the Forest Way. I didn't stop at home. It was well dark by the time I got there. As before, when I was unannounced, the gate across the driveway was closed. I parked my car in front of it, and, using my cell phone for light, floundered through the snow around the fence and back onto the plowed drive. I trudged through the cold darkness toward the warmly lit, inviting-looking lodge.

I banged on the door until someone came and answered. It was the giant man, Cliff. He looked at me, and thankfully, I don't think he recognized me.

"Who are you?" he said. "What do you want?"

"I want to talk to whoever is in charge when Tree isn't here," I said.

"Who are you?" he asked again.

"I have important news for the Forest Way," I said. "I think you'd better let me in."

He grunted, and slammed the door in my face.

I stood in the cold for a minute, wondering what that meant. He might be going to get someone. He might be off to do yoga, with no more thought of me left in his giant, empty mind. When I lost feeling in my lips, I knocked on the door again.

This time it was opened by the slim, balding man called Twig. He looked like he recognized me.

"Hmm. Well," he said. "Yes?"

"I need to talk to whoever is in charge."

"Our leader is not here right now," he said. "He is away in the Twin Cities on a mission."

"Actually, I've come to bring you news about your leader," I said. "Who is in charge when he's gone?"

Twig's face grew eager. "You have news of Tree?" He opened the door a little wider.

"I do," I said. "Can I come in?" While Twig hesitated, I stepped into the warmth and light. "Who is in charge when Tree is gone? I need to speak with that person."

"That would be me," said a thick-set, dark haired man, striding into the room in front of Cliff. I remembered now that this was the man called Rock. Vargas' file had said he was Herman Brown's lieutenant. "How can I help you?"

Cliff stood massive and silent behind him. Twig hovered off to the side.

"I have news for you," I said. I hesitated, looking at Cliff and Twig, and then decided, the more, the merrier. "Tree is dead."

Twig looked surprised and shocked. Cliff smirked. Rock's face remained immobile. Only his eyes betrayed any emotion, and it looked like he was doing some sort of calculus in his brain. It wasn't the reaction I had expected.

"Twig," said Rock, "go do something useful."

Twig hesitated, and then skittered out of the room. Cliff remained where he was, a huge, menacing hulk of a man.

"Why are you telling us this, Pastor Borden?" asked Rock, when he was gone.

"It's true," I said. "The police had him in custody in Grand Lake. He was killed in a jail fight last night."

Rock shook his head in irritation. "I don't mean that. I know that. I mean, why did you come out here to tell us this?"

"I came to get my fiancée, Leyla Bennett," I said. "Wait," I added. "You *knew* about Tree?"

Rock waved his hand dismissively. "Why do you think Ms. Bennett will want to leave now?"

"Tree is dead," I said. "He really is. I can't imagine that you all will want to keep on without him. Wasn't he the Spirit of the Forest, or something?"

Rock regarded me coldly. "You have no idea what you are talking about. Of course we'll keep on. Some few may choose to leave, but only because they never understood what this is all about. The rest will continue in the Forest Way." He added, with emphasis, "*Ms. Bennett* will continue in the Forest Way."

"No," I said.

Rock looked at me some more, like he was calculating again. Finally, he nodded to Cliff. "Throw him out," he said.

I was never one to wait around when I knew violence was coming. I hit Cliff before he had moved six inches. I hit him in the throat with my open hand, and then drove a side-kick into his knee. He went down wheezing and gasping for air, and clutching his leg. I turned back to Rock and looked at his big chrome revolver, which was pointed directly at my chest.

"Pastor Borden," he said, "if you ever come back here, I will personally make sure you die a painful death." He glanced at Cliff, who was still straining in panic to breathe, his face red, his expression agonized. He looked back at me and shook his head with a trace of something like respect in his eyes. "You're fast on the draw, I'll give you that." But his face quickly hardened again, and he wiggled the gun at me. "Get out."

CHAPTER THIRTY-FIVE

Dan Jensen called me the next morning.

"Did you get her?" he asked, as soon as I said hello.

"No," I said. I didn't feel much like talking about it.

Jensen swore.

"I know," I said. "I feel the same way, only more so."

"It's not just that," he said.

"What now?"

"Some people from the Forest Way came in this morning. They brought in a Remington 700, chambered for the .308 caliber. Two witnesses are willing to say they saw Tree with the gun the day Vargas was killed. A third says he saw Tree with it on another occasion, maybe close to the time John Doe was killed. They all say that it was common knowledge that the gun belonged to Tree."

"What about the conversation I overheard? That wasn't Tree's voice."

"Remind me about that," said Jensen. "Did either of them actually talk about killing anyone?"

"No. I guess I thought it was implied, from the conversation."

Jensen sighed. "I don't know what to tell you, Jonah. With this new stuff, our evidence is a lot more solid than a conversation with a lot of innuendo that you overheard while you were hiding in the woods."

I was quiet.

"I'm not discounting you, Jonah," said Jensen. "But try to think of it like the D.A.. On the one hand, you've got someone who overheard something from some distance away, someone who didn't even *see* the speakers. On the other hand, you have three solid eyewitnesses, plus several more to claim it was Tree's gun."

"So Tree was the killer? How does that make sense?"

"It might make a lot of sense. Maybe that's why he came in and was talking immunity."

"But if he was the killer, what was he going to trade for the immunity?"

"Leyla," said Jensen.

Now I felt like swearing. It did make a kind of twisted sense. If Tree thought he was about to be busted, he would come in and trade for immunity before anyone had any actual evidence on him. He knew I was connected to the police – Jensen had come out to the Forest Way with me to talk with Leyla. He knew that she might be a bargaining chip.

"What about fingerprints on the rifle?" I asked.

"The gun was wiped," said Jensen. "But prosecutors like eyewitness testimony. Without Tree here to explain this away, the D.A. is likely to consider this case closed."

"So you got your killer, anyway," I said.

"I guess so," said Jensen. "It's up to the D.A. now, but he'll probably close the case. That's why I was so upset when you said Leyla didn't come home with you."

"What do you mean?" I asked.

"As of today, with the gun and eye-witness testimony, we have nothing more on the Forest Way. We've got our killer. There's no further excuse to hassle them. There is no leverage to put pressure on them to release Leyla. As far as the law is concerned, they're free to do what they want. Unless someone can produce evidence that

Leyla is being held against her will, we're back to square one. We've got nothing, Jonah. So, if they didn't let her go last night, I don't know how we'll get them to let her go now."

My mind thrashed around. "How do we know the shooter was really Tree?"

"They're testing the gun right now. If it's a match to Vargas' bullet, we'll know we have the murder weapon. We have eye-witness testimony that it is Tree's rifle. We have eye-witness testimony placing Tree with the murder weapon the day of Vargas' death. I'm telling you, Jonah, the D.A. is going to like this. Case closed, no expensive trial."

I felt like I was drowning. "What about motive? Has anyone thought of why Tree would shoot those guys?"

"They were snooping around his private kingdom," said Jensen.

"Sure, but I don't shoot people who snoop around my cabin," I said. "Isn't that a little bit crazy?"

"Jonah," said Dan gently, "the man claimed to be the spirit of the Forest. He surrounded himself with nutcases who practically worshipped him. Sanity was not one of Tree's strong points."

I was quiet. "So, because the case is solved, you can't help me get Leyla back?"

Now Dan was quiet. "I'm sorry Jonah. I'm really, really sorry."

"Yeah," I said. "Me too."

CHAPTER THIRTY-SIX

Somewhere in the back of my mind, I knew Jensen wasn't really going to give up. He had struggled through a few tough days, and he was disappointed and discouraged. After he crashed for a bit, he'd come back around. Still, his basic point was pretty hard to argue with. With the capture and death of the shooter, all of the legal approaches to the Forest Way were dead-ends. A search-warrant was out of the question now.

I was going to have to save Leyla without help from Vargas, or Jensen, or Jaeger, or even Alex Chan.

I drove home from the church, my mind churning with possibilities and plans. Vargas' approach still seemed like the best one. His death wasn't due to a flaw in his plans. How was he to know that Tree was a homicidal maniac shooting people for fun? And if Tree was the killer, then now, I was safe from him. I tried not to think about Rock's big chrome revolver, and his threat to kill me if I came back.

On the other hand, though the police had no further grounds for investigation, any anomaly at the Forest Way was sure to get their attention. Another incident at this point would bring hordes of police swarming over every inch of the Forest Way property, and Rock must know that. I figured that made me pretty safe.

Back at my cabin I made supper, and ate it standing up at my kitchen counter, looking into the great room at the fire burning in the stove. I was too keyed up to sit down.

Was I wrong about Leyla? Did she really want to be there? Was she staying there of her own free, but brainwashed, will? Reluctantly, I decided I had better plan for that possibility. That brought me back to the original plan: take her out of there, and get her deprogrammed, if necessary.

I cleaned up the kitchen, banked the fire, and found my backpack. Vargas had used a brand-name Taser, which can only be used once, so that wasn't an option for me, and anyway, I probably couldn't have actually brought myself to tase Leyla. If necessary, then, I'd restrain her and carry her out. I got out a sheet of paper and began to make a list of some things I would need from town. For one, I'd need some large cable ties, the kind with the one-way zipper that can function as handcuffs in a pinch.

I regretted the loss of the night vision glasses, which were still out on the slope somewhere near where I had fallen, but I would make do. I didn't anticipate spending a lot of time outside, so I didn't bring a tent or any of my camping gear. Even so, my outdoorsman's conscience made me pack a tarp with rope, a small axe, a good clasp knife, a lighter and some fire-starters. In Minnesota in the winter, those things could mean the difference between life and death.

When I had packed all I could before going to town, I sat down in front of the fire with some hot-cocoa and brandy, and started reading *Beat to Quarters* by C.S. Forester. It was a novel of nineteenth century sailing adventures, excellently done.

The next day, after lunch, I called Doug Norstad, the owner of Norstad's North Shore Resort, which held the cabin where Vargas had been staying.

"Hi Doug," I said, "this is Pastor Jonah." Some members of my church are comfortable simply calling me by my first name. For others, I will always be "pastor Jonah." I didn't mind either way, but I knew that for Doug, it would always be "pastor."

"Hi, Pastor," he said. "Merry Christmas! How can I help you?"

I was jarred by his greeting. I had forgotten it was Christmas Eve. "Merry Christmas," I said mechanically. "Hey, do you still have the stuff belonging to Nick Vargas?" I asked.

"As a matter of fact, I just finished boxing it up yesterday. I was going to ship it to his relatives in the Twin Cites today."

"Can you hold off on that for about an hour?" I asked. "I may have left something there."

"Sure thing, Pastor," he said.

Twenty minutes later, Doug showed me a suitcase and two boxes.

"I'm sorry, but I'm going to have to go through them to look for it," I said.

"No problem, Pastor Jonah," he said. "I've got a few things to take care of. Just let me know when you're done."

I thanked him, and started with the suitcase. I was looking for anything that might help me. I was wondering if Vargas had another Taser or something else that would be helpful in kidnapping the one you love from a cult. I didn't find a Taser, but right away, in Vargas' toiletry kit, I found the sedative he had used on Ann. I stuck the bottle into my coat pocket.

There wasn't anything else useful in the suitcase, or either of the boxes. Probably, he had more gear stored in his car, but the police had impounded that, and I was pretty sure that Jensen and Jaeger would stop me, if they found out what I was planning, so I couldn't risk trying to get at it.

I thanked Doug, and then went to the hardware store. Christmas music was playing, and I was again jarred by the fact that tomorrow was Christmas Day. If not for the wedding, I would have been working on extra sermons to preach for Christmas Eve and Morning. It's a great time of year, but not much of a holiday for pastors. Even so, I was unusually out of the Christmas spirit this year.

I bought some cable ties and a few other things, wished the storekeeper a merry Christmas, and then drove out to the Forest Way.

As with our first attempt, I decided it was impractical to get Leyla through two miles of deep snow to the trailhead parking area near the Flintlock Trail. So I parked in the snow-machine parking lot, about half a mile past the main entrance to the Forest Way.

The day was cloudy, and it was about two in the afternoon when I strapped on my snowshoes, shouldered my pack, and stepped into the forest. I figured I had maybe two hours until dark.

I made my way carefully through the dimness under the trees, and came to the little ridge that overlooked part of the compound. I found a spot opposite the second building from the lodge, and crawled through the snow to the lip of the slope. I pulled out my binoculars, arranged myself comfortably, and settled down to wait.

It began to snow.

CHAPTER THIRTY-SEVEN

It was Christmas Eve, and it was snowing. It was my first Christmas off from work in six years, and I was spending it lying in the snow and the gathering dark, waiting to kidnap the woman who was supposed to marry me in eight days.

The falling snow grew denser, and the darkness came on faster. When I first remembered it was Christmas Eve, when Doug Norstad greeted me, I had wondered if it was a good idea to try and rescue Leyla tonight. But the more I thought about it, the better it seemed. I was counting on the fact that the Forest Way was an environmental cult, and if they were serious, as they certainly seemed to be, it was unlikely that they would observe a traditional Christian holiday like Christmas. If Google, which was just a business run by liberals, wouldn't even acknowledge Easter, I figured the least a full-fledged cult could do is to snub the birth of Jesus.

If I was right, this would be like every other night at the cult. Even more importantly, if Rock was worried about me or anyone else trying anything, tonight was the least likely night for it to happen. I ought to be leading worship services tonight and tomorrow morning. All but essential law-enforcement would be at home with family, or with me, in church. If the Forest Way would ever let down their guard a little bit, it would be tonight.

Lights were on in the Forest Way buildings, but I saw no Christmas lights. I watched as the cultists came out of the fourth building and made their way to the lodge for the evening meal. The next hour seemed to drag on. A few people came out of the lodge and went into the first and second buildings down. Perhaps I had been wrong. Maybe they wouldn't try to compete with Jesus for attention this night.

Suddenly, I felt, as much as heard, the throb of the big drum I had heard before, while watching with Vargas. The people who had entered the sleeping quarters came back out, and went into the lodge. My gamble had paid off. The remaining Forest Way leaders didn't want people to remember what this night really meant.

I felt the sudden rush of adrenaline, and my heart began to pound, but I held still for ten more minutes, just to make sure everyone was back in the lodge. Then I got up, and made my way through the flying snow to the edge of the circle of light cast by the spotlight over the door of the first building. I hesitated. This was a big deal. I was almost certainly going to break the law. Considering Rock's threat, I was also putting my very life at risk. But if I didn't go soon, I might as well slink home in defeat.

I stepped boldly into the light and walked through the door into the building.

This was the place where I'd had my interview with Leyla. I was standing in a little lobby with some cheap, commercial stuffed chairs. A hallway led off to my left, with nine or ten closed doors on either side.

The first door on my left was the room where I had sat with Leyla. When I was here then, it had held a table, three chairs, and the big mirror on the wall. I walked towards it, until I saw a light shining under the bottom of the door.

I froze, and then cursed my own stupidity. Standing like an idiot in the hallway would not save me from detection. The next door along on the same side appeared to be dark. It was not locked, so I stepped quickly and silently into the room. As I gently closed the door behind me, I turned only to realize that there was a light on in this room as well. I froze again, listening, but I heard nothing.

The light in my room was dim, as if it came from a television or computer monitor. I was standing in a short entry way, with a closet or something blocking my view of most of the room. The light came from the other side of that. Trying to move like Melanchthon, I stepped carefully forward and looked around the corner.

Like the interview room I had been in next door, this space was small. There was a table in it, and several chairs. The light emanated from the connecting wall between the two rooms. There was a big rectangular object on that wall, and it glowed. The room was empty and quiet.

At first, I thought I was looking at a large, flat screen television. But as I stepped further into the room, suddenly many things became clear.

The rectangular object on the wall was the back side of the mirror in the other room. The light coming from it was actually coming from the next room. It was a one-way mirror, and I could clearly see into the other room, where the light was on.

The other room was as I remembered it, and it was empty. I looked at the table and chairs, and thought of me sitting there, across from Leyla. Then I thought of someone standing here, where I now stood, watching us, listening to us as we talked.

In my mind's eye, I saw Leyla shift her gaze to the mirror. I heard her whisper, "I hate you."

Like an unexpected right hook, it hit me. At the time, I had thought she was meeting my eyes in the mirror. But she wasn't. She wasn't talking to me at all, not that first time. She was speaking to the person who stood behind the mirror and watched.

Although I was warmer now than I had been for several hours, I could not suppress a shiver. Who was it that had stood here? It wasn't Tree. He had been in the other room with us. Who was the mystery man whom Leyla hated so much?

I knew that after that, Leyla had looked directly at me, and repeated her hatred. But there was a look of inspiration in her eyes just before she said it, like she was sending me a message. She had looked at the mirror, and said "I hate you." Then she had looked at me, and repeated it, and then "Do you understand?" I kicked myself for not understanding until now. Someone had been watching us. That someone was the reason Leyla couldn't just walk out with me. I still did not understand completely, but I knew I wanted to find that someone and hurt him badly.

I opened the door to the hallway and stood listening. I could hear nothing except the distant sigh of the heating system. The door across the hall was also unlocked. It held another interview room, and another mirror. The mirrors were not built-in and obvious, like the observation rooms at a police station. They actually seemed to hang on the wall. The room next to the second interview room was locked, but it seemed pretty likely to hold the back side of another one-way mirror.

I found one more interview room, and again, the observation room next door was locked. On the other side of the presumed observation room was another unlocked door. I opened it onto darkness. Digging a small flashlight from my pack, I snapped it on. This looked like a small bedroom, maybe twelve feet long by ten wide. There was a built-in wardrobe, a chair and a bed. On the left-hand wall, adjoining the locked room next door, there was a big mirror.

I drew a breath. Since the room next door on the side of the mirror was locked, I didn't know for sure what it held. But my guess was that it looked both into the interview room next door, and into this bedroom.

I opened the wardrobe, and found two sets of the Indian-like garb worn by the cultists. There were some sexless sweaters also, and thick socks. It wasn't until I looked into one of the built in drawers and found underwear that I knew this was a man's room.

Continuing down the hall, I found another bedroom next door, this time with a big mirror on the opposite wall to its neighbor. There was male underwear in the wardrobe. Back out in the hall, I discovered that the next door down was locked. The room past that was open, with a mirror on the wall adjoining the locked room.

It began to look like a pattern. The rooms came in sets of three. There was apparently one observation room that looked in to a bedroom on each side. I felt slightly sick. The cultists could be watched while they slept, while they dressed and undressed. So far, however, I had found only rooms belonging to men.

I paused in the hall, listening. I couldn't recall how long I had been in the building. I couldn't hear the drum beat from the lodge, and I didn't remember if I had heard it before from inside the building I was in.

To save time, I walked down the hall, trying doors. Every second door was locked. I stopped to look at one of the unlocked knobs, which went to another bedroom, and found that there was no locking mechanism. At the end of the hall, I went into the final unlocked room. There was a man's underwear in the wardrobe.

At the end of the hall there was a stairwell going down, and an exit. I went down the stairs. It looked like the hill kept falling away, and so the lower level was essentially a walk-out basement. The hall at the bottom of the stairs looked pretty much like the one above it. In the first unlocked room at this end of the building, I found another mirror, and women's underwear. I thought of hidden men, watching Leyla undress, and my rage grew.

I found a locked room on the other side of the mirror, and then an open one again. Each room held a single bed, so unless children were separated from their mothers, this first building was for the single adults. After trying a few more rooms, I realized the flaw in my plans. Everyone's clothes looked the same. The rooms seldom contained any personally identifiable possessions. And because of our commitment to biblical mores, I wouldn't recognize Leyla's underwear, even if I came upon it. That would change, of course, once we were married, but that didn't help me now. There was little chance of me finding her room.

I paused in the hallway. I suspected myself of wishful thinking, but truly, deep in my heart, I believed that Leyla was a prisoner here, against her will. The discovery of the one-way mirror bolstered that theory. If she was a prisoner, they would either have to watch her twenty-four hours a day, or keep her locked up when they couldn't watch her. Locking her up was far more efficient, and less onerous, though I myself thought I could probably enjoy watching her constantly. But they couldn't lock her in any of these sleeping quarters, since there were no locks on the doors. So she would be either locked in a mirror-observation room, or somewhere else.

I had no idea how much time had passed since I had entered the building, and anyway, I didn't know for sure how much time I had to start with. I was going to have to start making guesses, and Leyla's fate might depend on me making the right ones.

If Leyla was locked in an observation room, most likely it would be one with no occupants in the room on either side. Even so, I thought it unlikely that they would keep her in such a place. She might bang on the door and make noise as people passed in the hallway. The cultists may be blindly obedient to Tree, but it would be easier for him not to have to explain the yelling and banging to the others. Therefore, I could eliminate this entire building, which seemed to be made up of one or two interview rooms, and sleeping quarters.

Hesitation could be fatal. I turned, and rushed up the stairs, and out the back door. The next building was only a few yards away. It had the same layout: two levels, with the upper level on top of the slope, and the bottom, a walkout basement below it. I tried a few doors, and found the arrangements to be basically the same as the first building. Feeling more and more concern about being caught, I quickly checked the bottom level, and finding nothing new or different, moved on to the third building, which was the fourth and final building of the compound, including the lodge.

It was more square than the two sleeping buildings. This was the structure that Vargas had assumed housed the cult's artisan workshop, and perhaps the laundries. There was a side door near to the building I had just left. It was open and I entered. I was in a hallway again, but this one was unlit. A dim light filtered through from the floodlights outside. I tried the first door to my left, snapped on my flashlight, and found myself looking at a nursery. There were cribs, and toddler-toys and two diaper changing stations. It made me sick to think of little children being raised to become mindless followers of Tree's twisted ego.

To the right, the door opened onto some kind of schoolroom. I closed the door, and shut my mind off from all but finding Leyla. I couldn't afford to be distracted by the tragedy of those children. I kept moving through the building. I came to the middle portion, where the main doors were. Beyond that, a large room opened up. It was lined on two sides with tables, and at the back there was a large, industrial-sized kitchen. The kitchen surprised me, since Vargas and I had assumed that the cultists ate in the main lodge. But then I saw the jars stacked on a table at the opposite end of the room, and I understood that this is where they made their artisan preserves and jams.

Almost as soon as I noticed it, I was overwhelmed with the smell of cooked berries. I went over and looked at the jars. They were labeled with a hand-drawn print of a large, majestic tree, with the words "Fresh from the Forest" underneath. Then there was a hand-drawn representation of what was in the jar, which in this case was a pile of blueberries. Underneath that, printed text confirmed that this was indeed blueberry jam. On the back, per USDA regulations, was a label of ingredients, and then a little blurb about how the Forest Way was giving me the freshest, most natural produce of the Forest, procured in only sustainable, nature-friendly ways. In addition to the wild-blueberry jam, there were jars of blackberry and raspberry preserves. Larger vessels held rhubarb pie filling. I found three different sizes of honey pots.

On another table were boxes filled with empty jars, and sheets of printed labels. I picked up a loose label and looked at it as I moved through the room. I stuck it in my pocket and went into the kitchen. In the kitchen, I found a big, closed door. I opened it to find a large pantry with shelves of various food items. Prominent on the shelves were dozens of gallon-jugs full of honey. They were labeled with the logo of one of those big shopping-club stores, where you can buy breakfast cereal by the pallet, or canned pears by the ton.

After that, I couldn't help looking into the large, walk in freezer. Sure enough, on the shelves were huge sealed plastic bags of blueberries, raspberries and blackberries, purchased at the same shopping club store. Well, at least they were using real berries.

I went back out of the kitchen and the canning operation, and found a large laundry. After that, I took a stairwell down to the level below. Here I found a wood workshop, and also a sewing room, where apparently they made their pajama-like clothes. Huge bolts of the same rough beige cotton were stacked against one wall. I bet they got a discount on that, too.

I also found the room which housed the heating unit, but no evidence that Leyla was being held there. Either my premise was wrong, and Leyla was here of her own free will, living in one of the dorm-type rooms with a mirror, or, she was in the lodge. If she was being held in the lodge, the best time to get her was now, while everyone else was in their group meeting. I ran up the stairs and outside, heading toward the lodge.

CHAPTER THIRTY-EIGHT

The patio door to the lodge, the one at the back, facing the other buildings, seemed to be the most commonly used entrance by the cult. It would be normal to see people coming in and out of that door. If anyone saw me, I might blend in and escape notice by entering that way.

As soon as I had the thought about blending in, I stopped in my tracks. In Northern Minnesota, in the winter, you do literally stop in your tracks if you are walking outside. I hesitated, and then turned and ran back to the first building.

In the first room I tried, the clothes were too small. The same was true of the second. In the third room, in the wardrobe, I found a set of the cult-clothing that seemed like it would fit me pretty well. I stripped off my outer clothes, leaving on my long-johns, and pulled the loose cotton tunic and trousers on. I stuffed my own clothes into my backpack, apologized silently to the owner of the clothes I was now wearing, and went back toward the lodge.

There were large glass windows looking out on what would be a patio in summer time. The room behind the windows was mostly dark. I opened the door and tried to walk in naturally, as if I belonged. The room was empty. I could no longer hear drum beats, but I thought I heard a muffled murmur, as if a group of people somewhere was chanting something in unison.

Deciding to go ahead and hope my disguise might count if no one looked at my face, I unslung my pack, and put it in a corner. I threw my coat on top of it, but I kept wearing my knit cap.

Directly in front of me was the hallway that led to the front entry area. I'd been through here when I had my interview with Leyla. To my right was another stairwell going only down. As with the other buildings, the back side of the lodge was down the slope from the front, and I assumed there were rooms or other usable space down there. Perhaps there was a room there, where Leyla was kept as a prisoner.

As I approached the stairs, however, I could tell that the chanting sound was coming from below. So much the better, I'd search the upper lodge first, and then wait for everyone to leave before checking the lower level.

I moved along the hall into the familiar entry area, where just the night before, I had confronted Rock and Cliff. At the moment, it was deserted. To my left as I faced the door was the small office area. It was unlocked and I went in, but it did not seem promising as a place to hold a prisoner. It wasn't. In addition to the little reception area, there were three offices off a short hallway. Each held computers, desks, books and filing cabinets. I started to scan the book titles, but quickly I kicked myself. I was here to get Leyla.

I went back into the entryway with its fireplace, sitting area and bookshelves. On the other side of it were stairs leading up to an open walkway that disappeared into either side of the building. I ran lightly and quickly up the steps, thankful for the solid, thick Minnesota lumber that didn't creak. I turned left into another hallway.

There were several bedrooms at this end of the building. They were large, and luxurious and well-appointed with nice log-frame beds, pine-paneled walls, thick carpeting, couches and flat screen televisions. Each space also had its own bathroom and built-in

Jacuzzi tub. As far as I could tell, there were no one-way mirrors on the walls. A room like that on the Shore would have belonged in a four or five star resort. All but two of the rooms were also very messy, with clothes strewn on the floor, and plates of half-eaten food on dresser tops. I noticed a pizza box from a Grand Lake Pizzeria in the corner of one of the rooms.

I supposed these must belong to Tree's favored leaders. They did not seem to be particularly in harmony with the forest to me, except for the log-beds and wood paneled walls.

None of the rooms was locked. There was no sign of Leyla. I began to feel the pressure of time, like a weight across the back of my neck. Any moment now, the meeting downstairs would be breaking up. The people who lived in these rooms would be coming upstairs, and as yet, the only way out I had discovered was back down the stairs in the open entry area of the lodge.

I went back across the open walkway in the entry area, and found two more rooms similar to those on the other side. But the corridor here ended much sooner, at a locked door. Aside from the mirror observation rooms, this was almost the first locked door I had discovered that night. I got a dry taste in the back of my throat. Maybe Leyla was behind this door.

In order to get my black-belt in Tae Kwan Do, I had broken bricks, and many-thicknesses of lumber. It was going to be noisy, but I was getting desperate. I took a step back and did a spinning back-kick, smashing my booted-heel into the door next to the lock. My foot broke through the door, but got stuck as I pulled it back. I hopped on one foot, thinking how foolish I would look if someone found me like this. At last, after scraping up my shin considerably, I extricated my foot. I reached through the splintered hole, but found no release mechanism on the doorknob. That meant that someone could be locked in from the outside.

Throwing caution to the wind, I smashed my foot at the door repeatedly, all around the lock, until I had effectively separated the small area holding the latch from the rest of the door. It swung open, leaving a little splintered section in place around the stationary doorknob.

Inside was an opulent apartment. I was certain I had found Tree's living quarters.

Immediately to my right was a very modern-looking kitchen with appliances that appeared brand new. I opened the fridge, and immediately felt hungry. I would have been proud to have that kind of food in my own fridge. The freezer held, among others things, a good supply of steak, and roasts and pork. Whoever lived here ate plenty of meat. The floor was some kind of reddish-brown stone.

It wasn't exactly a surprise to find that Tree was a hypocrite in his eating habits, but it didn't make me any sorrier about his death, either. I wondered if he had cooked for himself. I decided not. I didn't want him to be like me in that way, and anyway, it would have been easier and more convenient to have one of his slavish followers do it for him.

In front of me was a living room holding a furniture suite that would have cost a working man a month's wages. It looked out onto three walls of windows with patio doors, black in the night, but I could imagine the view during the day. I supposed the doors opened onto a deck. The lighting was sleek and muted, and the carpet smelled like lots of money.

His bedroom suite was to my left, looking out the back of the lodge. It was giant, with a separate sitting room, a Jacuzzi tub and a king sized bed with a canopy over it. A walk in closet held several very expensive suits. The whole place felt like a penthouse suite at some Las Vegas casino.

But it was empty. There was no sign of Leyla. I returned to the living room, and did a quick check for closets and secret passageways. I found nothing. As I stood there, staring at the black windows, I felt a soft breeze behind me.

I turned, and the door to the hallway swung open.

CHAPTER THIRTY-NINE

There were three of them, and appropriately enough, they looked like forest-creatures, but not the cute, fuzzy kind. More like the fierce, meat-eating kind. Two of them were very lean and kind of grey and dangerous looking, like wolves. As soon as they saw me, each one of them produced a pistol.

One of them smiled a vicious kind of grin, and his teeth looked black and rotten. "What have you gotten yourself into here?" he asked in a dead-sounding voice. With a shock I realized it was the voice I had heard on the hill above me the day I had gone looking for Vargas. The voice that had implied that he had killed Vargas and John Doe.

I was a great believer in seizing the momentum when faced with a dangerous situation. They all had guns pointed at me, but they were thirty feet away, just inside the door, and I was in the living room. If I moved fast, they might not even think to shoot. Without hesitation, I ran.

I flung open the patio door, and found myself knee deep in snow on a balcony. More snow was falling thickly, and it was dark. I grabbed the cold iron railing and flipped my body over, allowing my hands to slide down until I was dangling over empty space. The snow and dark hid what was below. Above me, I heard a yell, and footsteps pounding toward the balcony. I let go.

I dropped about twenty-four inches. My feet hit a sloped surface and slipped out from under me, and I found myself skidding face down on a portion of the roof. Deep snow on the roof slowed me, but

I still slid inexorably, and before I could figure out what to do, I was grasping at the gutter, and then falling again.

I didn't fall far. With my hands at the gutter, it was only three feet or so before my feet hit the ground. I fell back onto my rear-end, and then flopped backwards. I landed in a heavy snow bank. Some people get the idea that falling into snow is painless. That's not true, but it certainly cushioned the fall. I thought about making a snow angel.

Above me I could hear the voices of my pursuers on the balcony. They could obviously tell that I had jumped, and they wasted no time running back into the building, shouting for reinforcements as they went.

I decided against the snow angel. I was a little scraped and bruised, but otherwise unhurt. Soon they would come out of the lodge and circle toward me. If they were smart, they would come from both sides.

Snow is great for snow-angels and cushioning falls. It is also great for tracking fugitives. If I ran off into the woods, they would just follow my tracks, and sooner or later, they were bound to catch up.

I struggled upright and floundered through thigh-deep drifts to the front of the lodge. I bolted past the entrance, around the side to the shoveled walkways between the buildings. There was more risk of being seen here, but my tracks would be lost among dozens of others going to and fro between the buildings.

There were several people in the walkway between the lodge and the first building. It was dark, and snowing, so I hunched up my shoulders, slowed to a brisk walk and moved through them. No one really noticed me. I glanced at each of them, hoping vainly to see Leyla, but of course, if she was a captive, she wouldn't be among them. I kept walking, fairly fast, past the first building and then the second. As I passed the third and last building, I saw the light of flashlights coming towards me, up the plowed drive that I assumed led to a machine shed. I ducked back to the third building, went in, and down the stairs and then out the door on the lower side and into the woods. Hopefully, no one would think to look for tracks down at the lower side.

I was safe from dead-voiced men with rotten teeth, but I was outside in the cold and dark with no jacket, no pack and no light, and it was snowing hard. I bitterly regretted my decision to leave my pack and parka in the main lodge. The wind had picked up also, and was whipping the snow sideways. I had to squint to see. I decided to move parallel to the line of buildings, but back in the woods fifty yards or so.

I walked straight back away from the building, and then turned to see the lights, but the trees and snow, and possibly the slope, obscured them. I moved back the direction I had come, but at an angle, to come out nearer to the lodge. After walking for a hundred yards, all I could see was darkness. I stopped to listen, but could hear nothing over the wind. I turned the other way and walked a few yards. Still nothing. I was wet from my fall into the snow, and I was very cold. In these conditions, it would be a matter of an hour or less before I was in very serious trouble. I tried to follow my tracks backwards, but it was almost impossible to see them in the dark, and I had wandered enough to make the trail unclear in those conditions.

I stopped. I had always heard that freezing to death was a pleasant way to die. I didn't have a death wish, but death holds no fear for me. I have too much waiting for me on the other side. Even so, I knew then that I also had much unfinished business on this side of death, so I decided to pick a direction and keep walking until I found something, or I met Jesus face to face. Either outcome would be good.

I turned until the wind was blowing on my left cheek, and kept walking. As time passed, I started to stumble frequently. At one point, I found myself on my hands and knees in the snow. I couldn't feel my fingers. I pushed myself up and kept going.

Hours passed, so it seemed, though it could not have been that long. The wind whipped the snow at me, and blood slowly retreated from my skin, and I became numb all over. Soon, my brain felt numb also. I quit thinking, and just kept walking.

I found myself on my hands and knees again. Warm air was blowing up from the ground into my face. I shook my head. That couldn't be right. I pawed at the ground, but I could barely feel anything anymore with my hands. After a minute the air warmed me enough to bring some feeling back into my fingers, and I could tell that I was kneeling on some kind of steel grate. It must be the exhaust for some kind of heating system. That meant I was near a building. Slowly, my mind cranked into gear again. I could get into the space beneath the grate, I could warm up. It took me some time to locate the edges of the grate. When I did, I tried to pull it up, but it remained where it was.

Think Borden! A building must be nearby. You don't need to climb in the exhaust tunnel. Just find the building. I staggered to my feet, standing on the grate, and looked around me. Above and to my right, maybe twenty yards away, I thought I caught a glimmer of light. As I moved through the trees, the light grew stronger, and I could see it was placed above the door of a large, rectangular metal building. I must have stumbled upon the machine shed at the far end of the cult property. It was sided in metal, and looked like a typical newer machine shed of the kind you'd see on farms and country properties all over the Midwest, only maybe bigger. I went to the door, praying that it was unlocked.

It was the side door, a door for people, not trucks or equipment, and it was unlocked. Heedless of who might be inside, I flung the door open, and shuffled in. The warmth enveloped me like a blanket. Truthfully, I probably would have considered it cold under normal circumstances, but it was at least fifty degrees warmer than outside, and I was deeply grateful.

I looked around me. Orange phosphorous lights, of the type you find in old gyms, glowed from the rafters. I was in a large room with a cement floor. Some distance to my left was the far end of the building, which featured a large roll-up door for vehicles. Just inside of that sat a pickup truck equipped with a snow plow. Behind the truck was a tractor with a front-loader attached to it. To my immediate left were several bays for vehicles. I walked toward the tractor, and turned around, and I could see several cars parked in those bays. No clearing snow and scraping ice for the drivers of the Forest Way. Along the side across from the cars, and also along the back wall, were workbenches and tool boxes. About a quarter of the space, near to where I had entered, had been walled off, presumably into a few rooms. As I warmed up, I realized that the building was kept at maybe fifty degrees, which was perfectly fine to keep engines in good working order. But I was already wanting more heat. I walked toward the walled off section. Presumably, one of the rooms there was an office for record keeping, and it was likely to have a space heater. There were three doors. The first opened to a bathroom, one however, devoid of a heater. The second door was locked. There was only one more door. As I laid my hand on the handle, I heard a squeak, and felt a breath of cold breeze as the outside door behind me began to open. The knob under my hand turned, and I stepped quickly into the space behind, and closed the door quietly after me. It was dark, but as I reached out with my hands, I could tell I was in some sort of supply closet. I knocked a long pole, and quickly grabbed it before it fell to the floor. Exploring with my now-warmed hands, I realized I was holding a mop. Carefully, I set it down. I hoped no one wanted to do any cleaning at this hour on Christmas Eve. Just in case, I moved slowly toward the back of the closet. Now that my eyes had adjusted, I could see some things in the faint light coming underneath the door. Only, I was turned around somehow, because the door was in front of me.

I swiveled back, and found another thin line of light glowing from the other side of the closet. *That* must be the door, so what was the glow from the back of the room? I turned again. My eyes were adjusting to the dim light, and the faint illumination seemed to show a rack of shelves in front of me. I reached out, and sure enough, I touched shelving. My right hand slipped off one shelf, and bumped into a metal canister. Out of curiosity, I tried to pick it up. It wouldn't come. I rocked it back toward me and I heard a faint click, and then the wall in front of me swung aside, revealing a short vestibule, and a staircase descending downwards into darkness.

CHAPTER FORTY

Most machine sheds in the area have slab foundations, and no basement. Every indication was that this one was the same. And yet, this machine shed had a secret door in the back of a closet, and steps going down, presumably to a basement.

The vestibule was lit by a bare fluorescent bulb. I would have expected nothing less from an environmentalist cult. In the light, I could now clearly see the back of the closet, complete with shelves, swinging on cleverly concealed hinges. Even with the light on in the closet, I would not have suspected it was a door. The canister I had grabbed looked like any other can of WD-40. I grabbed it again, and saw how moving it worked the latch. On the other side of the door was a lever that activated it from that side. I moved it, just to make sure that worked also, and then, stepping into the vestibule, shut the door gently.

I could feel warm air moving up the staircase. That, and the possibility of another way out, spurred me down the steps. The bottom of the staircase was in darkness. I felt along the wall and finally found a bank of light switches. I flipped them all. Bright white fluorescent bulbs fluttered on. To my left was a giant room, underneath the machine shed. To my right, a passage led away, apparently underground, to somewhere else.

I stepped into the room. At first, I couldn't understand what I was looking at. The area was fully as large as the building above. Every wall was lined with waist high workbenches, interspersed with racks of metal shelving. There were also large, stainless-steel sinks hanging from every wall at regular intervals. On the workbenches were gas burners of the type people use for portable cooking with propane, and also glass beakers and bulbs, some hanging from stainless steel arms, some with red liquid in them. There were pipes running along the walls above the work benches, presumably carrying the gas for the burners and the water for the sinks. On the shelves, and under the workbenches, was a profusion of jugs, and plastic five-gallon buckets, and bottles and stacks of coffee filters and bales of paper towels. Against the left hand wall was a massive, industrial-style refrigerator.

I started looking more closely. Some of the jugs were labeled "muriatic acid." I noticed containers of acetone, cans of engine starter, bottles of drain cleaner, bags of rock salt and lye, measuring cups and blenders. Near the fridge, two of the workbenches held dozens of empty, glass pint-jars, and what looked like canning equipment. Scattered around the place were many large garbage cans. Taken as a whole, the room looked like a massive, oversized laboratory for a dozen mad scientists.

Perhaps they were making explosives. Maybe they intended to rid the world of those who did not live in harmony with the forest. That might explain the Guardians, and the plethora of guns I had seen waved about at the Forest Way. I moved into the room, staring at the confusion of materials around me. I had heard somewhere that ordinary fertilizer was used to make the bomb that killed so many people in Oklahoma City.

I didn't find any fertilizer. But I did see, in the mad jumble of unrelated chemicals, stacks upon stacks of boxes containing nasal decongestant. I looked at them more closely. There were many different brands, but they all contained pseudoephedrine as a main active ingredient.

Slowly, like an old television warming up, the light began to dawn in my brain. I was looking at the world's largest crystal methamphetamine-lab.

A chill shuddered through me, and it had nothing to do with my recent exposure to the blizzard outside. It was like discovering the proto-type for a nuclear bomb. I was standing in the epicenter of destruction and death for thousands of souls. What was made here would ruin untold lives; not just the lives of the addicts, but also the lives of those who loved them. I was standing at the edge of a crack that led all the way up from Hell, and heartache and devastation were leaking out like poison gas.

I walked numbly toward several tables that were pushed together in the center of the room. All my assumptions about the Forest Way were crumbling, and I didn't know what would be left behind. Surely this lab, this *factory*, created far more meth than the sixty-odd members of the cult could use. What was going on here?

Stacked on one of the tables were several cardboard boxes. I opened one of them, and found it was full of jars of blueberry jam. Suspicion blossomed in my head. I removed one of the jars, and looked closely at it. The label was slightly different from the labels I had seen in the other building. There was the hand-drawn picture of the tree, as with the other jars, but on this label, beside the tree was a large boulder. Everything else was the same.

It was sealed. I broke the seal and opened the jar. Inside, as advertised by the label, was blueberry jam. I dipped my finger into it and put it on my tongue. I have always liked blueberry jam, and this was pretty good. I had never been high, but I didn't feel like I imagined it would feel. I wondered how long it would take, if I had just licked 3 grams of meth-infused blueberry jam.

I carried the jar over to a sink along the wall. Sticking my fingers in it, I started scooping jam out, and dumping it in the sink. In the center of the jar, surrounded by jam, I found a small plastic baggie. I took it out, and rinsed off the jam. There seemed to be plenty of paper towels about, so I used them to clean up. The baggie was clear, and contained something that looked like rock salt, or ice cream salt, except the crystals were longer and thinner. I stared at it for a minute, and then went back and counted the number of jars in a box. It was twenty-four. There were about ten boxes stacked on the table. Two-hundred and forty little baggies of meth. I wondered how much was in the baggies, and how much it sold for on the street. Pastors were always wondering about "the street."

Except, in this case, "the street" was probably little kiosks at malls where innocent-looking cultists sold their products of the forest to environmentalists, people who felt sorry for them, and ordinary people who liked blueberry jam. But obviously, they sold to customers with different tastes as well.

I looked at the label again. The rock by the tree was artfully done. It looked like it belonged in the picture. But it distinguished *this* blueberry jam from the blueberry jam produced in the other building. Certain customers of Forest Way products probably knew to look for the special label preserves; Forest Way vendors probably knew that some people were to get ordinary jam, while others got the jam that made it the breakfast of drug addicts.

Certain things began to make sense at last. Amaryllis, or Ann, had been high when Jensen met her. Probably, she had been high on meth. I remembered how skinny she looked, and the few small scabs on her face, which I now remembered, were typical of meth-addicts. Heidi too, had been a bit too skinny, and her otherwise flawless face had also shown a few small scars. The dead-voiced man who chased me out of Tree's apartment had rotten teeth – another hallmark of meth addiction.

I glanced around the lab again. It looked like they were producing an awful lot of the drug. I wondered if the growing meth problem in the Northland started right here. It seemed likely. There was probably some sort of storage area somewhere around. I saw several heavy-duty stainless steel cabinets that turned out to be locked. Perhaps there was more meth in them.

I was trying the second cabinet I found, when I realized that none of this was helping me to find Leyla. I turned abruptly, and started walking back toward the passage that led away from the giant meth-lab. At that moment, I heard a rush of feet on the stairs, and before I could find a place to hide, Rock stepped around the corner. Behind Rock, Cliff towered sullen and ominous, a semi-automatic pistol in his right hand. The rotten-toothed man with the dead voice was there too, also holding a gun, and behind them, little Twig stood hesitantly, shifting from one foot to the other. Rock looked at me the way an uncle might look at a nephew that he is mildly exasperated with.

"Well, Pastor Borden," he said. "I really wish you had not seen all this."

CHAPTER FORTY-ONE

I looked at them. "So this whole thing, the Forest Way – everything, was just a front for the drug business?"

Rock shook his head. "Brown – that's Tree's real name – had his cult thing going before we met. It was real, from their perspective, I guess. He was small-time though. He was looking into drugs as a way of expanding his influence over his followers, and that's how we connected. That's when I got my bright idea, and we partnered up. I gave him a bunch of money, and he gave me the world's best cover, and a terrific money-laundering outlet as well. There are about thirty fruitcakes here, who are true believers. It helps to have some of the genuine article, makes the whole thing more believable." He turned and nodded at Twig. "Twiggy here is still a true believer, but I've convinced him that we need to keep the drug-thing going in order to keep the Forest Way out here, saving the world. We'll keep going as we were. Brown is not necessary. The others can carry on the Forest Way, and we'll carry on with our business, just as before."

It hit me then, like snow down my back.

"That's what happened!" I exclaimed, almost involuntarily. "Leyla discovered this. That's why you can't let her go."

Rock looked at me without blinking, his grey eyes flat and dangerous. At last he nodded. "That's right. She was poking around, and she poked her nose into the wrong corner. We were going to just kill her, like that stupid hunter who came around before her. But then we found your notes, and your clever little drop-box, and we knew that if she ended up dead, there would be no end of trouble, and cops everywhere, and our cover would be blown. So we converted her."

"You didn't convert her," I said flatly.

He snorted. "You were too smart for your own good, Borden," he said. "Or too dumb. You just couldn't let it go. Not even after Heidi."

"You sent Heidi."

"Was she good, Pastor? Even if Leyla forgave you, we could ruin you with that, you know."

"Nothing happened," I said.

Cliff snorted. Rock said, "Yeah, our photographer told us. Are you sure you're straight? Maybe we could put *that* rumor around your little congregation."

I just shrugged.

Rock hesitated. "How about it Borden? You keep quiet about this, and no one in your church learns about Heidi."

I stared at him. "Are you serious?"

He looked at me closely, and then slowly shook his head. "No," he said. "I guess you aren't the kind of man who gives in to blackmail."

I just glared back at him.

"You know the score now," said Rock, like he was thinking out loud. "How about your silence for your girlfriend's life? You keep quiet or she dies."

I looked around the lab. Thousands, maybe tens of thousands, of lives would be thrown into ruin and desperation as a result of what was made here. Murders would be committed over it. Girls would hire themselves into prostitution for it. Bodies would be broken by the drug itself. Others would be beaten and bruised in the violence that went along with it.

"How long?" I asked.

"How long what?" asked Rock.

"How long are you going to keep doing this?"

Rock was silent.

"You expect me to be OK with Leyla being a prisoner for the rest of her life? You expect me to stand by and watch you destroy people with this stuff?" I gestured at the room around me, and then I shook my head. "How about this: You give me Leyla, and we'll give you a forty-eight hour head start. You'll lose all this," I said, waving my hand again, "but you'll keep your freedom."

Cliff snorted again. The dead-voiced man was looking at me with a kind of intensity that I didn't like. Rock just laughed mirthlessly. "You expect me to just take your word for it, that you'll give me a sporting chance? What do you take me for?"

"Apparently, the same thing you take me for," I said. "Do you expect *me* to believe that you'll let me go free, knowing about all this, with only Leyla's life keeping me from talking? You'll wait until things settle down a little, and then some day, I'll go fishing and never come back, and no one but you will know what happened."

Rock nodded. "Like I said, Borden, you're too smart for your own good."

"So what now?"

"I'm a businessman, Borden. A very rich businessman, making a very large amount of money. It's too much of a risk to leave you around to blab about this."

"It's a risk not to. The cops know where I am."

"I doubt it," said Rock. "But no doubt they'll be suspicious of us anyway. We weren't very smart with that hunter, or that guy you hired."

The dead-voiced man grinned with his rotten teeth, but not his eyes, and said, "That guy liked to talk, didn't he?"

Cliff smirked. "Sure did. After I was done with him, you had to shoot him to shut him up, huh, Boggs?"

"Shut up, both of you," said Rock. "That's wasn't smart. But we can get smarter. After a few months under the ice in a lake up on the border, no one will know who or what you were, come spring. We get the right lake, maybe it's July before anyone even goes there. Won't be much left by then. No body, no crime."

He nodded to himself, apparently coming to a firm decision. "I'm sorry Borden. In other circumstances, I could use a man like you. You're smart, fast and hell-on-wheels in a fight. But you've got too much honor, or something like that. It's nothing personal." He turned and nodded at the others. "You know what to do. No need to pretend it's another hunting accident, so you can use the pistols." Without another look at me, Rock swiveled on his heel and walked out.

CHAPTER FORTY-TWO

Cliff and the dead voiced man, who was apparently called Boggs, moved slowly and menacingly toward me. There was a little bit of open space here at the entrance to the room.

"We talked about this," said Cliff. "We can both get our fun, but it's me first."

Boggs glanced at Twig, who still stood uncertainly near the entrance to the room. "Not a word of this to Rock, or you're next." Twig nodded hastily, several times.

He nodded at Boggs, and while the latter covered me with his gun, Cliff, deliberately turned and laid his own pistol on one of the nearby workbenches. He turned back to me, and spread out his hands, waving them slowly in the air in front of him, shuffling forward in a fighter's stance.

"Now," he said. "Let's see what happens when I'm ready for you."

He was about five inches taller, and maybe a hundred pounds heavier than me. I swallowed and took in a few deep breaths. Many people don't realize it, but martial arts skill does not confer the greatest advantage in every fighting situation. It's hard to overcome someone who is bigger and stronger than you are, no matter how skilled you may be. All other things being equal, it is usually the bigger man who wins the fight. And there was no doubt here about which man was bigger.

I turned my left shoulder toward Cliff, lifted my hands, and shuffled backwards and to my left. Cliff swung his left leg in a great wide arc at my groin. He would have felled a tree with it, had it connected, but given what I had done to him in our first encounter, I was expecting something similar, and danced out of the way.

Someone as big as Cliff probably didn't get into too many fights. Most people likely submitted meekly to whatever he wanted, without violence. In addition, when it did come to violence, my guess was, things didn't last long with Cliff. One or two solid punches from those softball-sized fists, and it would be over. My only hope was to stay out of range, and make this last as long as possible. Then, if I beat him, all I had to do was jump the man who was holding a gun on me, and get out faster than Twig could call for help.

I grinned at Cliff, not letting them see my despair. "You're slow."

Something exploded on the left side of my head. I snapped my right fist out, connecting with something soft, even as I staggered backwards.

"Not as slow as you think," said Cliff, and then called me a very unchristian name. He spat blood, and his lips began to swell. I shook my head to clear it. I couldn't wait around for him to pick his spots, or I wouldn't last long at all. Still side-on to Cliff, I hopped once and drove my left leg in a side-kick at his knee. As he danced out of the way, my foot came down, and I turned right, lifting my other leg and drove my shin into his body. I could hear the air whoosh out of him.

As he backed up, I stepped after him, sending my left fist at his temple. He chopped my arm down. I ducked my head and his counter-punch whiffed through the air above me. I straightened and circled away. Cliff knew more about this business than I had hoped. I feinted a kick and smashed my fist at his neck. He hunched up and took it on his shoulder. I blocked his counter-punch, but my forearm ached from the contact.

"You thought I was just some slow, dumb big-guy, didn't you?" said Cliff. He circled towards me. "Maybe I am. But maybe you're dumber and slower. You sure aren't bigger." He threw a looping right hand that was indeed a little slow. I threw up my right elbow to block, and staggered when his left hand connected with the side of my head again. As I reeled he kicked me in the stomach. I retreated dizzily. Dimly, at the edge of vision, I could see Boggs and Twig, watching intensely like a couple of lean wolves.

Cliff stepped deliberately toward me. He looked like he was starting to enjoy himself. I backed up until I bumped into one of the steel shelves that lined the walls. Pushing off, I twirled and caught him in the jaw with the back of my fist, with the torque of my spin behind it. He stumbled, and I moved in. I threw a kick at his stomach, but he caught it with his hand, and threw my leg off so forcefully that I fell down. I scrambled desperately to my feet, but he was not following up. He was shaking his head a little.

We were both breathing heavily. There is nothing I have experienced, not even cross-country skiing, that requires the amount of energy that real fighting demands. He shuffled towards me, and I circled away again. He seemed to slow even more. I drove a front-kick at his face, and suddenly he moved smoothly to the side, and smashed his fist into my jaw.

Little sparks exploded behind my eyes, and the room seemed to grow kind of dark. I threw up my hands. There was another explosion as something hit me in the same spot, and then I was staggering away, my hands outstretched. I half-turned, and crashed into one of the metal shelves. My hands grasped at something to hold me up.

266

Cliff kicked me in the side, and I could feel myself sliding toward the floor. Another blow to my head. Distantly, I could hear his voice.

"Not so clever now, are you, Borden? This is how it ends for you. You are going to die here. I'm going to beat your life away, and the last thing you'll hear is my voice, telling you what a piece of scum you are."

He proceeded to call me every name in the book, and quite a few that were not, punctuating his foul language with blows from his hands and fists. He was standing mostly behind me. I grabbed at some support, and my hands clasped around a big jug. I brought my head down between my arms, but Cliff reached around, under my arms, and began to hit my chin with vicious uppercuts from behind. My mind screamed something at me as the blows and insults continued to rain on me. It seemed like I could hardly feel them anymore. Moving as if through a vat of molasses, my left hand crept up, and unscrewed the cap on the jug. Then, with the last of my strength, I straightened, and whirled, spraying the contents of the jug into the face of my adversary.

He screamed, and clutched at his face, and then fell on his knees, with his hands over his eyes. Not knowing what else to do, I looked at the jug. It was labeled "Muriatic Acid." I dropped the jug and stood there, shaking, heaving in big breaths, doing all I could not to collapse.

Boggs was walking toward me with firm purpose, gun up and out and pointed at my chest. I turned toward him. My main regret was that I had not saved Leyla. There was a tremendous boom, echoing throughout the big room, and I collapsed to the floor.

CHAPTER FORTY-THREE

Dimly, I heard the sound of a shout, and a scuffle, and then another boom. I could feel the warmth of blood seeping around me. I felt so much pain from the beating that Cliff had given me, that I was aware of nothing from the bullets.

I lay there, my ears ringing, and then I could hear someone talking.

"Borden," said the voice. "Borden, can you hear me?" Hands pulled at me, dragged me across the floor and pulled me up into a sitting position against a workbench. I opened my eyes, and slowly focused on the thin, ascetic face of Twig.

"What?" I said. I was irritated and in pain. I didn't want to spend my last minutes on earth talking to this nerdy little cult follower.

"Can you walk?" he asked. "We don't have much time."

It seemed like a stupid question, but as I slowly thought about it, I realized I didn't know if I could walk or not. Slowly, with Twig's help, I struggled to my feet, and swayed. I could feel Twig exploring my torso with his hands.

"Are you OK? Have you been shot?"

Another stupid question. Boggs had been scarcely five feet from me when he pulled the trigger. I realized then that things weren't making sense. Why was Twig helping me? And if he was helping me, why weren't the others objecting? I rubbed my eyes, and looked around me.

Boggs was on the floor in a pool of blood. He wasn't moving. There was a tremendous smear of blood leading from next to his body to where I stood – the path by which Twig had dragged me. Beyond Boggs lay Cliff, also unmoving, a gun in his hand.

"I had to shoot them," said Twig. "Enough is enough. But we have to go. Now." He walked over to Cliff's body, and removed the gun from his hand. Then, with some difficulty, he pulled Boggs' jacket off his body, and brought it to me. I numbly put it on, flinching away from the warm stickiness in the upper back. Twig checked the gun he had picked up.

"Neither one got off a shot," he said, thrusting the weapon into his coat pocket. I don't imagine you feel great, but you'll be all right eventually. We've got to go now. I'll explain on the way."

"What happened?" I asked.

Twig hustled me into the passage outside of the meth lab. "Boggs was going to shoot you," he said. "So I shot him first, with Cliff's gun. Then Cliff crawled over and grabbed Boggs' gun, so I had to shoot him too. They're both dead. I thought the first bullet might have passed through Boggs and got you too, but I think the blood on you is all his. You don't have any on your front." We passed the stairway back up to the machine shop on our right, and entered a long straight corridor.

"Keep walking," said Twig. "When you get to the door, wait for me. I'll be right behind you."

I noticed that he was not saying "Hmm, well," anymore. He went back into the lab, and I shuffled forward, slowly regaining a sense of where I was and what was happening. The corridor was long, with a cement floor, cement walls, and cement ceiling. It was lit with bare fluorescent light bulbs. Twig caught up with me before I reached the end.

"Now we really have to hustle," he said. We broke into a little trot. I tried not to grunt with every step.

"How do you feel?" asked Twig.

"Like I was run over by a steam-roller."

"Cliff is a big guy. But you held your own for a good amount of time."

"That's a great comfort." I realized belatedly that maybe sarcasm wasn't the best approach with someone who had just saved my life. "Thank you, by the way," I said. "Thanks for saving my life."

Twig looked back over his shoulder, and his face twisted in an odd, self-deprecating way. "I've screwed it up pretty badly up until this point," he said. "It was the least I could do. Anyway, we aren't out of the woods yet."

I didn't understand his comment. I didn't understand a lot of things just then. When a man who is six foot five and two-hundred-ninety pounds hits you in the head for a while, many things become harder to comprehend.

We came to a steel door. Twig stopped. He turned to me and held out his hand.

"My real name is Daniel Pershing, by the way."

"Nice to meet you, Daniel," I said, still bemused. I shook his hand. "My real name is the same as it was ten minutes ago. At least I think so."

Twig gave a tight smile, and turned back to the door. He produced a key from one of his pockets, and unlocked it. The other side of the door was cold, black winter. The wind howled, whipping snow into our faces. It wasn't pleasant.

"Let's go," said the man formerly known as Twig, now Daniel Pershing.

I stepped into the cold wind, and Twig turned and locked the door again. "Hold on to my coat," he said. I grabbed the back of it, and he turned, and led us into the blizzard. After three steps, I realized I had forgotten about Leyla again. Cliff must have hit me harder than I imagined. I tugged on Twig's coat, and we stopped. I stepped close, and spoke loudly, so he could hear me over the wind.

"You go on," I said. "I've got to find Leyla."

His face was a blur in the darkness. "That's where I'm taking you," he said, also speaking loudly. "I got her out, earlier."

I tried to see his eyes, but I couldn't. "What do you mean, you got her out? What's going on here, Twig?"

"Daniel," he said. "Daniel Pershing. We don't have time. I'll tell you when we're further away."

He turned away, and I grabbed his coat again, and followed blindly into the storm.

CHAPTER FORTY-FOUR

We descended quickly, and as we did, the wind lessened a little bit, though not the snow and the cold. I stuck my right hand in my pocket and discovered a mitten. I tugged on Pershing's coat, and we stopped while I put it on, and then the left hand mitten, which was in the other pocket. With surprise, I realized I was still wearing my stocking cap. All in all, I could have been much colder, and I was thankful.

Pershing led us on again for maybe fifteen minutes. I could see that he had a little flashlight, and was following some sort of trail. We weren't the first ones through, so some of it had been broken in, even so, we frequently sank into knee deep snow, and the going was rough work. I didn't feel too great, and my breath was coming in great, deep gasps. My side ached, and my face felt like one giant bruise. My right leg was sore. I didn't remember being hurt there, but memory was in short supply that night. When we came under the shelter of some large trees, Pershing stopped.

"All right, Borden," he said, "I know you're in tough shape. Take a breather."

"Sounds good," I said, still breathing hard. "Care to explain anything to me?"

"I am Daniel Pershing," he said. "Constable, Royal Canadian Mounted Police."

I couldn't see his face in the darkness, but he sounded serious.

"A *Mountie?*" I asked. "Where's your horse?"

"Don't be stupid," he said. "The horses and red uniforms are part of a great historical tradition, but that's not how we do things anymore. It's not exactly the same, but we Mounties are similar in some ways to your FBI. We enforce federal laws all over Canada."

I was disappointed. "A horse could have come in handy right about now."

"Sorry," said Pershing. "No horse. I've never ridden one in the line of duty, either."

"So what *is* your line of duty?" I asked. My brain fog was clearing a little, and I thought I might guess.

"Drug enforcement," said Pershing. Score one for the beat-up pastor.

"So what are you doing here?" I asked.

"Messing up," said Pershing. "I am neck-deep in what will probably go down as the worst screw-up in Mountie history."

I began to catch my breath. My head was throbbing.

Pershing went on. "A few months ago, I was transferred to Northwest Ontario, Thunder Bay district. We had word that meth-use was increasing, and we assumed that there must be a supplier in the area. Thunder Bay is a pretty small agency with the Mounties, and I am the only drug-enforcement constable there. I have a civilian criminal-intelligence specialist who works with me. He's pretty nerdy and weird, but he's smarter than Einstein. Anyway, he got the idea that this little cult was the point of contact for most of the meth-trade in Thunder Bay. I didn't buy it, and neither did anyone else. But I went undercover to one of the meetings, just to satisfy him. When I got there, I didn't see any evidence of drug-dealing, but the meeting was so freaking weird, that I thought I'd better check it out while I was there, in case it was a different kind of threat, you know.

"As the meeting went along, I decided to leave, but somehow it never seemed like just the right time. If the cult was the source of the drugs, I didn't want to blow my cover and alert them that someone was investigating them. So I stayed, and played along, and one thing led to another with no chance to leave without making them suspicious. It was freaky, the subtle way they applied social pressure. Suddenly I was in a van. I don't know if they slipped something into the food, or what, but the next thing I know, I wake up, and we're in the States."

"I think I can go on, if we move slowly," I said.

"Okay," said Pershing. "Anyway," he went on, as we started out again, "I'm in the U.S. now, an agent of a foreign government, with no permission to be here or operate. It's a major scandal waiting to happen. I'm gonna get egg smeared all over the face of the Mounties."

"So when was this?" I asked, struggling through the snow beside him.

"About four weeks or so ago. And we're out here in the middle of nowhere, and it's winter, so it isn't like I can just walk away. And the longer I'm here, the more I begin to think that my intelligence worker's theory might be right. Things seemed a little suspicious. I started poking around."

"That's right when Leyla joined."

"You've got it," he said. "Pretty soon, I noticed that she was poking around as well. I didn't let her know who I was at that time, because I wasn't sure of her. What neither of us knew is that Rock and Tree were getting suspicious of me. Either Leyla, or I, must have left a light on in the wrong place, or left a door unlocked, or something. Anyway, they set a trap for me, but they caught Leyla instead."

"What?" I almost shouted. "You got Leyla into trouble with the cult?"

"I know," said Pershing miserably. "As I said, the biggest screwup in Mountie history. I jeopardized a civilian. What makes it even worse, from that perspective, is that once they caught her, there was no more suspicion on me. They figured they had nabbed the snoop. She saved me, even if she didn't mean to."

I was quiet. It was still hard work, moving through the snow.

"I would have walked out with you the first day you showed up," said Pershing. "Except they had just caught Leyla a few days earlier. I had to stay and see if I could get her out."

We were quiet for a while as we struggled through the dark snowstorm.

I spoke at last. "So when I came to see her, they already knew she was a reporter, and they were holding her captive."

"You did save her life, you know," said Pershing after a while. "They would have killed her out of hand, but once they realized that you knew she was there under false pretenses, they couldn't kill her. Not with you coming around, demanding to see her."

"So that's why they tried to convince me that she had really joined the cult," I said. "They wanted me to give up. And just in case that didn't work, they used Heidi to try and convince me that it was all over between Leyla and me."

"Who's Heidi?" asked Pershing. Of course, he would not have been privy to all the workings of Rock and his minions. I told him briefly about Heidi.

Pershing nodded. "These guys are devious and nasty."

"What about Tree?" I asked. "Herman Brown, the cult leader. Rock said he really was a cult-guy. You had him fooled into thinking you were a true believer?"

He shrugged. "I don't know if Tree believed it all himself, but he was a world class persuader and manipulator. I think he believed he could convince anybody. It really wasn't hard to persuade him I was the real deal – he expected his powers of persuasion would convince anyone in the world. A lot of the folks back there are genuine believers. They were all shocked when he died."

I wondered about Tree's death. It seemed like a strange coincidence. Then, like a blast of caffeine to the brain, I had a thought. "I think Tree was going to blow the whistle on Rock and the drug operation," I said. "The police were putting a lot of pressure on him, and they suspected that someone at the Forest Way was killing people who came too close. He came in to the station and asked for immunity. Maybe he *was* the real deal."

Pershing shook his head. "You're probably right that he was going to blow the whistle. But when it was all over, he'd probably still have his hands on whatever money they had laundered. Depending on the deal he cut, he might have even been able to continue on with the cult. It was actually a pretty devious plan. Team up with the drug dealers until you have amassed money and property from them, and then turn them over to the police. I figure that's why he was killed. I bet it was a hit. Plenty of gangs and drug rings can arrange things like that, even in prison."

After maybe ten more minutes, he spoke again. "The only thing that puzzles me is why my intelligence guy hasn't told someone where I was. It shouldn't take this long for Canada and the U.S. to straighten things out, and send someone in here."

"Maybe he was afraid of the bad publicity, like you were saying. He's probably hoping you'll just show up someday."

From behind, I could just see the shake of Pershing's head.

"I don't know. Todd isn't really cued in to social things. He might not even think of the scandal until after it was too late."

A cold feeling that had nothing to do with the wind began to creep into me. "What does your guy look like?" I asked.

"Medium height. Reddish hair. Scraggly red beard. Mid thirties."

I grabbed Pershing's coat and stopped him. "I'm sorry, Daniel," I said. "Your friend is dead. I found him three weeks ago, about half a mile from the Forest Way property. He'd been shot in the chest, and he was gone by the time I discovered him."

Pershing swore. "The stupid fool. He came down here on his own, and got himself killed. The poor, stupid fool. He's probably got the highest IQ of anyone I know, but he doesn't have a gram of common sense." He looked at me with sudden hope. "Or? Did he tell someone?"

I shook my head. "I'm sorry. As of today, we still didn't know who he was. They took all ID, all labels off clothes. We had no way to trace him. No one made inquiries for him. I expect that's because he didn't tell anyone where he was going."

Pershing swore again. "He was single, didn't have much of a social life, and he would go weeks, sometimes, without talking to his family back in Toronto. And if he didn't tell anyone about me, that means we're still on our own. No one is coming to rescue us."

"It's Christmas Eve," I said. "No one is even thinking about us."

CHAPTER FORTY-FIVE

The temperature was falling. It soon got cold enough so that it was painful to take a deep breath. Any time I did, I felt a burning in my lungs, as if a thousand tiny pins were sticking into the inside of my chest. That isn't unusual in Minnesota in December, but it is a sign that the temperature is dropping lower than twenty-degrees below zero, or fifty-two degrees below freezing. The blowing wind could easily take the chill down to forty or fifty below zero, approaching almost a hundred degrees below freezing. If we stayed out very long in these conditions, we were going to get frostbite. And if we stopped moving for long, we would die.

About an hour and a half after we had left the meth lab, and about ten minutes after I first felt the burning in my lungs, we struggled through the deep snow to a clearing. I could see the dark outline of a small cabin, or shack. Suddenly, in the cold, keen wind, I could smell the invigorating aroma of a wood fire.

Pershing stopped. "When I first got to the cult, I sneaked out when I could, trying to find a town or even a house that I could escape to. All I found was this place. I've come here several times since then, but it's been deserted since before I came here the first time."

"Probably a summer place," I said. "Even if it's a hunting cabin, it probably doesn't get used more than once or twice between October and May. There are lots of places like that around here." Both of us had the strange frozen-lipped accent of outdoor conversation in the northern winter.

"I brought Leyla here earlier," said Pershing. "I don't know if I was followed or not." He dug into his pocket and brought out one of the pistols he had taken from the men in the meth lab. "Take this. Wait here to make sure that no one came along and laid a trap for us."

"What about you?"

"I'll go on in. If someone is waiting in ambush, they'll relax once they've got me. Then it's up to you."

"That's a great comfort," I said.

"Do you have a better idea, one that you can put into action before we freeze to death out here?"

"How will I know if there is an ambush?"

"If it's clear, I'll come back out and call you. I'll shout 'Border Cats' if everything is OK."

"*Border Cats?*"

"It's the name of the Thunder Bay minor league baseball team. How long do you want to talk about this?"

"Go already," I said. I was starting to shiver, standing still.

Pershing made his way across the clearing. I could barely see him in the snow and dark. After what seemed like a long time, I saw a brief light, and then it went out. That must have been the door opening. I paced around and flapped my arms, but I grew very cold. Nothing happened. Then the light flickered again. Faintly, across the clearing, over the heavy wind, I heard Pershing call, "Borden! Come on in." There was a short pause, then "Border Cats!"

I made my way through the thick snow. There were five short steps up to the door of the cabin. I went up and thrust the door open.

Immediately, a body slammed into me, grabbing me tightly, pinning my arms to my sides. Adrenaline raced through me. But even as I started to pivot to throw my attacker off-balance, I heard Leyla's voice, muffled in my shoulder, shout "Jonah!"

I relaxed. After a minute, she shifted her grip, and I could reach up and return her relentless bear-hug. I did not want to let go, not ever. At last we loosened the hug and pulled back enough to look at each other. The room was lit by firelight. Leyla's face looked a little too thin, but I still thought she was beautiful. We stared at each other a minute, and then hugged again. She stroked my neck.

"I'm sorry Jonah," she said. "So sorry."

"Shh," I said. "No need. I'm here now."

We broke apart again, and she had tears in her eyes. I pulled off my mittens, and took her hand, and she led me over to the wood stove.

The cabin appeared to be just the one room. Light from a fire filtered through the metal screen over the mouth of the wood burning stove. After the wild whirling darkness of the blizzard, it seemed brighter than a room full of lamps. Pershing was standing by the stove, warming himself. Beyond him, against the back wall, was a small kitchenette, with a few cupboards, a sink with no faucet, and a short counter. In the opposite back corner were two single beds. At the front of the room, opposite the beds and to the left of the door as you came inside, was a little sitting area with an old couch, a rocking chair and a comfortable-looking recliner. On the other side of the door was a cheap table set up to be a dining area. There were two windows in the front wall, one on each side of the doorway, and a third window on the wall of the little sitting area. All of them were heavily, but roughly, curtained by old blankets. Simple and functional. Some guy's hunting or fishing retreat.

Now that we were finally together, there was so much to say to Leyla, that it seemed there was nothing to say.

"Are you all right?" I asked her at last.

She nodded. "But what about you?" She gingerly touched my face. "You're hurt." I had momentarily forgotten.

"I had a disagreement with a big guy named Cliff." I shrugged. "I'll heal."

She shuddered. "I know him."

I hugged her to me with one arm. "Don't think about it right now," I said.

"Jonah," she said after a moment. "I'm sorry I said I hate you." She drew a deep breath, and shuddered, and then slowly relaxed under my arm. "I don't hate you, I love you. I was trying to send you a message."

"I know," I said. "I figured it out, but not until much later. Don't worry about all that now."

"It kind of helps to talk about it. I haven't had the chance to talk to anyone about it yet."

"Okay," I said. "But if it bothers you, then you can stop."

"When you came to see me that time, Rock and some men were watching us from behind the mirror on the wall. They were in the next room. They had guns, and Rock said they would shoot you unless I got you to leave and not come back. They said if I did anything at all to tip you off, they would kill you. The first time I said 'I hate you,' I was looking at the mirror. I was talking to Rock. But then I saw you looking at me in the mirror, and I had an idea. I thought that if I said I hated you, you wouldn't be able to believe it. It would bother you, until you figured it out, and they would never think of it as a tip off."

"It did bother me. I kept thinking about it, and I did figure it out. But I couldn't figure out how to save you."

She kissed me gently. "Knowing that you were there, that you weren't giving up, that saved me."

I met Pershing's eyes for the first time since we'd come into the cabin. "Thank you," I said.

"Like I said," he replied with a dull edge of bitterness, "it's my fault you're in this situation in the first place. And I hate to tell you, but we aren't out of the woods yet. Literally."

"What now?" I asked.

"It's too cold to go out again right now," he said. "We'd be risking serious frostbite, or even death. We have to wait until it warms up. Then, I guess the best chance is to get to your car, wherever you left it. We'll have to hope that Rock assumes either we've already escaped, or that we've frozen to death in the woods."

"One of us had better be on watch all the time, though," I said.

"Agreed," said Pershing. "I've been at the stove a little longer than you. I can feel my fingers and toes again. I'll take the first watch. I think if I get behind the curtain my eyes will get used to the dark again."

He walked over to the window that was by the sitting area, and slid his body between the glass and the rough blanket that served as a curtain, leaving Leyla and me in a kind of semi-privacy.

"Jonah," said Leyla. "I have to tell you something." She seemed agitated.

"Okay," I said.

She looked away sightlessly, and I could see tears forming in her eyes. When she spoke at last, her voice was shaky.

"They – they couldn't kill me because you kept coming around and bothering them about me. I heard them talk about it. They thought if I told you to go away, that might work."

"You told me about that," I said gently. "You said you hated me in order to save my life, and to try and get me a message."

"It's not that," she said, waving her hands. She took small paces around the kitchenette. "They thought they had maybe fixed it so you wouldn't come back. But that wouldn't stop me from running, if I could. They wanted double security."

I looked at her. She was crying, and pacing, and wringing her hands. Leyla could be emotional sometimes, but she was a lot more agitated than I had seen her before. "What did they do, Leyla?" I asked.

"They injected me with meth."

The room seemed deathly quiet. The words were clear, but I wasn't sure I believed them. I smothered my emotions, and fell back on my pastor-experience. "Tell me more," I said, far more calmly than I felt.

She stopped pacing and met my eyes. "They injected me with meth every day, Jonah. Every day for the past three weeks." She started moving again. "I hated it Jonah, I did. I still hate it." She turned abruptly and strode over until she stood right in front of me. Tears welled up in her eyes. "But I loved it too, Jonah. I still love it. The rush is wonderful. I feel so good when it hits. My captivity didn't bother me much when I was on the high. I started to look forward to my hit, every day. Sometimes they would play with me, and push back the time an hour or two, just to show me that they could control me, that they own me." She started sobbing in earnest now, her shoulders shaking. I took her in my arms and held her.

After a little while, she grew quiet. "What else?" I asked gently. Inside I was churning.

Leyla pushed back from me a little and met my eyes. "Isn't that enough?" she asked. "I'm hooked, Jonah. I'm an addict. Even right now as we stand here, I'm overdue. I want my dose."

"That's all?" I asked. "They didn't make you do anything else?"

She met my eyes questioningly, and then her expression softened. "Oh Jonah, no, nothing like that."

"Do you want to quit?" I asked her.

"Of course I do," she said. "But part of me doesn't. Part of me wants my high. Right now, in fact."

I held her again. "We'll get through it," I said. "We'll get through it together."

But it seemed to me like someone else was saying the words. Inside me, hate was blossoming like a deadly wound. My whole being began to scream for vengeance.

CHAPTER FORTY-SIX

"This is no good," said Pershing after about forty-five minutes. "If they find us, we'll be caught like rats in a hole. We need a plan."

"They might never even look for us," I said.

"They'll look for us," he said. "If we get away, the whole operation is blown. Millions of dollars down the toilet, with serious hard prison time to boot. There is no way they don't look."

"Maybe they won't find where we've gone."

"We can't know what the enemy will do," said Pershing. "So we have to plan for what he is *capable* of doing. They are certainly capable of following our tracks through the snow to this cabin."

"So you are saying this place isn't safe," I said.

Pershing nodded slowly. "Our only hope is the blizzard. It's full-on dangerous out there right now. If a man had to walk out here from the Forest Way, and then make the return trip without stopping in shelter to warm up, he could possibly freeze to death before he made it back."

"Do you think there's enough snow to cover our tracks?"

He shook his head. "Not snow. The wind may do it, though."

"So what do we do?"

"We make a plan, in case the wind doesn't cover our tracks, and they decide to risk the cold."

"Back at the Forest Way, I left a backpack with some survival gear in it," I said.

"Might as well be the moon," said Pershing.

"I'm not going back there," said Leyla. "Not ever." Her voice sounded shaky.

"We don't have your pack," said Pershing. "But I brought some things out here each time I came. Let's see what we've got. The owner might have left some stuff, too. I haven't checked everything."

Pershing and I began to go through every board and cupboard of the little shack. Leyla sat on the bed, out of the way.

We found two kerosene lamps, some matches, and a medium-sized can of kerosene. Between the hangings on the windows and the two beds, we had eight blankets. There were various cooking utensils, and pots and pans. A drawer in the kitchen contained a ball of rough twine and an old pocket knife. A small hatchet leaned next to a long axe by the woodpile just inside the door. There was some ground coffee and an old enamel percolator. I called a pause to the search, went outside and filled a pot with snow. While I was out there, I discovered two woodpiles, each covered by a thick tarpaulin. I came back in, and put the pot of snow on top of the wood stove to melt. When we had water, I put on the coffee to percolate, and resumed looking around the cabin.

We had a little bit of rope, some dried beans and rice, a can of spam, coffee, five cigars still in their plastic wrapping, some thick leather gloves, a poker from the stove and a package of hot cocoa.

We looked at our treasures in silence for a moment.

"Okay, now what?" I asked.

"We need a place to escape to, if they come. We only have two pistols, and no spare ammunition. We can't fight it out here."

"I've never been exactly here before," I said. "But on the map, it's all woods. Do you know of another house or cabin?"

Pershing shook his head.

"We can't spent the night outdoors," said Leyla. "We'd freeze to death. Besides, if they followed us here, why wouldn't they just follow our tracks from here to wherever else we go?"

"So we need to get out of here to another safe, warm place, and we need to make sure they won't follow us."

"Agreed."

We talked it over. We considered the various possibilities. Finally, we figured something out. It wasn't a very good plan, but it was the only one we had. At least we all agreed on the two major objectives. I kept the third objective, my own personal goal, to myself.

"I'm hungry," said Leyla when we were quiet for a bit.

"Good idea," said Pershing. "We ought to stock up while we can. If we have to do this, we're going to be burning a barrel-full of calories."

I put the rice and beans on the stove. The coffee was done, and I poured us each a cup. Leyla emptied the package of hot cocoa into her coffee.

"Sacrilege," I said.

"I'm craving something sweet," she said. Her hand shook as she lifted the cup to her mouth.

I opened the spam, chopped it into rough chunks, and fried it in a cast iron pan that I set on the stove top.

"We'd better get to work," said Pershing. "We'll have to move fast, in the cold."

On the right side of the clearing, looking out the front of the cabin, was a small river. Behind the cabin was a small, steep, tree-clad hill. I went back into those trees, and through them, down to the river. It was frozen, of course. I crossed it, and climbed a steep bank on the other side. With the aid of a flashlight, I quickly found what I was looking for.

As I had when I had gone looking for Vargas, I used the two tarps from the woodpile, and the rope, and made a snow-cave shelter. The only major difference with this one was that I lined the inside of the cave with one of the tarps. We didn't have waterproof sleeping bags this time. Snow is almost a perfect insulator, and no matter how cold it was outside, the snow cave would stay just below freezing. In this case, that made it eighty degrees or warmer than standing in the wind.

I came back the way I had come, pulling a pine branch behind me to obscure my steps. I caught a glimpse of Pershing, crisscrossing the clearing around the cabin, leaving tracks going in fourteen different crazy directions.

I smelled the kerosene as I climbed the steps and stamped my way back into the cabin, my face aching with the frost. Leyla pulled the blankets from the windows and beds, and bundled them up in three packages.

"I think the food is ready," she said. Pershing came in, along with a blast of frigid air.

"Any trouble, you two?" he asked. We both shook our heads.

"Snow cave is all set," I said.

Leyla gestured at the wood and the kerosene. "Does that look right?"

Pershing nodded. "It should work."

We mixed the spam with the beans and rice. It wasn't very good food, but there was plenty of it. Afterwards, we settled down to wait, straining our ears to hear over the whistling of the wind.

CHAPTER FORTY SEVEN

The sound came less than fifteen minutes later. Faintly came the clang and rattle of pots and pans and lids, banging together. Pershing had strung them on some twine, and lightly buried an attached line in the snow, where anyone following our tracks would trip on the twine and trigger the noise.

"Go!" said Pershing. He bent to light one of the kerosene lanterns, while Leyla and I each swung our blanket-bundles onto our shoulders. In less than fifteen seconds we were all standing outside, behind the cabin. I showed Pershing my pine branch, and we all stared into the flying snow, looking across the clearing.

"They might think we're going to ambush them, said Pershing in a low voice. They'll go a little slower now."

"Either that, or it was a moose," I said.

It wasn't a moose. About two minutes later we saw the glimmer of flashlights in the trees on the other side of the clearing.

I took a deep breath. "Okay, let's do it," I said.

Pershing went back into the cabin. I took Leyla's hand, and we moved down the same route I had taken earlier. We made our way across the river and up the bank into the snow cave. Once inside, I turned around and gazed out of the entrance hole, across the river toward where the cabin stood. I could barely make out its silhouette from here. Leyla slithered up beside me.

"Do you think it will work?" she asked.

"I hope so," I said.

"Jonah," she said. I turned, but I couldn't see her face in the dark.

"What is it?"

"There's a part of me –" She stopped. When she continued, her voice was very shaky, and the words all came out in a rush. "There's a part of me that thinks, maybe it would be okay if it didn't work, and we got captured, because then I could go back with them and get my shot of meth."

I turned to her and put my arms around her. Outside in the Minnesota winter, hugs are not as satisfying as at other times, because there is so much insulation from real human touch. My soul felt insulated, too. I wanted to comfort Leyla. But more than that, far more, I wanted to hurt Rock, to make him pay for what he had done to this lovely, brave, beautiful woman.

Suddenly, several shots rang out. Someone shouted. Another shot was fired, and then there was silence. I pulled Cliff's pistol from my pocket and continued to peer out into the darkness. After what seemed an eternity, I could hear the soft crunch of someone moving through deep snow.

"Border Cats," hissed a voice. I put the gun away, and we made room for Pershing to wiggle down into the snow cave.

"You really need a new code word," I said.

"I know," he said. "Hey, it's warm in here, at least compared to outside."

"Just like I told you," I said.

"I think maybe I got one of them," said Pershing. "Can you see anything?"

I looked back outside. For another minute, I could see nothing, and then suddenly a bright orange glow blossomed across the river. I breathed a sigh of relief.

"Looks like it took," I said. "The cabin is burning."

We couldn't see much while we stayed in the snow cave. Faintly, we could hear the sounds of shouting.

"They've probably been out there for an hour already in this cold," said Pershing grimly. "It's at least an hour back, and they have no shelter in between. They are in serious trouble. They won't have time to try and find us now. It will be all they can do to make it back alive."

It wasn't enough for me. "Wait here," I said, and crawled out of the shelter, ignoring their protests, and headed back toward the burning cabin.

CHAPTER FORTY-EIGHT

The cabin was blazing fiercely, flames roaring twenty-feet high and more, painting the clearing with a garish, orange glow. Even so, I could see that already the fire was past its peak. Most of the building was already consumed. I stayed back among the trees, in the shadows. Even from there, I could feel the warmth of the blaze. Two men were leaving the clearing, supporting a third between them. Two more stood, staring at the flames.

One of them said something to the other, shouting to be heard above the fire and the wind. I could just make out the words.

"We can't stay out here and search for them any longer. We need to get back to shelter!"

"Go!" said the second man, waving his hand. "I'll be right behind you." He turned face on to the fire, and I could see that it was Rock.

The first man left, making his way across the clearing, and into the woods. I could see his flashlight click on as he moved further from the light of the fire. Rock stood, unmoving. His face was full of anger and frustration. I could imagine how he felt. We had outsmarted him. We had gotten away, and taken away his shelter, and his ability to continue the search. I waited twenty more seconds and then stepped into the light, ten feet away from him. My gun was out, and pointed at him. He looked up, startled.

"Borden!"

"I don't know your real name, Rock," I said, "and I don't care to." I watched him carefully, but he made no move towards his pockets.

"I thought you'd be long gone by now."

"I will be," I said. "But I have some unfinished business first. Give me your gun. Slowly."

Rock carefully reached into his right hand pocket and brought out the weapon.

"Toss it into the snow, over there," I said, jerking my head to the right.

He did as he was told. I walked over, keeping my eyes on him, and retrieved his big chrome revolver. I moved back and laid it on the ground.

"Take your coat off," I said.

"What are you doing, Borden?" he asked.

"Take your coat off," I said. "The fire is plenty warm right now."

He took off his coat, and laid it in the snow.

Carefully switching hands, I took off my coat also. It was chilly, but the massive fire nearby made it tolerable. Then I laid my gun down next to his. I shook out my shoulders and looked him in the eye.

"Come and get it," I said.

He looked from me to the guns and then back to me. He licked his lips.

"Come on you coward," I said.

"What are you doing, Borden?" he asked again.

I took three quick steps, and kicked him in the stomach. All the rage that had been building for the past several hours went into that kick. He bent forward, and then fell to his hands and knees, and vomited.

I stepped back, breathing wildly. I felt like pressure was building in the back of my head and neck. I wanted to hurt him, to maim him, to kill him. But he just knelt there, taking deep breaths.

"Get up," I said. "Fight me."

He shook his head and stayed where he was, heaving.

I kicked him again and he fell back into a fetal position on the snow.

The pressure in my head hardened into cold ice. I felt impotent. I went and picked up my gun again, and pulled on my coat once more. I pocketed Rock's weapon.

"Get up," I said.

He slowly rose. Even in the orange glow of the fire, his face was pasty white.

"You pumped Leyla full of meth," I said.

His eyes widened. "So that's what this is all about?" Then he seemed to regain some equilibrium. "One good turn deserves another. You ruined my life, I ruined yours."

"I didn't ruin your life, you piece of rotten flesh," I said. "You chose to make and deal drugs. You ruined your own life, and then mine, and now it's time to pay the piper." I stepped forward, grabbed him, and jammed the gun into the side of his head. For some reason, I couldn't quite catch my breath. I felt my finger tighten on the trigger.

Rock's face changed instantly. "Please," he said. "Please, Borden. No." His eyes were wide with fear. "Please. I'm sorry. It was never personal."

It seemed to take a tremendous amount of effort to release the pressure I had begun to put on the trigger of the gun. Slowly, I did. The hard wall of ice still pushed at me from within my head. I shoved Rock away from me, and he stumbled a few steps toward the dark, cold forest. I waved the gun at him. "Go."

He looked at me uncomprehendingly, and then looked back at his parka.

"No," I said. "No coat. Go!"

He paused, slowly straightened, and then looked out into the cold, black night. "I'll freeze," he said. "You might as well shoot me."

"That can be arranged," I said. "I think I'll start with the knees, and then maybe the groin, and perhaps a low-stomach shot. You'll have hours of pain before you die. Or, you could try to make it back. If you move fast, you might stay warm enough to make it. And if you don't, I've heard that freezing is actually a pleasant way to die. It's better than you deserve, that's for sure."

I aimed the pistol at his lower body. He raised his hands, and then turned around and took three steps further away from the fire and into the frozen night.

My head throbbed, and suddenly the pressure seemed to burst open, and I heard a soft voice, gentle, but firm.

It said, "Stop."

I have never heard anything like it before. Some people might have called it my conscience, or my better nature, because to think of it that way might make them more comfortable. But I knew it at once as the beloved voice of my savior.

"Wait!" I called out. The sound in my throat was hoarse. I coughed, and then called again. "Wait."

Rock stopped. I walked over and picked up his coat. In the pocket, I found a flashlight, but no weapons. I went over and tossed him the coat. Now, I didn't know what to do. I couldn't keep him captive. It would be like bringing a live tiger into our snow cave. I couldn't imagine how Leyla would react. I didn't want to let him go either, but I couldn't kill him. I had no choice but to do what I did. These days, I tell myself that continually.

"I'm going to check my back trail frequently," I said, as he pulled on the parka. "If you follow me by so much as one step, I'll shoot you down like the dog you are. Use the flashlight so I can see where you go as you leave. I'll be in town soon, and I'll send the police after you even before that, just as soon as I get back in cell phone range."

"You have a car nearby?" His face was pinched.

"Get out of here," I said.

I didn't need to tell him twice. He started quickly through the snow. Once, he glanced back over his shoulder, his face a pale blur in the darkness. Then his flashlight flicked on, and his light slowly dwindled into the distant woods and out of my life.

CHAPTER FORTY-NINE

I found another pine bough, and made my way slowly back to the snow cave, brushing out my tracks behind me. A careful search would reveal that the snow was disturbed, but no more than that. The cabin still burned, but with less fury now. About halfway back, I began to shake, and I had to stop while my body was wracked with tremors.

"I'm sorry," I said. "I'm sorry, I'm sorry."

After a while, the shaking stopped and I realized the pressure was gone inside my head. I felt exhausted. I stumbled wearily back to the snow cave and slid inside.

"What happened?" asked Pershing. "Where did you go?"

In the darkness, I could feel the silent force of Leyla's gaze on me.

"They left," I said. "They're gone."

"Jonah, what did you do?" asked Leyla.

I took her hand. "I wanted to —" I paused. "I was going to kill Rock. But I let him go."

There was a long silence in the shelter. Leyla gently touched my face. At last Pershing said,

"What if he comes after us?"

"I waited for a while. He wasn't following me. If he wastes time searching for us, he'll freeze to death. He has to get back to the Forest Way. I also allowed him to think that we had a car, parked on a back road nearby, and told him to expect the police. I don't think we have to worry about him tonight. Tomorrow, after the police fail to show up at the Forest Way, we may have a problem."

There was another silence. At last, Pershing said, "I'm getting cold. Let's try to get some sleep."

We spread three blankets on top of each other on the ground, and then laid on them, pulling the other five over the top of us as we huddled together for warmth. It was a cold and uncomfortable night, but we were not in danger of freezing to death.

When I awoke in the morning, I felt like I had been rammed by an ore-freighter. Light filtered into our shelter through the snow. Leyla was snuggled against my side, with her left arm around me. As I watched, she opened her eyes and smiled at me. From somewhere, warmth began to creep into my heart, for the first time in what seemed like forever.

"Merry Christmas," I said.

Her eyes widened. "It's Christmas already? I lost track of time, all those days being locked up."

On the other side of her, Pershing stirred, and then pushed himself up onto an elbow and looked at us.

"Good morning," he said. "Merry Christmas."

I looked at Leyla. "Never in my wildest dreams did I imagine that the first night I spent in bed with you would involve a snow-shelter and another man."

She touched my face and smiled sadly. "When I was held captive at the cult, it got so bad that I even imagined I missed your smart remarks."

Then she shifted herself up and kissed me, seriously, on the lips. "You won't even remember this after our first real night together," she said huskily, and then gave me an impish grin. I felt a warm glow. Leyla seemed like Leyla again.

"Speaking of that, Jonah," said Leyla. "They showed me some pictures, and told me you had already found someone else. I figured the pictures were photo-shopped or something, but they looked really bad."

"They weren't photo-shopped," I said. Leyla looked at me steadily.

"Nothing happened though," I added, and I told her about Heidi, not leaving out anything.

She was quiet for a long time.

"Nothing happened, Leyla, seriously. My clothes stayed on the whole time."

She shook her head. "It's not that. It's just how *wicked* they were to try and do that to us. You must have felt terrible, knowing that they showed me those, not being able to explain."

I nodded. "I hoped you would trust me, even when the evidence said otherwise."

She met my eyes. "I did. I do," and then she kissed me again.

Pershing cleared his throat. "Maybe you two could hold off the festivities until we really are safe," he said. "Odds are, it's still fiendishly cold out there, and we've got a lot of ground to cover without freezing to death."

"What's the plan?" I asked.

"We have to find either a house, or a car that we can drive," said Pershing. "Where did you park, Jonah?"

"In the snow machine parking area, about half a mile from the main entrance to Forest Way."

He frowned. "That's pretty close to the compound. If Rock and the others made it back safely, they've probably been looking for it, and likely they've found it already. They'll be watching it, waiting in ambush."

"How will they know it's my car?" I asked.

"How many people will be parked there on Christmas morning?"

"Good point," I said.

"The other thing is, once they figure out that it is your car, and the police haven't showed up, they'll know we're still out here. They're going to come looking for us. Do you know of any houses or farms or anything around here?"

I shook my head. "Almost all this land is national forest. A little further north and you have the Boundary Waters wilderness, and Voyageurs National Park. Someone may have a little plot of private land here and there, but mostly it would be just seasonal cabins, like the one we burned down last night."

"Hey, that was the only way to be safe from them."

"I agree," I said. "I'm just saying, that is as much civilization as we are likely to see in a twenty-mile radius, besides the Forest Way, of course."

"We could make for the county road," said Pershing.

I shook my head. "There's not much traffic out here on a normal basis. On Christmas day after a snowstorm, we could walk on that road all day and not see a single car."

"And Rock and the others might expect us to do that," said Leyla. "They might send cars up and down the road, looking for us. We could end up flagging down the very people we're trying to escape from."

"You said there was a back-way into the Forest Way. Some sort of trail, where you found Todd?"

"Todd?"

"My civilian criminal intelligence worker."

"Oh," I said. "I might be able to find that trail from here. If we went that way, it's probably four or five miles from here to the trailhead. After that, it's back roads to town for twenty miles or so."

"Twenty five miles, altogether."

I nodded. "The first five through deep snow. In summer, we could do it in a day. But if it's still cold out..."

"Let's find out," said Pershing.

We scrambled out of our hole and stood on the bank of the river, looking across at the clearing and what remained of the cabin. The day was bright and sunny, which, in winter in Minnesota, usually means a bitterly cold arctic air mass. The hulk of the cabin had collapsed in on itself, and a pillar of thick gray smoke still trailed into the cloudless sky.

I took a deep breath, and regretted it instantly. A thousand tiny icicles stabbed into my lungs. I covered my mouth and coughed as gently as I could.

"It's definitely still dangerously cold," said Pershing.

"Let's get back inside," said Leyla.

Back in our shelter, we discussed it more.

"We could kill ourselves out there, trying to reach town," said Pershing.

"Maybe we should just hole up here for the day," I said. "If we don't show up on the roads or by my car, Rock might think we're long gone, and he may even pack up and leave to get out before the police get him."

"I want to get away," said Leyla. "I haven't felt safe for almost a month." I grabbed her hand and squeezed it. She seemed like she was slipping back into the tight, burdened place she had been in the night before.

Just then, we heard the first snow-machine.

CHAPTER FIFTY

"What do we do?" asked Leyla.

It was a terrible dilemma. Minnesotans are irrepressible in the winter-time, and it was entirely plausible that some intrepid family had purchased new snowmobiles for Christmas, and were now trying them out. If that was the case, all we had to do was flag them down, and we were saved.

On the other hand, maybe it was Rock and the Forest Way, out searching for us. I tried, and failed to remember if I had seen snowmobiles in the machine shed at the compound.

"Does the Forest Way have snow machines?" I asked Pershing. He shrugged. Leyla shook her head to show that she didn't know either.

We could clearly hear several of them now, and they were drawing closer. While we sat there, we heard the roar as they entered the clearing just across the river.

"They might see us if we stick our heads out now," said Pershing. "There's not much brush in front of us, and we're pretty high on the bank here."

We waited. The awful thing was that if they were friendly, the only way we would know it is if they left without searching for us. Only if it was Rock or the others, would they hang around the clearing and try to pick up our trail.

I could hear the sound of the machines as they idled, and then we heard voices shouting to each other over the throb of the engines. One by one, abruptly each time, the engine noises ceased, until it was quiet. They were staying.

Pershing eased his gun out of his coat, and nodded at me. I pulled mine out too, and checked it. Across the river we heard more yelling, and then silence punctuated by the occasional distant voice. The tension grew. Suddenly, after maybe twenty minutes, we heard someone much closer, shouting again. Other voices called back, and then came closer. I motioned Leyla to the back of the shelter, and moved to one side of the door hole. Pershing crouched against the wall on the other side.

We heard footsteps, heard them clearly, approaching through the snow. And then a voice, clear and crisp, no nonsense.

"You in there! Come out now, with your hands on your heads, no weapons. We see a weapon, we'll shoot you on sight." Something about the voice was familiar, and unpleasant.

Pershing put his finger to his lips. We waited in perfect silence.

"Ahoy the snow cave!" said the crisp voice again. "We know you are in there. We can see your fresh tracks right outside the hole. Come out with your hands on your heads, no weapons."

They were going to kill us anyway. I was never one to submit meekly to my fate.

"You come and get us, you cowards!" I shouted. "We'll take a bunch of you lowlifes with us!"

There was a brief silence. Pershing was staring at me in shock. "They saw our tracks," I said quietly. "The game is up. I'd rather go down fighting."

"Borden?" shouted the crisp voice. "Is that you, you scumbag?"

And then I knew the voice.

My face split involuntarily into a huge grin. "Jaeger?" I shouted back. "What are you doing here, you lazy excuse for a public servant?"

I stuck my gun in my pocket and wormed out of the hole, and stood up on the bank with my hands in the air. Jack Jaeger was standing on the river below me, and two Sheriff's deputies had rifles lined up on me from the right. He waved them off, winked at me, and motioned for me to come down the bank. The deputies lowered their rifles until I passed, and then aimed them at the hole again.

"Are you alone?" he asked.

"No," I said. "Two more good guys. No bad guys."

He waved at the deputies to stand down. "Call them out," he said to me.

"Leyla, Pershing, come on out. It's okay. It's Jack Jaeger and the sheriff's department."

I climbed back up the bank, and helped Leyla out of the hole. Pershing followed.

"Merry Christmas," said Jaeger. He looked at Leyla. "I've read your stories in the paper. I have to say, your press picture doesn't do you justice. No wonder Borden wouldn't quit."

"Nice to meet you," said Leyla. "And thank you so much."

Jaeger turned to Pershing. "This is Daniel Pershing," I said to him. "Royal Canadian Mounted Police."

They shook hands.

"Where's your horse?" said Jaeger.

Pershing rolled his eyes. "I don't have one. Most Mounties don't, anymore."

Jaeger looked at the hole we had crawled out of. He nodded at me. "Smart," he said.

"Thanks. I surprise myself sometimes."

"I can see you guys have a story to tell," said Jaeger. "We do too. But let's get you out of the cold, first."

"How did you find us?" I asked.

"Some of the suspects up at the Forest Way compound told us several people had come down this way. Plus, we saw the smoke, and thought we should check it out." He indicated the column of smoke that was still rising into the clear air from the smoldering remains of the cabin.

"Wait," I said. "Why were you out here in the first place?"

"Long story," said Jaeger, "and it's freaking cold out here. Let's get you guys back to some warmth first, and then we'll talk."

We each rode on the back of a snow machine. They took us to Forest Way, first, and we found it crawling with law-enforcement personnel. Jaeger brought us into the lobby of the main lodge, and sat us down on the couch in front of a roaring fire with steaming mugs of coffee.

"I need to get some other people in on this," he said, "and then we'll have to go over what happened. Do you need anything else?"

"I'm sorry to be a bother," said Leyla. Her arms were crossed, and she held herself tightly, looking at the floor. "But do you think we could go into town and do this at the Justice Center? I don't want to spend a minute longer here than I have to."

Jaeger looked at the comfortable couch and roaring fire and then at Leyla. Like gears turning in his head, I could see him imagining one of the bare, cold, soulless conference rooms at the county sheriff's office, and comparing it with the cozy lodge. "Absolutely," he said without hesitation. I felt a tremendous rush of Christmas spirit toward him just then.

They drove us the short distance to my car, and then Leyla and I drove into town together. Pershing rode separately with Jaeger.

After that followed hours of going over our stories, answering questions, retelling certain parts and dredging our weary minds for anything else we might have forgotten. Halfway through, Leyla's parents and brother came in, and we all hugged and cried.

Towards evening, Dan Jensen showed up.

"You are one lucky son-of-a-gun," he said.

"Thanks," I said. "Much later, and we might not be around to appreciate it." I looked at Jaeger, who sat relaxed with a self-satisfied smile on his face. "We've been so busy talking that no one has told us what happened. Why were you guys at the Forest Way? How did you find us?"

Jensen smiled and put a small cardboard box on the table. "It was this," he said. He opened the box and pushed it over to me. Inside it, in a clear, sealed plastic bag, was a half-empty jar of blueberry jam. In another bag, was a piece of paper, laid flat. The jam came from the Forest Way, and the label on the jar had a picture of a tree and a boulder on it.

"What's the paper?" I asked.

Wordlessly, he pushed it over to me. It was handwritten, and it said:

Merry Christmas to the Grand Lake Police Department! Please open this gift right away. You will notice that the jar is sealed, and that it comes from the Forest Way. Look inside for the gift that will keep on giving. You will know what to do when you find it.

-- A friend.

P.S. Please tell Jonah Borden Merry Christmas, from "Heidi."

"You opened the jar, of course," I said.

"I didn't. I wasn't here. It was Christmas Eve last night. But the desk sergeant was hungry, and opened it up. From your testimony, obviously, you can guess what he found. He called me, and I called Jack, and we called a judge, and the State Police and half of the federal departments, and one thing led to another, and we raided the Forest Way at about five this morning." He looked from Leyla to me. "We called you too, Jonah, but you weren't there. We kind of figured we might find you somewhere out there."

"So did you guys find Rock?" Jensen, of course, had met him once, and the others had heard my description of him sixty-eight different times as we had gone over my story.

Jaeger shook his head. "We didn't find him. But we will. And in the meantime, his organization is busted wide open, and the meth operation is over. You did good work Borden." He slapped me on the shoulder.

I stared at him. "It's the Christmas spirit, getting to you. You don't know what you're saying."

He actually smiled. It was a smallish grin, but it touched his eyes. "Probably so," he said.

CHAPTER FIFTY-ONE

The day afterwards, I picked up Leyla, and brought her back to my place for brunch.

"Jonah," she said. "You know I love you. But we can't get married next week."

"I know," I said. "I didn't know what to do. I didn't know if you would get out in time, and then I worried about how you would feel about me when you did. So I didn't make any decisions about the wedding. We probably don't have a band, cake, or a meal, or anything, now."

"I'm not worried about all that, darling," she said. "But I can't do it. Not right now." She began to tear up. "I'm a meth-addict Jonah. Even now, I want more. I don't want to spend our honeymoon wishing I was shooting up."

"What do you need?" I asked.

She smiled. "You are so good to me," she said. Her face got serious. "I need to come to terms with what has happened to me and I need to deal with my addiction."

"I am here for you, darling," I said. "Whatever you need."

"Wait for me?" she said.

"Forever."

She frowned. "I hope it won't be that long."

That is why, on New Year's Eve, instead of getting ready to start our life together, Leyla and I had dinner and a movie night with Alex Chan and Julie. Julie came early, and I gave up my kitchen so that she could cook dinner for us all.

"This is really good, Julie," I said after my first bite.

"I told you I make a mean steak," said Julie.

Alex lifted his entire piece of meat on his fork, waved it around, squinted his eyes, and said in a funny voice, "Hey suck-uh! Yo momma is dumb as a bag of rocks."

We all stared at him.

He put the meat down. "A mean steak," he said. "That's a mean steak."

No one stopped looking at him. Finally Julie turned to me. "Have you been trying to teach him your humor?"

After dinner we watched movies until almost midnight. Then we turned on the TV and watched the ball drop in New York City.

"This already happened an hour ago, you know," said Alex.

"I know," I said. "All those people aren't even there anymore."

"You guys have no sense of fun," said Julie.

When the New Year started, I kissed Leyla. Out of the corner of my eye, I saw Julie and Alex look at each other uncertainly, and then exchange a quick peck.

Alex left shortly after midnight.

"So what's going on there with you and Alex, Julie?" asked Leyla when he was gone.

She shrugged. "Nothing. We're friends. Alex is fun to be with. He has a good sense of humor."

"*Mean steak?*" I asked.

"Well, *most of the time,* he has a good sense of humor."

"So it's not serious?"

"No. Gosh, no!"

"I think he kind of likes you," said Leyla.

"I'm not dumb," said Julie. "I guess I know that. But I'm not ready to get serious with him."

"You are both my friends," I said. "Try not to hurt each other."

She saluted me. "Aye, aye, Boss!"

~

Five days later, Leyla checked into a drug rehab facility in Duluth. It was an outpatient program, but it ran all day, five days a week, so she decided to stay with her parents for the duration of the program. It was going to be a long month, only seeing her on Saturdays. I felt like I had lost her all over again.

During the second week of January, I got a phone call. It was Daniel Pershing.

"Jonah," he said. "I'm in town to clear up some paperwork. I wondered if you'd like to grab a cup of coffee or something."

We met at Dylan's that afternoon.

"So how are you, Daniel?" I asked. "Are you still a Mountie?"

"I am," he said. "But I'm suspended, pending the result of an investigation." He cleared his throat a little. "I...ah..." he said, and for just a moment, I saw Twig, the diffident little cultist, once more. "I wondered if you would be willing to come up to Thunder Bay and testify on my behalf," he finished.

"Absolutely, I said. " Did they ever find Rock?"

He shook his head. "Nope. No one seems to know what happened to him after he left you. They've questioned all the gang members, and even the legitimate cultists. No one has seen as much as his five o' clock shadow."

I hoped he had died a slow and painful death. Even as I thought it, I knew I would have to address that bitterness inside me.

"What's happened to the cult?" I asked.

"What you might expect. They've fallen apart and gone back home. There wasn't much to it, without a leader holding them together. Your lieutenant Jaeger tells me that the place up there is empty now."

"You know," I said, "what happened to your civilian intelligence agent is not your fault. He should have told someone right away."

"I know that, I guess," said Pershing. "All the same, if it weren't for me, he'd still be alive."

"If it weren't for you, *I* wouldn't be alive. Neither would Leyla, probably."

"Let's hope the investigative committee sees it the same way," he said, grimacing.

"I'll make sure that they do."

He nodded. "Thank you, Jonah. I appreciate it."

On my way home, I dropped by to see Chief Jensen. After I had accepted a cup of awful police-station coffee, I sat down in one of his office chairs.

"Dan, whatever happened with that woman, Ann, who tried to get us busted for kidnapping?"

"We held her for a while, until she detoxed. Eventually, she admitted that Herman Brown had cooked up the scheme for her. She's got a trial date for obstruction of justice."

"I've got to admit, she caught me off guard. I thought she was a true believer."

Jensen shrugged. "Maybe she was. We got a little bit of information from her, and some other things we can only guess at. My thinking is, Brown figured you might try to rescue Leyla, so he put Ann out there as jail-bait. We think she met up with someone from the Forest Way when she and Julie went to the store for snacks. That person probably gave her the drugs, and maybe told her to get you and Julie in trouble."

I shook my head. "Brown sure knew how to mess up a person's life."

Jensen sipped his coffee, and nodded. "Between him and Rock, they screwed up an awful lot of people."

~

I drove up to the Forest Way on a gray, blustery day. The warning signs were down and the gate was open. The buildings were locked, and the windows were hollow-eyed and empty. I wandered between the buildings, and walked along to the machine shed. The little service road was unplowed now, and choked with snow. At the shed, the remains of some yellow police-line tape flapped in the cold wind, held in place on one end by the closed door. The door was locked. I had seen Leyla twice in the past few weeks. I thought about Rock, holding her captive, forcing meth on her until she didn't know if she loved it, or hated it.

I knew I hated Rock.

I almost hoped I would see him darting furtively among the buildings, still hiding out from the law. I began to fantasize about what I would do. But it came to me then that I was here for the opposite purpose. I needed to forgive.

I'd preached on it often enough, but that didn't make it easier to do. Even so, I knew that I needed to forgive Rock if I was ever to be free of him. Forgiving wasn't letting him off the hook. But it was letting him off *my* hook. I had to do it, not for his sake, but for my own sake, so that I could let him go, so he didn't have to be part of my thoughts and feelings anymore. My forgiveness would set me free from him. Until I did, I would be his captive, just as surely as Leyla had been. I knew that was true, but even so, it was hard.

I shouted into the wind. I shouted my anger, my hate. I pounded on the locked steel door of the shed. I finally wept, the tears freezing on my cheeks in the wind. When my emotion was spent, I stood for a moment, looking into the dark trees. I imagined Rock there, watching me.

"I'm done with you," I said. "I forgive you. You don't owe me anything anymore. You're in God's hands, now."

Out in the cold forest, for some reason, the shouting and talking did not make me feel foolish. A lone wolf howled in the distance, and a little seed of peace took root in a corner of my cold heart. I turned, and went home.

~

About four weeks after Christmas, I got a card in the mail. It said:

> Dear Jonah,
>
> I want to thank you for not sleeping with me, and for talking with me about life and God. That night changed my life.
>
> I guess I was a meth-whore. I was hooked, and I ran out of money, and then one day my dealer offered me more meth if I would go to your place and seduce you. They told me that they wanted pictures, so I assume they tried to blackmail you about something. I hope it didn't work, and I'm sorry that I was part of it.

Anyway, after you were so nice to me, it made me think a lot. I got help, and went to rehab, and I'm doing a lot better now.

You told me that night to 'pay it forward.' Well, I did. I blew the whistle on my dealer, and I think, his whole operation. I told the police to tell you about it, but I don't know if they did. If you watched the news around Christmastime and saw some stories about a giant meth lab and a drug-ring being busted up...well, I think that all started with the evidence I gave the police. The stories say they got an anonymous tip. That was me.

Thanks again,

Love,

Heidi

I showed the letter to Leyla on my third Saturday visit.

"It says, 'love'," she said. "She loves you."

"That's just an expression," I said. "I told you all about it. Nothing happened."

"But why would she say she loves you?"

"She didn't say she loves me," I said. "It's just a way to end a note. Come on, Leyla, you know me. Nothing happened."

She put her hand on my cheek and smiled. "You're too easy, Jonah," she said. "I'm teasing you."

I glared at her. "Don't do that to me," I said.

She smiled again, but all her smiles these days had a touch of sadness or tiredness to them.

~

Two weeks later, Leyla and I were thick in the middle of wedding plans.

"Do you want to serve Walleye Fingers at the reception?" she asked.

"I didn't know Walleye had fingers," I said. "I thought they were fish. Do they have opposable thumbs, too?"

For some reason she threw one of the small couch pillows at me.

"Is that why they call that a throw pillow?" I asked.

Another one followed shortly.

"Watch yourself, young lady," I said. "Never bring a pillow to a tickle fight."

"What tickle fight?" she asked, like a little girl who had just heard she was about to get a present, and then gave a little scream as I jumped out of my chair, my fingers seeking fertile spots on her rib cage and under her chin.

There was a certain amount of laughing and wrestling around that somehow became kissing. After a minute, the kissing got serious, and then we broke apart.

"Time for that later, Buster," she said, pushing me away. "After the wedding. Which is why," she said with emphasis, "we need to decide whether or not to serve little pieces of fish called Walleye Fingers."

"How can you think about fish at a time like this?"

"What time? What are *you* thinking about?"

Contrary to popular belief, my faith isn't negative about sex. It was God's idea first, after all. My faith just teaches me the context for it, which led to my reply. "After the wedding," I admitted.

"Okay," she said. "Don't think about fish. Think about fish-*ing*."

"How well you know me," I said. "But that won't eliminate the problem. It will only take the edge off."

"Well, then," said Leyla relentlessly, "let's finish this planning, so we can have a wedding, and that way, we can have an 'afterwards,' too."

"Can we have a cake shaped and decorated like a trout?" I asked.

"We cannot," she said.

"Just trying to take the edge off," I said.

She gave me a dangerous look.

"Okay," I said. "That's a 'yes' on the Walleye Fingers."

~

It wasn't all fun and games. Leyla had never been particularly moody before, but after her experience with the Forest Way, she often seemed to fall into a kind of funk. One day I showed up at her house with home-made caramel rolls.

She let me in with little enthusiasm.

"Caramel rolls," I said. "Made with love and lots of sugar."

"Thanks, Jonah," she said.

I brought them into her kitchen, and then put two of them out on a plate.

"Mind if I make coffee?" I asked.

"Go ahead, if you want," she said.

I brought the rolls and coffee into her little living room.

"I'm not really hungry, Jonah," she said.

"Caramel rolls are not really related to hunger," I said. "Just as coffee is not related to thirst."

She smiled a weak, listless kind of smile. "You go ahead," she said.

She didn't have much to say, and neither did I. Normally, one of the things I loved about our relationship was that we could be together without talking, and it was comfortable, even joyful. Just being together was a pleasure. But that day was different.

"I'm tired," she said, after a while.

"It's two o'clock in the afternoon," I said.

"I know. But I think I need to sleep," she said.

I let her sleep, and went home and stared out at the lake, held two miles distant from the shore by her chains of ice. I understood that Leyla had been through an incredibly difficult and traumatic ordeal. I understood that it would be some time before she was her old self all the time. But that didn't stop me from wishing it was all over right now.

Overall, it was a long, difficult, lightless winter. The wind blew and the snow fell through the bare, bud-less branches, and the earth lay as dead as a desert underneath its cold, monochromatic blanket. Leyla fought her demons. At first she didn't sleep. Then, it seemed, all she did was sleep. She binged on sugar, and then spent days hardly eating. She spent weeks feeling, she said, absolutely nothing at all. No joy, no pleasure, not even the intensity of despair. After that, she spent more weeks wallowing in and out of depression. She battled the traumatic memories of a month of being held captive against her will, being force-fed a drug she didn't want, yet came to crave.

Some mornings, she woke crying from nightmares, and the crying never quite stopped until she turned in, exhausted, for another restless night. She battled, just as I did, to forgive Rock and Tree.

319

I tried my best to be patient, but I was not good at being happy during this time. I prayed with her. I prayed *for* her. I took her out on joyless dates, and we made plans to which she seemed indifferent. I did not leave, and I did not give up, but I grew very weary, and my hopes were bruised and beaten down.

At last, a young, yellow sun began to suck away the lifeless snow, and thaw the frigid earth. The days grew longer, and hope returned from its long sojourn in the south. The air lost its bite, and the tips of the branches swelled and burst, and flowers shook themselves out of their wintery graves.

And then finally, one fine spring day, Leyla said at last that she was doing better. She put on a pretty spring dress, and did her hair, and even wore make-up for the first time in weeks. We went outside and stood hand in hand on the fresh new grass, and Leyla took her shoes off. She turned to me and smiled, a real smile, full of real joy.

Someone standing nearby asked her a question, but she never took her sparkling, dark eyes off of me.

"I do," she said.

Did you enjoy this book?
Would you like to see more like it?
You can help!

- Post about the book, and link to it on Facebook, Twitter, LinkedIN and other social networking sites
- Review it on Amazon, GoodReads and anywhere else people talk about books
- Tell your friends and family about it. Blog about it.
- Check out the other books in the series!

The *Lake Superior Mystery* series depends upon you, and others like you, to keep it going and growing!

Acknowledgements

As always, I want to thank the Ultimate Author, for giving me stories to tell, and letting me tell them, though very imperfectly.

I also need to thank (once more) Kari, Noelle, Isaac, Alana and Elise, for putting up with me all those days and nights when I was only half-there with you, while the other half of my mind was trying to sort out some particularly witty piece of dialogue. I'm also sorry for the thirty minutes I ignored all of you when I was thinking about how to write this part of the acknowledgements.

To my readers, I highly recommend Kari's music: http://www.reverbnation.com/karihilpert Jonah loves her stuff, and so does Leyla. I also warn you to be on the lookout in the next decade for three or more aspiring new Hilpert writers. I am so proud of each one of them!

I owe many thanks to the League of Literary Gentlemen, a grandiose name for our humble little club: Mark Cheathem, Michael Kosser, myself and sometimes, Rob Shearer. Your feedback and encouragement is vital to me. Thank you also, for putting up with my insecurities, which so often masquerade as conceit. I highly recommend to you, my readers, that you Google-search each of these names, and check out their writing also.

Lyn Rowell, as always, provided much-needed, extremely valuable feedback on the story. Thank you, Lyn!

The cover design was done by the lovely and talented Lisa Anderson, who happens to be married to my cousin, Matt. Lisa is a talented photographer, and a brilliant designer. Check out more of her work at http://www.opinedesign.com

My office assistant, Tigger, continually lobbied for me to put more of Melanchthon into the story, and gave me a good deal of loud-purring as feedback.

I have more encouragers, supporters and fans than I can tell, and I owe thanks to each one of you for keeping me going. Without you, there would not have been a third *Lake Superior Mystery*. Keep it up, **spread the word to others**, and perhaps we'll have a fourth!

Odds and Ends

A JONAH BORDEN WEBSITE

Learn more, keep up with news, and sign up for *infrequent* informational emails at www.tomhilpert.com

If you sign up for the email list, I promise I won't give your email to anyone else, unless I can get, like, $700 for it (just kidding, of course.)(I think. $700 is a lot for one email address.)

A JONAH BORDEN RECIPE - Peanut Chicken

Simple, but delicious. Don't bother serving the pasta to the cat.

1 lb chopped chicken

14 oz chicken broth

½ cup peanut butter

Linguine noodles

1 medium onion, sliced into rings

1 tsp grated ginger

1 TBL cornstarch

2 TBL dry white wine

2 cloves garlic

1 TBL soy sauce

¼ tsp red (cayenne) pepper

Whisk together into a sauce: chicken broth, peanut butter, soy sauce, white wine, cornstarch, pepper and ginger.

Stir fry chicken in 2 TBL of hot oil. Add garlic and onion. When onion is soft, add sauce, and stir until hot and thickened. Serve over cooked linguine.

A JONAH BORDEN PLAYLIST

Adagio in G minor – Albinoni

Do it Again – Steely Dan

Prairie Town – The Wailing Jenny's

Underneath the Star – Kari Hilpert (great Christmas song)

Jolene – Ray Lamontagne (this is *not* the same song as the one by Dolly Parton)

Everything and Nothing – Matt Maher

Element – Moses Mayfield

Over You – Miranda Lambert

The Part where You Let Go – HEM

How He Loves – The David Crowder Band

Colder Weather – The Zac Brown Band

Disappear – The Gabe Dixon Band

A JONAH BORDEN MINISTRY

Some of my fans have said, in one way or another, that they wish there was a real pastor like Jonah Borden, or that there were churches where Christians like him really hung out together.

I want to assure you, I know many living Christian people who share Jonah's values and commitment to being authentic. It takes more time to get to know real people than it does to read about a character in a book, so you might have to give it time and patience. But Christians like Jonah are out there, all over the place. My own ministry association, the Alliance of Renewal Churches (http://www.allianceofrenewalchurches.org/) is full of people who would fit right in to a Jonah Borden novel.

No one is exactly like Jonah Borden, of course, not even me. But one of my passions in writing his character is that I want people to know there are, in fact, many Christians who are a lot like him. If you really want to find fellowship with such people, I humbly suggest you ask God to help you. After that, the ARC website (above) is one place (but not the only one) you might start.

I try to keep my preaching separate from my writing, because I don't want my readers to become too disappointed, or my listeners to have fictional expectations. If you think you're ready for the potential let-down, and you are truly interested, you can hear me preach at http://revth.wordpress.com

About the Author

Tom Hilpert grew up in the tropical paradise of Papua New Guinea. When he was ten years old, he knew he wanted to write books. In fact, he began writing several novels at that age. Thankfully, they are lost forever.

However, his more recent works are available in print and ebook formats. His fiction features strong, memorable, quirky characters who face mysteries and adventures with humor and persistence.

Hilpert has visited more than 17 countries, and has lived in three of them. In the U.S., he has lived in six different states, including Minnesota, the setting for the Lake Superior Mysteries. Currently, he lives in Tennessee with his wife, children, and far too many pets and farm animals.

Learn more at http://www.tomhilpert.com

Made in the USA
Charleston, SC
21 August 2014